To Joa

Grandmother's Footsteps

Hope you enjoy this
lockdown read.

Love

Anna

March '21

Grandmother's Footsteps

ANNA ANDERSON

Matador
9 Priory Business Park,
Wistow Road, Kibworth Beauchamp,
Leicestershire. LE8 0RX
Tel: 0116 279 2299
Email: books@troubador.co.uk
Web: www.troubador.co.uk/matador
Twitter: @matadorbooks

ISBN 978 1800462 311

British Library Cataloguing in Publication Data.
A catalogue record for this book is available from the British Library.

Printed and bound in Great Britain by 4edge Limited
Typeset in 12pt Adobe Jenson Pro by Troubador Publishing Ltd, Leicester, UK

Matador is an imprint of Troubador Publishing Ltd

To my blind friend Mavis.
A wonderful listener to this tale.

'Had we never lov'd sae kindly,
Had we never lov'd sae blindly,
Never met, or never parted
We'd had ne'er been broken hearted.'
                    Robert Burns, Ae Fond Kiss

'It's a joy to be hidden,
but a disaster not to be found.'
                    D.W. Winnicott

PROLOGUE

THE JOTTER

March 31ˢᵗ 1921.

The final pages…
Does this augur the end for me?
Another slippered footstep towards my demise?

Most days I wish it could be so. But then the voice of my education speaks to me.

It reminds me that 'there is a divinity that shapes our ends, rough hew it how we will.'

So another beginning beckons. This time without the companionship of this, my secret friend. My confessional will now lie snug in the cocoon of its lining in this old bag made of crocodile leather. I will entrust it into the custody of Mistress Niven in the hope that she will keep her promise to pass it on to Tam when my departure from this world comes about. That is of course if it is not stolen. Most things get stolen here, including time.

I will leave the last page blank. A symbolic gesture

for what may be to come, I fear. One day now passing much like another. And yet I must not complain. Today the rough winds of winter have been softened to a gentle breeze. I am permitted to sit in the grounds when my work in the Linen Room is done for the day. I can see Donald Niven at work digging the garden. New borders for the spring he says. He tips his hat and hands me an early bloom. A beautiful red tulip. It opens its beak to the pale sun now peering through the sandstone turrets of the East Wing.

When the flower has wilted I shall press its petals into this album of shame.

And Lily promises to join me when her travails in the kitchen are over. She may indeed bring me a morsel to eat. Perhaps a rare treat? Maybe a scone, left over from the 'Friends of the Asylum' social gathering held here this afternoon.

So we will sit together biding our time, rough hewn as we are, until that divinity which shapes our ends eventually comes to pass.

Jeannie Anstruther (nee Logan)

PART ONE
AUTUMN

ONE

MOVING ON

If only she'd kept a diary, she might be writing now in that forward sloping hand of hers:

Tues 19ᵗʰ November 7pm 1990

> *Today I have a new address. But how can I be sure I've moved on to somewhere else?*

And then stopped. Put the pen down. And before the ink was dry on that trembling question mark, she would have closed the diary up, leaving an unsightly blot between the two sheets of paper.

What she wanted now was certainty. Or perhaps a kindly assurance that there could be a life to come.

Bella Cavendish, nee Anstruther falls to her knees and crouches over yet another cardboard box. In the shadow of the unshaded light bulb she makes out the label: TRASH AND

TREASURES she had scrawled on the top in an attempt to stay cheerful. In the box lay the miscellaneous objects she had picked up at the last minute, going from attic to cellar in that vast rectory she had called home for over thirty eight years. Stuff that the removal men had left or thought she was throwing out – an assortment of odd shoes that hadn't quite walked to the Charity shop, a soup ladle, an old handbag reeking of moth balls (where had that come from?)- plant pots, seeds for summer flowers, a pack of cards…

Her hands reach down and touch the contours of a mirror. As Bella's fingers trace the pattern round the frame, an ache of a memory shifts her heart's beat. She feels it take up a staccato rhythm inside her chest. She knows where this came from. The mirror was an old companion. An impulse buy she remembers. Bought from a junk shop in Beeston, the first of her many extravagances at the beginning of her life with Don. She recalls the hours of scraping off layers of paint from the slender wooden edge of the glass until the first grain of oak was revealed. Then patiently scouring round the delicate pattern of leaves and fruit with a toothbrush before buffing the whole thing with a rag, until the rich golden patina shone through.

'What in Heaven's name made you buy that old thing?' he had quizzed her.

'Because I do daft things sometimes Don. You'll have to get used to it. But it is beautiful, isn't it?'

And the two young faces that looked back at them agreed that perhaps she might have been right.

Bella lifts the mirror from the box. She blows off the dust that has gathered in the hollows of the carved acorns and stares at the glass.

Who was this old lady?

Then reaches out to touch her. The hands she sees with some relief are familiar; strong practical hands that could grasp nettles in the garden of Swallow's Rest without even flinching. These hands were used to hard work. They could pummel dough that rose to a crispy loaf. 'Jam Maker's hands' her mother had called them, well practised in a lifetime of plunging in and out of the tasks of daily life.

But she couldn't recognise the face that looked back at her now; it's features so grey and indistinct.

A ghost of a face!

'Is that why you left me Don?'

Bella sighs. Small seeds of anger begin to swell up in her stomach. They rise and stick in her throat, fermenting at the back of her mouth like undigested cud. In their juices, the spittle of her last fight with Don. Not so much a fight as a spat, because you could never really fight with him. Not once did he ever take his gloves off and really wrestle with her. Nor with anyone else come to think of it.

'At the first hint of disagreement, you'd always return to your corner, wouldn't you? Putting on that hard-done-by look you've perfected over the years.'

'If you say so Bella.'

'There what did I say? You're doing it again.'

'Am I?'

'You know you are.'

She feels the puddle of tears gather and pool behind her eyes. Maybe she's done enough today.

Move on!

Rising from her knees she stumbles over a packing case, snagging her tights on its jagged edge. Walking into the kitchen she sees the ladder run from her thigh to her ankles.

Heigh ho!

Elvis, the cat, asleep in the soil of an old rubber plant, yawns and stretches before following her, his soft pads falling quietly over the bare stone floor. Bella finds the gin bottle amidst the cat litter and pours a tumbler full before picking Elvis up. Clutching these two sources of comfort she crawls upstairs to an unmade bed, praying to a god she no longer believed in for the oblivion of sleep.

~

Morning comes with a clatter of sleet on the uncurtained window.

'Mercy!' she cries, drawing the cat closer to her for warmth. Elvis stretches out before obligingly tucking himself into the hollow of the mattress where Don had so recently lain.

The sound of footsteps up and down the stairs thump through the walls of her bedroom, a reminder that she now had neighbours at close quarters.

Must be the boys getting ready for school.

Their heavy tread takes up an insistent thud-thud thudding in her head.

She gets up quickly, shooing Elvis off the bed. Standing by the window she gazes down at her front garden.

A lone laburnum tree, now skeleton white, shivers up a greeting. Underneath its canopy, a mosaic of city life shifts and settles on the bare soil: scraps of newspaper, uneaten chips, a gathering of butt ends burrowing down to take their root.

'What have I done?'

No time for questions now. No turning back.

Bella bosses herself into action. Opening the wardrobe door she cannot help let out a groan.

Half of this stuff should have gone to Oxfam.

'I know. I know.'

She closes the door and seeks out the well-worn jeans with patchwork pockets and puts them on. Over her head goes a blue sweater that her mother had made in her 'knit and natter' years. She feels it mould itself into her new shape. A forgiving friend at this time in her life. The time she has labelled: INVISIBILITY.

'I wasn't always like this though, was I Elvis? You've seen me in my prime. Me in my glad rags, with my long leather boots and all those hats and scarves…I was a bit of a stunner, wasn't I? And my hair…'

Bella puts up a hand, splaying her fingers to comb through the thick auburn tresses of her memory and feels only the russet and white tufts of cygnet down growing unevenly on her head.

'Oh Elvis, what happened to my hair?'

No time for self pity. That way lies… she shudders to think.

Get a wiggle on girl!

Going downstairs she clears a passage from the hallway to the kitchen. She forces herself to eat a slice of toast. And then makes another list:

— *see bank manager and check that D's standing order has come through*
— *ring for new entry in the telephone book (should I go ex directory?)*
— *call Julia and Evie*
— *query solicitor's bill- it can't be that much- bloody lawyers!*
— *confirm appointment with consultant next Thursday*
— *change my name by deed poll (when I feel there might be a ME that's worth naming!)*

By ten o'clock she had ticked off several items. She was solvent

7

for another month. Don was as good as his word. She mustn't forget to book the taxi to the hospital next week.

Fingers crossed!

Bella looks up from the phone and the scrawl on the pad.

The place was a midden!

Her new house , like herself, was in a state of disarray.

But it would be lovely in the end!

Crooning thoughts, like lullabies, come into her head and she allows them to stay. These thoughts meant no harm. They seemed gentle in their assurance and positive about the future. She feels their welcome embrace of congratulation for the work she has done so far. The wall between the dining room and the kitchen had to come down to create more space. And that large window, now ready for painting, at the back of the house would let in so much more light. Outside she could see the first straggly rays of winter sun streak down on a small back yard, now rank with weeds and rubbish.

A few tubs would work wonders there. And a small tree where she could sit under in the summer. What about a rocking chair by the kitchen range? Too much of a cliché perhaps? Maybe those two nice Polish builders of hers could build some bookcases into the walls when they had done all the heavy stuff.

Bella takes in the imagined scenarios and adds the aroma of coffee, freshly baked bread, the smell of beeswax on the polished furniture… it could all just happen. In the meantime she would have to hunt for mugs, buy some sugar and milk and take all that stuff to the local charity shop.

The sounds of the city assault her as she steps from the gate of number 36. She was not used to traffic. At Swallow's Rest all had been birdsong when she opened her front door. A large front garden with fruit trees and shrubs. Bees humming, butterflies round the buddleia…

Ah well!

She looks up the street along the neat row of terraced houses stretching into the distance in uniform regularity. Mill homes once she guesses, built in the industrial heydays of the last century. Good, serviceable, no-nonsense dwellings – modest yet built to last. Several of them she notices were undergoing facelifts like her own. People seemed to be reclaiming the city and it felt exciting, if just a little daunting to be part of this renaissance. And now, instead of always having to use the car, she could walk to the shops for all the essentials.

At the corner store, the elderly Indian couple introduce themselves and asked her how she was settling in to her new neighbourhood.

Nice people she thinks. Their gentle lilting voices offering their welcome to her new surroundings.

On impulse she buys some vegetable samosas as well as the basics. Walking on down the street, she finds a branch of Barnados and is greeted by an elderly volunteer called Shirley.

'Well my duck,' Shirley says, picking up the old crocodile bag, 'this is an interesting item to be sure. I bet it has some history to it. Or provenance as them posh blokes with their bow ties on all these antiques programmes on the telly, would have us call it. This is a real find love. Can you see Joan Crawford wearing that in those wonderful black and white films? I can! Swaggering around in her fur coat with this magnificent bag swinging from her shoulders in 'Mildred Pierce'. Oh yes duck, oh yes indeed!'

Bella grins. She likes the look and the sound of Shirley. Maybe when she has sorted herself out she could help Shirley in the shop?

Perhaps...

'Where did you find it love?'

Bella frowns. She can't remember. She thinks it could be something her mother picked up in a jumble sale at her church. Ailsa had a soft spot for things like that.

And remembers that Iona and Evie once played with the bag in their dressing up days but the smell had put them off.

The same pungent whiff of camphor hits her now as Shirley opens the clasp. She pulls out an old paisley shawl and holds it up to the light, checking for signs of the moth. No holes that either could see.

'I'd hang on to this my love. It would be wasted on the likes of those around here.'

One hand wanders into the cavity of the bag.

'And summat else if I'm not mistaken. A proper little treasure trove this.'

Shirley is holding a small brooch in her hand in the shape of a claw with a golden stone at its centre.

'That's a cairngorm isn't it? Worth a bob or two. Take it home with the shawl love, I'll keep the rest.'

For the remainder of the day Bella escapes from the sound of the drill and the blare of rap music, fleeing from one job to another. Feeling defeated she gives up and starts to strip away the multiple layers of wall paper off the living room walls. The latest two-toned stripe unfurls easily to reveal a classic Laura Ashley pattern in pale blue. She likes that and could have lived with those flowers in their day. But it wasn't what she wanted now. Under the pale forget-me-nots she hits on a stubborn layer of hessian. This would take some shifting. Chipping away at the knobbly furrows, she catches a glimpse of some roses from another era. They open up their blooms and the first traces of raw emulsion peep through.

Bella sighs. She would lay it all bare again. A soft white paint with a hint of apricot perhaps? It would lend the room light and make it seem bigger than it actually was. She and Julia had plans. They were going to hunt for bargains at the auctions and she just might take another look at that pretty Victorian fireplace she'd seen at the reclamation yard on Derby Road.

The phone rings. One of those modern contraptions you could pick up and move around while you are speaking, then put down somewhere and never find again before the bleep and a message stutters out a greeting.

'Hi, sweetie, it's me, just checking you are still in the land of the living. Give us a buzz, I'm worried about…'

'Julia!'

' Bingo!'

'This must be serendipity. I was just thinking about you.'

'Good thoughts darling?'

Bella hears in her friends drawl, the long pull of a Turkish cigarette.

'I'm trying to sort out the front room. Wondering which wall to hang your picture.'

'Don't you mean the parlour? Isn't that what the working classes call those pokey little places where they kept their aspidistras and never used except on high days and holidays? Come into my parlour said the spider to the fly…'

'Julia!'

'Hang it on the wall opposite the window. That way it will catch the afternoon light. What light there is in that little rabbit hutch. You're mad Bella. Quite bonkers, even to have considered moving there.'

'No I'm not!'

'Oh yeah? Same old impetuous Bella, never looking before she might take a leap.'

'Less of the old.'

'Have you seen the crime figures for your part of the city? Your mother's ashes will be jingling in that little urn of hers.'

'We can't all afford a big flat in The Park. Don's settlement didn't amount to that much.'

' But he's given you half his pension, hasn't he?'

'Research academics aren't the best paid Julia.'

'Academics! My giddy aunt. Too high-minded to go for that Professorship when he could have had it on a silver salver. That was your Donald! Yet the same one was not so pure as the proverbial white stuff when the rich widow Twankie snapped her fingers at him.'

Bella hears her friend chuckle.

'A little sparrow tells me that she's known as 'the-brisk-and-bracing-Brenda' in some quarters. Good name eh?'

'I wouldn't know.'

'Oh come on Bella. Don't get all high and mighty with me. Anyway that's not why I am ringing. I've been in touch with Iona. It's time your eldest daughter pulled her finger out to help you. She's treating you to a make-over with that woman she and Rosie consulted. Did wonders for them and there is no reason why she couldn't do the same for you. Get your sparkle back my girl!'

'I don't suppose I've any say in the matter?'

'None at all. And by the way I've seen some curtains that will go very nicely with my abstract in John Lewis'. Dots and swirls in red and black. Very Kandinsky.'

'We'll see,' Bella replied, already feeling quite defeated.

TWO

'THIRTY DAYS HATH SEPTEMBER...'

'Shirley! I'm just about to put the kettle on for a brew. Fancy a cup?'

'Love one my duck. I'll be with you in a minute. Just let me finish sorting out all these videos.'

The old woman mutters to herself as she works. What could they do with all these videos? Who had a video machine now anyway? It was all DVD's now and mobile phones which took pictures and told you what you should be doing in half an hour, and things they watched on the internet. What was the world coming to? Give her a good three and six penny seat in the stalls at the Essoldo any day of the week. In amongst the smokers on the back seat with all those young men who bought her chocolates and wanted no more than a squeeze of her breasts when their hands fell south from her shoulder as the main film was on. She's hang on the the copies of 'Titanic' though, lovely music it had, but not all that rude stuff and violence. She's had enough of 'Diehards.' Come to think about it, there were too many diehards round here thank you very much.

Then she spots an old exercise book on a shelf amidst all the clutter. She can't remember for the life of her how it got there. Didn't someone leave it inside a bag? She picks it up, one arthritic hand hovering it over the black bin liner. The red cover falls open, a few papery flower petals fall out and Shirley notices some faint writing in a beautiful copperplate style on the front page.

The bin liner falls to the floor.

Now where did she put her glasses?

'Shirley? Teas mashed!'

'Mmmmmm? In a sec.'

The Jotter

Lily Cochrane has bought me this jotter. From a sale of work in the reception hall. She tells me that they are held every month on Friday afternoons from two to three thirty. I haven't been to one yet. It is too soon to show my face in public.

The red exercise book is unusual. On the back is printed all the tables I used to learn by rote: 5 x 12=60. Eleven sevens are seventy seven. Are there still four pecks to every bushel? Eight furlongs to a mile? Lily says the jotter is a good place for keeping my deep thoughts: 'you're a deep one, aye so you are Jeannie Logan.' she says. However I am not sure about keeping my thoughts anywhere but in my head. I know they are deep, but I'd rather bury them than have them exposed to the rest of the world. But she means well, does Lily. Lily Cochrane with her large slack body and her raw-boned look of simplicity. When she smiles her one tooth sticks out from her upper gum. A solitary nail in the head of a flotsam creature, blown up on a tide of misfortune like me.

So I will keep her gift. And use the pencil Mistress Niven gave me for calculating the lengths of material I will require for the new curtains in the Staff dining room. Twelve inches to the foot. Three feet to every yard. 30 days have September. April June and November. All the rest have 31, except February alone...

I think the month is now September. I know I have been here some time. Lily tells me that this is the year of our Lord 1920. There is a king on the throne. I recognise his whiskery features on the back of a penny piece. He has a wife called Mary. Her name is above the ward where I am now placed. I must remember it it is called a ward and not a cell. There have been 5 kings called George. 8 Henry's and 7 James' if you live in Scotland. Hang on Jean! I must hang on to something that is me!

20th SEPTEMBER.

THOUGHTS AT DAWN.

I have had another disturbed night. Lily was screaming again and others joined in with her caterwaul. I think she must be due for her menses, so her nature will be contrary for a week. Sister Jewell was roused in the wee small hours and I heard her swear and hit Lily across the face. Slap, slap, repeatedly on and on. It seemed to have little effect.

I can see the light streak through the high windows to the east. There is not much sunlight that gets into this room that is like a long corridor, leading on to another passageway and beyond. The colours within it are sombre. Dark green tiles clad the walls. They come up to my shoulders. When I stand I sometimes fancy that I could be touching moss. The black shadows cast by the iron bedsteads make this ward an eerie place and those who sleep here seem haunted as well. I have counted over sixty beds and Lily tells me there are more yet. Across from me Maggie Lennox cries out for her mother every night. She is an aged crone Maggie and I fear that her mother has been dead a long while. I have noticed Irene Parkes sleepwalking again. When she strays up and down the corridor she often forgets which bed is her own. Sometimes she will lift my sheet and place her frail body next to mine. When she does this, I let her stay. It is the only warmth that we are able to share together in this place.

I must think where I am to put this jotter. In here no one can call anything their own. We only have a small cabinet kept by the bedside in which to place personal items and they are often stolen.

My dentifrice tin lies within my drawer, along with a comb with many of its teeth missing. The ivory handled brushes belonging to my mother disappeared shortly after I came here, as did my purse and my wallet containing my Teachers Certificate of competence. Maybe I shall use this bag made from a reptile's hide and given to me by Mistress Niven to keep my needles and thread. I shall keep this slim book within its lining and ask the good lady to lock it up in the Linen cupboard at the end of each day. Only she has the key.

There is one piece of small good fortune to be thankful for.

I have hung on to the brooch that Tam gave me on our wedding day. I grasp it under my pillow at night and pin it by day to whatever piece of clothing comes my way. It has seen me through many trials and tribulations and I would certainly mourn its loss if it were to be stolen from me.

~

'Oh my!' says Shirley, 'wherever did I see that brooch?'

THREE

THE MAKEOVER

She is awake in the early hours. Dreaming again.

But this time, the first time in years, Bella feels a pleasant moistness between her legs. The first patches of light were coming through the bare window and she was there, in bed with Don, and 'going all the way'.

Closing her eyes, she wills herself into that narrow bed of yesteryear with its lumpy mattress and its sheets, stale with the sweat of other bodies. There in that shabby room over the pub. Don had bartered with the landlord; a ten shilling note buying their first night of illicit pleasure. All evening after their graduation ceremony they had filled themselves up with cheap wine. Inebriation made them bold. When they left her mother and Don's parents at their hotel after the degree ceremony they couldn't wait to be on their own.

'Bugger them! Bugger them all!' they had laughed.

Still giggling, climbing up the narrow staircase, opening the door of the darkened room... and then, she remembers fondly, all was a clumsy confusion. Clothes tossed on the floor, a swearing at bra straps and suspenders, then gasps of incredulity with the wonder at that first sight of their naked bodies.

He entered her and she held on to his shoulders as they moved together in the urgent quick-step of sex. It was over all too soon. He shuddered and spilled himself into her. She found herself rocking in seconds of delight and pain. For a moment she was out of time and out of herself. Her ferocious mother could have stomped into the room and she would not have noticed; stranded on their island of unfamiliar joy.

Then the strains of a Procul Harem song floated up through the floorboards. She began to sing along to its dreamy organ accompaniment. Images tumbles into her head as her heart slowed back to its normal pulse.

'I've never worked out what the lyrics of that song meant, all that tripping of light fandangos and cartwheels on the floor,' he said sleepily.

'You are far too literal Don. Its the stuff of poetry.'

Seconds before sleep and the tender wrapping of euphoria began to unpeel.

Panic!

'Don, what if I'm pregnant?'

The voice from the other pillow was calm.

'Then we'll just have to get married, don't worry.'

'Will that be alright?'

'It will be fine.'

'Okay then. Goodnight', then shyly, 'sweet dreams Don.'

~

Tears of tenderness come into Bella's eyes. And she lets them flow.

~

19

Her mobile phone is buzzing in her pocket. She reaches inside her coat and switches off the noisy interruption.

'Don't worry, it will only be my daughter Iona sending me another text. She and her, er, partner are treating me to a 'makeover' later on.'

'Lucky you!'

Bella makes a face.

'I know it is kind of them, but really I don't want to go Shirley. I wish I was thirteen again and could forge one of these notes from my mother saying I had to be excused from PE.'

'The old period pain standby eh.' Her new friend clucks in sympathy.

They are chatting by the counter at Barnados whilst sifting through another pile of leavings from Bella's cupboards. Despite the swellings in her finger joints, Shirley's hands are deft in picking out potential buys.

'I see you are wearing that pretty cairngorm brooch. It goes well with that coat Mrs Cavendish.'

'Call me Bella, please.'

'Right you are my duck. Short for Isobel, is it?'

'Isabella. But my mother only ever called me that when she was cross with me as a child.'

Bella nods to the window where Ailsa's bag is draped on the arm of a bald headed dummy.

'I see you've still got the old alligator then?'

Shirley's eyes follow her gaze.

'Yes and if it doesn't go this week, I'll put a few bob in the tin and get it from my granddaughter. She's into all that retro stuff. Spends her life going to vintage shops and goes out at night looking like some teddy boys moll. Daft I call it. But hey-up love, I mean Bella, I've just minded myself, I've got so forgetful recently, but there was summat else in that there bag. I didn't find it until you had gone.'

'Oh?'

'Don't get yer hopes up – no great treasure trove, just an old exercise book that somehow had got lodged in the lining. I think I kept it in the stock room on the chance that you might pop in again.'

'Don't bother Shirley. Dump it in the bin if you like. I'm trying to shed all my unwanted clutter now. Any day I might be seen wandering round in the saffron robes of a Buddhist monk with nothing to my name but a begging bowl of rice.'

'Oh my lord, you are a one! A one-off I should say. But I wouldn't fancy your chances round here with a get-up like that.'

~

Gaynor, style guru and self-appointed mentor and coach, didn't look like one of the bossy brigade that were either loved or hated on the television. Bella looks across the table and sees a woman in her early forties, dressed modestly in layers of autumn colours. So this was the Gaynor who helped Iona make the most of her large frame and had given Rosie the permission she needed to indulge in her zest for dressing in bright primary colours. Bella looks down at her own hastily assembled outfit, then tightens her coat for disguise.

Over coffee they discuss her tastes and habits and history of shopping for clothes.

'I should tell you that my mother is a real squirrel,' Iona is saying. 'Charity outlets mainly. Buy it, wear it, recycle it, that's her motto. My brother and sister and I used to dread Parents Evenings at school, wondering what on earth she would wear to show us up.'

'Really!' Gaynor puts down her pen.

Rosie's round face had two spots of bright pink high on her cheekbones.

'But Bella always looks great, what ever outfit she puts together.'

I may as well not be here, she thinks. They could do this without me.

'So how do you see yourself now Mrs Cavendish?'

The question was aimed directly at her. She would have to respond.

But the guru presses on not waiting for an answer. Bella hears a cool professional tone in her voice, each word weighed and spaced before it falls.

'You've been through a lot of changes recently, I hear. Personal circumstances, life events and so on.'

So that sums up the loss of a parent, a life threatening illness, the end of a marriage and a house move. Very neat. Very succinct. 'Person circumstances, life events' and of course don't forget the ubiquitous 'and so on.' I must remember that.

Something within Bella tightens and coils. She wills her mind back to those days of reckless joy; rummaging for bargains … and sees herself in that Jeff Banks designer skirt bought for nineteen shillings and eleven pence. It went well with those thigh length boots of Spanish leather even though they were one size too big and she had to put tissues in the toes to stop her tripping over.

'I am therefore not surprised, Gaynor continues, 'that you may have felt that you have lost some of your identity in that process. And so I am left wondering how a new wardrobe will help you on your journey to a new self?'

Every phrase a cliché, words so well polished before they leave her mouth.

'I'm not altogether sure.'

Bella can feel her voice fall, then get up again and toddle itself into the shape of an answer.

'For some time,' it stumbles, 'I felt like it didn't really matter. Best not to be noticed, if you see what I mean.'

Rosie has taken her arm and gives it a gentle squeeze.

The first salted droplet falls on Bella's sweater. She sees the stain settle and spread to a darker one. Gravy perhaps?

Iona hands her a tissue with a gesture of impatience.

She takes it and crumples the soft membranes in her hand.

'But now,' she adds, taking a breath to strengthen what was to come next. 'I'm beginning to resent what I can only feel is being… oh what is the word I want Rosie?'

Rosie stares at Iona. They both look blank.

Then a word come to the rescue with a clarity that she did not expect.

'Unregarded. Yes that's it. That's the word I've been looking for.'

She says it again, stressing the first syllable.

'**Un**regarded. I am leading an unregarded life. I've become the sort of wallpaper that people have in their hall. It's been there for years and no one can remember the pattern any more.'

Iona butts in: 'But mother, no one has ever disregarded you.'

'That's not what I said Iona.'

And finds with a growing sense of her own power that there is no stopping her now.

'I've got this picture in my mind, no please don't interrupt, it's a painting by Gustav Klimt, called 'The Three Ages.' I saw the original with your Dad when we went to Rome a couple of years ago. The last time we had a holiday together in fact. Let me paint it for you now. There is a young mother in it, all clad out in blue and gold chiffon. She's holding a child in her arms and its all very romantic and dreamy- very Klimt.'

Bella stops for a moment, casting a glance round the busy restaurant.

'But what makes the picture interesting is the grandmother beside them. She's leaning on her daughter's shoulder. Mother and baby in full frontal beauty and the old lady standing in profile.'

She allows herself another pause and sees that all three women are giving her their full attention.

'An old woman sideways on and totally naked and bent over the young woman. Not a pretty sight at all. She has a dowager's hump on her back, a flaccid stomach and big hands and feet. Her hair is grey and long and it covers her face so we can't see her expression. I've no idea what it could be. Sadness perhaps?'

'Or maybe a sense of shame.'

Bella settles back in her chair. She looks around the room again, this time noticing all the tables occupied by Saturday shoppers; middle-aged women mainly, smartly dressed, all caught up in everyday chatter: husbands, children, the special offers in the kitchen department. She looks across to Gaynor. The guru has nothing to say.

'I've rambled on, haven't I? Probably not made much sense to you. But what I am trying to say is I feel that I am getting to know that old woman now, naked, imperfect and covering her face from the world, yet when I tried to get a print of the painting I found that time and time again she had been air brushed away. Can you believe it? All that is left is an image of such sentimentality- mother and child in swathes of golden light- but I know it is what's missing that gives the painting its meaning: that old woman. The sad thing is no one wants to buy it with her in the frame.'

Silence.

No one says a word.

Bella catches the quick glance that Gaynor was giving to an elegant watch on her wrist.

She's paid by the hour of course. Like a whore. Earning her living by tending to the needs of the insecure, the vulnerable, those who have lost their sense of self.

'That's quite a story, Mrs Cavendish. Who was the old lady in the painting? Do you know?'

'I'm not sure,' Bella replies, 'some one said that the model was one of Rodin's discarded mistresses.'

'No wonder she wanted to hide herself away.'

And now Bella feels the knot inside her stiffen and snap.

'I don't actually think that's the point!'

A hot flush begins its rise at the base of her neck. In a few seconds her face is suffused in a scarlet glow.

'Let's get down to business, shall we?' Gaynor was poised for action. 'Why don't you two ladies leave us for a while? Come back later in an hour or two when we've done some work.'

'Forget fashion,' she commands, directing the instruction to the back of her client. 'At our age it is just a little absurd to dress like the young. We'll concentrate on style, shall we? A good sense of style never dates one. What say you Mrs Cavendish?'

Now would be the time for Bella to make her escape- a good sense of style never dates one- the woman was talking like the Queen!

'Good luck Mum, you'll be fine.'

She sees Iona and Rosie leave the table. Then she stands up and follows her Svengali obediently into one of the dressing rooms on the first floor. In the changing area her eyes are drawn to a notice over the mirror: Customers are requested to keep on their undergarments when trying on swimwear. In her mind she reads it as another instruction she had seen many times before in the hospital cubicles- PATIENTS ARE REQUESTED TO REMOVE THEIR

JEWELLERY BEFORE EXAMINATION. Bella's hand strays automatically to the fourth finger of her left hand before stepping out to face the x ray eyes of her new consultant.

' Your eyes are a lovely shade of grey, Mrs Cavendish, very unusual, and your skin is still smooth. We should emphasis these features. Soft colours, shades of dawn. Can you wait here while I show you what I mean.'

~

'I felt like a waxwork!'

Bella giggles to the girls over a second glass of wine.

'All I did was raise my arms every now and then when she told me to.'

' But was there anything that you liked, mother?'

Iona could not disguise the impatience in her tone.

How could she tell them? Would her daughter ever understand?

All those rails of pinks and lilacs and soft shades of grey...

In the hospital bed the colours of dawn she saw every morning weren't painted in cashmere or silk- raw silk maybe: violet, purple, cobalt blue, the jagged colours of pain.

'Yes I was tempted to get one outfit. A dress with lovely suede buttons on it.'

'Then why didn't you buy it? It would have been our shout.'

'Yes, I know, and thank you. Don't think I'm not grateful to the pair of you.'

'Well then...'

'I don't know.'

She stops, waiting for a moment of clarity to arrive.

'Yes I do. At least I think I do. Because I didn't recognise the stranger wearing it.'

'Mother!'

'Sssh Iona', Rosie was saying. 'Let Bella speak for herself.'

'That wasn't me, Iona. The person I saw in the mirror was one of these cardiganed women I used to meet at your Dad's faculty parties. You know the sort; understated, unobtrusive, well camouflaged for every occasion.'

'So you didn't get anything?'

'No. And what is more that little girl inside me who was holding my hand, agreed with me.'

'Now you are not making any sense. Is this some of your 'therapy' speak, mum?'

'Maybe. But let me tell you something. The whole experience reminded me of the last time someone dressed me. I must have been four or five and your Gran is getting me ready for Sunday school. She always warmed my clothes by the fire. That bit I loved. First the vest, then the liberty bodice- what an invention that was with all its fumble of hooks and eyes – next one of her fair-isle creations that you wouldn't dress your dolly in, then the socks, the pleated skirt, the elastic knickers that cut off the tops of your legs. And I was ready; all trussed up for Jesus!'

'What a sight,' Rosie is amused, 'but what has all this got to do with Gaynor?'

'Everything, Rosie. I was wearing an outfit that someone had chosen for me and that little girl in her Sunday best told me not to do it. She wanted me to run away and get into my dungarees and scamper down Grandfer's garden and not to conform to someone else's idea of what I should look like.'

'So it was all a waste of time?'

'No I don't think so Iona. I think it helped me in a funny kind of way.'

'How?'

'To stand up for myself again. I haven't done enough of

that lately, too much passive drifting. But as my Grandfer would have said: "you've got a tongue in your heid lassie. Use it!"'

'Good for you!' Rosie claps her hands. 'Anyway how dare she say you haven't got style, Bella. You've got bags of it. And a great figure too. Have you noticed,' she points to a group of teenage girls standing around the bar, 'that the young have no waists at all? They just let their midriffs bulge over their jeans and have to put on an extra layer of blubber in the winter to keep out the cold. Not like you, though,' she hesitates, 'we might have to do something about your hair. How about a crop? Annie Lennox meets Judy Dench perhaps?'

They keep the tone easy for the rest of the day. Talk of soft furnishings for the new house. The girls would take her to a retail park out of town where the price of curtains were a fraction of the big department stores.

Bella found that conversations were always more relaxed when Rosie was around. She looks across and smiles at the two young women sitting opposite her. Iona had been the cleverest of her children. Don's pride and joy, working hard at school before getting a first class degree at Cambridge, 'in a science subject,' he was fond of boasting. 'That takes real brains.' She dutifully followed in her father's footsteps into the laboratory world of research for a while, but then got bored. There followed a brief spell in London working for an investment bank. She made lots of money but was not happy there either. A cycling holiday in France brought Rosie into her life. The recognition of Iona's sexual preference sent waves of alarm through the family at first. Bella kept it a secret from Ailsa and Don's parents. 'They just wouldn't understand,' Bella had said. And Don had never understood either. Having his favourite child tell him she was a lesbian was baffling enough, but abandoning a scientific career was for him way beyond the pale. Father and daughter rarely met now without the acid air of resentment between them.

'Mum, we've got something to tell you.'

Iona's serious tone brought Bella into the present.

'Really?'

'We've decided to get married. Well, not married exactly as we don't go along with all that patriarchal nonsense, but as good as – a civil partnership. What do you think?'

For a brief moment Bella felt the disapproving scowl of her mother flit across her face.

'Just a small affair, no big deal,' Rosie butts in.'We'd love you to come and Evie too if she wants. My sister Fay will be there and a few friends from work.'

'No men!' adds Iona.

'Not even your father or your brother?'

'Definitely not Dad. He wouldn't know where to put himself. And certainly not the 'brisk and bracing Brenda' – no way! I'd really like Tom to come but he's in Canada, he wouldn't want to leave his precious prairies and come back for us.'

'I suppose so,' Bella says, and then finding the spirit of her true self, she reaches out and clasps their hands together. 'I'm really happy for you both. You have my blessing. And whilst we are on the subject of good news, I saw my consultant on Thursday. He tells me I am in the clear, for a while, at least.'

~

'For a while.'

The exact words he had spoken.

'How long was 'a while?' she had wanted to ask.

Otherwise the white-coated interview had passed without too much pain.

~

She sat obediently amongst the whey-faced hopefuls handing over the still warm specimen to the waiting nurse. She even found some small talk when a cheery vampire punctured her arm for blood. Then waited patiently for her name to be called.

'Mrs Isabella Cavendish to see Mr Clark.'

He had been, as ever, abstracted in his manner. His attention absorbed on a computer screen. Bella looked round his office. Not much had changed since her last appointment. A monk could have lived here, or an anchorite. No photographs on the desk. No calendar on the wall. How she used to long to rest her eyes on a picture of the lake district, a copy of a Monet print... even a nude would have been distracting.

Nothing but the glare of a neon light shining down between them.

'So how have you been? Any problems? Need another prescription?'

'Fine so far,' she said, ' giving his back her Sunday school smile.

'Three months on ... urine's clear as far as I can see ... bloods okay. I don't think we'll be needing to see you for a while.'

Clicks from the mouse, his fingers flicking up the whole of her medical history up and down the monitor.

And stopping.

'I see you've had some bouts of depression in the past.'

Squinting at the screen, his voice slowing down to catch up with the clinical notes.

'A post natal episode after the birth of your second child, quite a bad one it says here. Valium prescribed in '83, anti-depressants a year ago...'

'My mother had just died.'

'You responded well to the Prozac. Want it again to get you through this time?'

'No I don't think so.'

'Can you tell me why not?'

Still looking at his notes. Not so much a glance in her direction.

'Because I'd rather feel something now, even if its painful, if you don't mind. Rather than being wrapped up in cotton wool and feeling like a zombie.'

And now she had his attention. His forehead rutting into a deep frown.

'Go on.'

And finding her voice at last.

'I just think I've been pathologised enough by you medics, with the best intentions. Don't get me wrong Mr Clark. I've had it all! Too much black bile? Not enough serotonin? Hormones gone haywire? Plus a couple of years in therapy excavating my rackety childhood … forgive me if I have a hand in diagnosing myself for once and let me say that perhaps I may have suffered from a surfeit of sadness at certain times of my life. It may not be listed in your directory of mental illness but it feels very real to me.'

The computer screen now switched off.

'Well then, let's see how the scar is healing, shall we?'

The moment she had been dreading. Her whole body shaking as she pulled off her top, undid her brassiere, catching the jelly mould in the right cup before it fell to the ground.

'I don't want to boast, but I think I've done a good job with this one. We might even get round to some reconstruction work on the breast in the fullness of time. Give it eighteen months and we'll see. What does your husband think?'

Swallowing hard through the lie.

'I think he'd be all for it.'

'Good show!'

Then dressing quickly, out of the clinic, into the corridor, anxious to be rid of the antiseptic whiff of destiny that had been around her all day.

FOUR

PICASSO

Driving home, slowly, savouring the remains of the dull autumn day, Bella can feel the darkness come down and gather her up.

A long evening by herself lay ahead.

A real gloaming!

And she begins to sing the first verse of the old Harry Lauder song that Grandfer had taught her as a child. The words came back as fresh as those late Saturday afternoons when they would sing together in his garden.

> *'Roamin' in the gloamin' by the bonnie banks of Clyde*
> *Roamin' in the gloamin' wi' a lassie by my side*
> *When the sun has gone to rest, that's the time I love the best*
> *Oh it's lovely roamin' in the glohohohomin'…*

She extends the last word up and down the scale as old Tam had done. Then she starts to giggle. Today, the day she had been dreading, had not as been as bad as she had expected.

'You would have been proud of me Grandfer. I stood up for myself like you always told me I should. And my wee girl Iona is getting married!'

She wonders what Don would say when he got the news. The family tom-tom of communications was bound to spread to Sleaford somehow or other. And what would the 'brisk-and-bracing' think when he told her that his beloved daughter had chosen a partner of the same sex to spend her life with? Oh to be a fly on the wall when that happened! This thought quite cheered her up.

She must write to her son Tom soon. He and Iona had always been close as children. Sensitive siblings the pair of them. So very different from their sister.

She begins to look forward to the evening ahead. Now there was no one there to account for her actions. The kitchen was almost finished. The lads had done a good job in installing that second hand range. Her thoughts ramble on... she'd polish up the stove when she had the energy. Buy some of that blacking stuff they'd used in the past. A bit of elbow grease and it would look lovely! Maybe she would make some soup with the left-over vegetables.

She tells herself that she is not lonely. She is in fact enjoying solitude.

And parks her car carefully outside number 36. Then taking heed of Iona's parting words, she checks that she has not left anything valuable inside.

'This is the city. You can't be too careful, mother.'

Stepping back, she presses the tab that locked all four doors at once. The 'clunk' gives out a reassuring sound. Now she fingers the fob for her house keys. Turning to the gate...

Then almost bumps into them on the pavement. Five, or was it six boys in a bunch padding quietly up the street in a tightly packed group. A shapeless shroud heading towards her in the failing light: blue jeans, loose tops, hoods over their heads. She thought she recognised one of them by his luminous trainers. Darren, or was it Dean? Sent to her for counselling after a shoplifting spree on St. Anne's Well Road. A nice boy, she recalls, for all that mischief he got up to.

Bella hesitates to let them pass in front of her. The lights in Darren's heels go out. She opens her mouth for a friendly greeting to emerge. But her words are swallowed up in that first gulp of fear. Now she feels the downy tufts of the new growth in her hair rise and tremble.

Slowly they begin to gather round her car.

'Nice motor,' says one.

'A bit girly,' another replies, his voice cracking from soprano to base, 'for Grandma here. I wouldn't let my Nan have a car like that.'

'We know what girlies are good for!'

Communal sounds of sniggering and snorts.

'Let's give it a face lift!' The smallest one joins in.

'Yeah.'

'Yeah!'

'YEH!'

The little one takes out a penknife from the pocket of his jeans. A Swiss Army model, she remembers later. Tom had been given one as a present when he joined the cubs. Her son had used it for whittling sticks and cutting ropes to make a ladder for the tree house.

This cub had other ideas. He pulls out one of the blades with a black and broken thumb nail. A long thin piece of metal with a serrated tip at the end. He feels its sharpness with his left thumb and gives out a 'WOW' of appreciation whilst moving slowly towards her, his heels flashing on and off. The others follow, forming a semi circle round his pint-sized frame.

Then he turns to her car. Her brand new two-toned mini with its alloy wheels, bought six weeks ago as a symbol of her independence.

'Great model, madam. Retro, but classy, like yourself,' the salesman had said, clinching an easy deal.

The boy begins running the blade along its body, testing its strength. He looks back at her every now and again, calculating the effect he was having on his audience. Then casually, and with a nonchalance that seemed so well practised, he bends down and starts to work.

She watches him as he uses the knife like a paintbrush. A young Picasso, swiftly etching silvery whorls on the nearside doors. The pattern stands out in pale relief against the dark blue of the trim. He moves to the back of the car and signals to the others to come and surround her.

Bella sees them closing in. She can feel the heat off their bodies coming through their cheap, thin clothing. She watches their breaths rise into the air. Long, thin trails of life vaporising above her head. She wills herself to stay still. One hand fastens round her handbag; the other grasping her keys. She feels the metal dig into her palms, braking the surface of the skin and coming to rest on the bones beneath. And doesn't see the tiny droplets of blood fall onto the pavement in the fading light.

For all the while her eyes are on him.

Hunkering… up and down, forwards and back. He begins to sketch undulating waves along the boot of her car. When he finishes the first line, he goes back to the beginning and starts another surfing motion. If his face could wholly be seen at this task, she imagines a brow in furrow and a tongue working round his lips in an effort of studious concentration.

When he rises from the eddying tide, he walks down besides the roadside panels to the front of the vehicle, the lights from his heels flashing a festive wink.

Then she sees him look up at her. Under his hood, she feels his stare.

He takes one step back.

'Pleea…' she begins.

Now he is standing still. He takes his time putting the long blade back into its furrowed groove.

'Wicked!'

And he is holding the knife up to her, his body stretched out to his toes.

Then back to his task.

She sees him take out a stubbier blade and raising his fist again he begins to gouge out chunks of metal from the bonnet of the car in short tourettic stabs.

The boys beside her start to titter. One of them belches loudly in her face and the whiff of stale cigarettes and rancid beer catch her high up in the throat.

'Nice one!'

'Cool!'

'Finish her off!'

'Fucking finish her off!'

'Fucking finish off the cunt!'

'CUNT!'

'Does Grandma have a cunt?'

He stops what he is doing, flicking the knife shut and putting it back into his pocket, pushing it out into a bulge and pointing it towards her.

'Maybe Grandma would like to show us her cunt.'

'Pppleaseee!'

'Oh Grandma does wants to show us her cunt,' he sniggers, 'but only if she says "please" again. Say "pretty please" cunt!'

Bella's protesting mewls rise high in the cave of her mouth, filling her sinuses with their pain.

'Grandma has lost her tongue as well as her cunt,' he sings in a high voice, sticking out his tongue and flicking it from side to side.'

Her mouth opens and to her surprise she hears herself speak .

'How old are you? Nine? Ten?'

At the sound of her voice he comes nearer, his hand now raised in action. She blinks, ready for the blow, but now she sees a small boy; a child at the back of the class straining his arm to answer a question in order to please her. Her trembling knee takes a step forward but now he has thrown his head back. She hears a soft guttural sound coming from deep in his throat. His lips forming a perfect rosebud.

A freeze frame of stillness before he pitches himself forward.

His mouth opens and he throws himself at her.

Bella feels the warm spittle on her face, landing on her blinking eyelids, running down her cheeks; a dribble passing her mouth then onto her neck: soft globules of mucous hardening to wax on the cold night air.

He is smiling, dimples playing at the corners of his mouth.

Before raising his questioning hand again, this time in a high five of triumph.

She is aware of the Babel of noises around her.

Snorts and farts, the giggling obscenities...

Then he turns away. The others follow. They form a ragged line, lolloping in that ungainly way as young males are prone to do as they strive to master the unpredictable spurts of growth that erupt and confound a wayward adolescence.

And they were gone. Padding down the pavement, darkness swallowing up their shapeless silhouettes. She smells their musk and sees pinpoints of light blinking morse-like signals into the heels of the night.

She can't stop the violent tremors that run through her body as she gets through the door. And something else churning at the base of her belly. Letting out a cry, she feels her bowels give way.

Under the shower, his spit melts back to moisture.

Bella puts out her tongue and tastes him, fancying that the droplet of a tear had turned to a pebble. She swallows the stone and then it comes to her with the pain throbbing in her left hand. She worked with young boys like Picasso. She earned her living by listening to the stories that he and his like told her, giving them her compassion and her trust.

And this is what they do when they leave me! How the hell am I going to feel when I walk into the Children's Centre again and **he** may be there to greet me? Ready to regale me with his latest adventure.

Closing her eyes she sees him again. He comes up to her: closer, close! Bella can feel him exult in his power.

It couldn't have been Darren, couldn't it?

'OH DON!'

All plans of soup abandoned. She pours herself a large brandy. Perhaps the distraction of some Saturday night television could calm her. Some escapist nonsense. A dance programme where a rugby player learns the tango with a beautiful woman in a spangled costume… the harmless prattle of the judges' comments to make her laugh.

But when she switches on the box, it was a 'maker-over' show. Cheap and cruel. A woman of forty or so stood in the middle of a busy shopping mall as if she was in the stocks. Passers by were asked to guess how old they thought she might be. Each one gave out a number well beyond her chronological age. Then a crisp young woman with a clipboard and a Swedish accent took her off for cosmetic surgery. Shots of skin being lifted right off her face then stitched tightly behind her ears. When the victim came to, her smile seemed to be held in a permanent rictus of submission. Now Gaynor, in another guise, appeared and dressed her body top to toe in the latest skimpy fashions. "Mutton got up as lamb", Ailsa would have said.

And she would have been right. One of these hairdressers Bella hated, with stuck on nails and a fake tan, held up hanks of hair, then cropped and sliced it with disdain.

Snip, cut, scar, transform.

When the woman stood in the stocks again to repeat the humiliation, she was told by the same passers-by, or different ones selected for effect, that she looked her age, or thereabouts.

Why? What was all that for?

Bella feels the familiar blanket of hopelessness tuck itself around her. If she stayed there long enough it would have her in its grip. She gets up, shaking the feeling off with an exaggerated fervour. Should she ring Iona and tell her about the car? What about the police?

No, not now, tomorrow is another day.

Finding Elvis curled up and warm beneath the kitchen range, she climbs the stairs with him tucked under her arm. She had recently discovered the works of D.H. Lawrence and had marvelled at some of the early passages in 'The Rainbow'. Moving near to the old Lace Market led her back to 'Sons and Lovers.' She gets into bed and and tries to settle in to the novel, willing herself to walk down the same lanes as the young Paul Morrell had done before. And then stepping into the factory where he worked, up to the office where Clara would be waiting. When she closes her eyes Bella forces herself to imagine the steady thrum of bobbins on the loom.

But she can't concentrate tonight. Other thoughts intrude. She hears the distant 'ting' of trams and rises to close the window, averting her eyes to avoid looking at her car.

Getting back into bed she can't help straining her ears for the lifting of her latch at the gate. Would she ever feel safe again? When she picks up the book, heart pounding, palms clammy, her eyes drifting to the window, Lawrence's prose begins to fall off the page in yawning, pretentious chunks.

FIVE

GRANDFER

It was the darkness that brought comfort these days. An escape from the nightmare of daily living.

So when Grandfer beckoned to her in her thoughts tonight, she was happy to follow him, skipping up the slopes of her past to the comfort of his world.

Every week Bella longed for the gift of Saturday. Early in the morning she would rise and dress, tiptoeing past her parents bedroom where the sound of her father's snores gave out the signal that he had been drinking the night before. Bella couldn't bear looking at her mother's bruised face over breakfast, so it became her pattern to escape. Down the stairs and out of the house, so careful in closing the front door, her small fingers easing the latch to cause little noise. And she was away. Along the road to the bus stop with the threepenny bit held in her hankie all week long; the bus taking her to the bottom of Burnbrae where she knew he would be waiting.

'My how you've grown, my wee pet lamb! Do a twirl and let me look at you.'

The old man bent down for a kiss and she took in the smell of his Harris Tweed jacket and the tobacco breath of his pipe. Then clasping his strong right hand they would walk past the row of sandstone cottages hunkering into the steep brae. With every step away from her mother and father, Bella's bidden tongue would loosen. Soon she was prattling on about her adventures during the week. 'Blether time,' he called it. He stooped to listen to her, allowing her stories to be punctuated with an 'aye', or a 'fancy that', or his favourite 'mercy on us!'- reserved for a special piece of news. At his gate, she ran ahead to the house, throwing off her gaberdine coat in the dark hallway. Then into the kitchen where a ginger biscuit and a glass of Iron Bru would be waiting.

Now in her dream, she could feel the tiny hairs in her nostrils stand up to attention in protest against the fumes of the paraffin stove in the centre of that room. Steam rose up from the weekly wash hung on the clothes horse around it. Bella counted the milky grey long-johns, the row of boiled handkerchiefs folded neatly in half and the woollen socks with darns on the heels.

Moses, Grandfer's ancient cat scurried away, no doubt fearing being dressed up again in dollies clothes and being taken for a walk in the wheelbarrow, up and down the path of that carefully tended garden.

In her sleep, Bella feels herself relax. She knows that this will be a day of blissful routine. She was just content to follow the old man around. 'My little shadow' he called her and taught her the song that Judy Garland and Fred Astaire had sung in, oh what was that musical called?

'Easter Parade'?

'Meet me in St Louis?'

Grandfer couldn't move his left arm properly, so her nimble little fingers were useful; trailing behind him with the seed potatoes, dropping them into the grooves in the soil he had made with his good hand.

He kept all the fiddly bits for her: tying back the raspberry canes with the green ball of string that he kept in his jacket pocket, picking out seedlings in the greenhouse; the ones she left had magic in them he said. They would grow big and strong. On rainy days inside the house she became adept at threading needles so he could sew on buttons to the collarless shirts he wore underneath the rough wool of his jacket.

She listens in the night and his voice comes back to her as clear as day.

'Mercy on us, if you hadn't come by this weekend, my wee lassie, I don't know how I would have managed.'

And she would primp with the pleasure of his praise.

'What happened to your arm Grandfer?'

'Oh that was an accident, pet lamb, in the shipyards at Clydebank. A long time ago. A girder fell on my arm and crushed it and that brought the end to my welding days. I gave my soul to John Brown lassie. He was the maister and we we were the slaves. But you mind this, it was always the slaves who built the most beautiful things in the world.'

'But I don't want to be a slave, Grandfer.'

'Then I'll see to it that you don't become one, my wee lass.'

Once he took her to the shipyard where he had worked. A big boat was being launched on the Clyde. She climbed onto his shoulders for a better view when the vessel was loosened from its chains and floated off down the river.

'I name this ship...' the lady in the pink hat and the English accent had said.

She noticed that on that day the men would either embrace

or shun the old man when he walked beside them, holding her by his side with his strong right hand.

'Is that wee bairn one of your own, Tam?'

'She's George's wee lass.'

'My but she's bonny. She has the look of her, doesn't she?'

'Aye,' he rejoined quickly, glancing down at her with an expression of pride and something else unknown to her at the time, a look she would later identify as a high blush of shame.

Bella stirs in her sleep. She hears the chimes of a clock from a church somewhere in the city. It penetrates into her dream. At five o'clock in Grandfer's time it was always: 'stop what yer doing and haud yer wheesht.'

And they'd go inside, leaving their muddy boots in the kitchen. The old wireless, kept up on the mantelpiece of the tiny living room would be switched on for a few minutes, to heat the valves up he said.

Feet up, a pipe lit and the sonorous voice of someone called Raymond Glendenning taking centre stage with the football results.

Bella loved to hear rhythm of his cadence rise and fall as he went through the weekly litany:

Queen of the South 2 Forfar Athletic 1
Cowdenbeath 3 Partick Thistle nil
Hamilton Academicals (she thrilled to that name,
tripping round her mouth as if it were a tongue teaser)
Hamilton Academicals 1 Heart of Midlothian 4
Rangers 2 Celtic nil

A big cheer if Rangers won, but he never got angry, like her father did if his favourite team was beaten.

'It's only a game, lassie. Only a game.'

Then it was time to get out the special tablecloth for

their tea; the one that was beautifully embroidered with little flowers round the borders.

'Who sprinkled these daisies on here, Grandfer?'

'Oh that would be a fairy I used to know. She had beautiful fingers… just like you in so many ways.'

And tonight Bella can feel his sadness come down to her through the years as he spluttered into his handkerchief and she hears him cry.

~

He presses the digits of the unfamiliar code, mouthing each number as his fingers touched the keys.

A long ringing tone.

'Hello, Bella, is that you?'

'Don!'

Silence.

Clearing his throat he continues.

'Are you there?'

'Yes I'm here.'

'How are you?'

'Fine. And you?'

'Getting by. It's all a bit strange at the moment, but well, I guess.'

Another pause, then…

'I had a spot of bother with the car, Don.'

'Oh? It was brand new. Wasn't it? What happened?'

'Just some kids having their idea of fun. I might sell it when I get it fixed. I don't need a car living here.'

Don feels the beginnings of a tic take up a blinking motion at the corner of his left eye.

'You'll lose a lot of money in depreciation if you do.'

'It's my money!'

Here we go again. He mustn't let this conversation drift into the usual thrust and parry of accusation and rebuttal.

'I hear Iona is getting married?' he says, attempting a breezy tone.

'Yes she is.'

'I wonder what your mother would have said?'

'Stop it Don before you get that -'where did we go wrong?'- note in your voice. I'm actually very happy for them. Rosie is a lovely girl.'

'Mmmm…'

He is stuck for words. The right words. Words that would bounce the conversation into an easy sequence of to and fro.

'Anyway I am glad that you called in a way. Perhaps you can help me. I've been having all these dreams about the past lately. Such vivid dreams. Maybe the drugs I've taken after the radiotherapy. Last night I had an amazing one about my Grandfather Tam. You met him once Don. Don't you recall? I took you to see him before our wedding.'

'The old man in the Home that smelled of cabbages and pee?'

'That's right. But can you remember what he said when we were there? I woke up in the night and could see him as clear as clear when I was a child but that last meeting with all three of us together was mainly just a blank.'

'Gosh, that's a tall order Bella. Your mother said he was 'gaga' by then.'

'Maybe but I can just about picture him in a misty sort of way, all wrapped up in a tartan rug with those milky white eyes of his.'

'Cataracts,' he corrects her.

'I can't remember his voice.'

'It was quite rasping wasn't it?'

Don frowns in recollection. He stands stock still, straining to retrieve an ancient polarised shot shunted to the back of his memory bank. He and Bella in their old mini minor car taking a pilgrimage back to the land of her birth.

'He didn't call me by my name, did he? What did he call me Don?'

'Does it matter?'

'Yes it does. I bent down to him and sang the verse of an old song we used to sing together. He joined in didn't he? At least he tried to. And then he said something.'

'Hang on. It's a long time ago but I seem recall that he called you Jean or Jeannie, didn't he?'

'That's right Don. Well done! It's beginning to get a bit less foggy now. And then didn't he say: "Have you brought my Jeannie home," to you. It's coming back.'

'I remember asking you who this mysterious Jeannie could be.'

'I know but it doesn't matter now. I just wanted to hold that last memory of him in my mind, that's all. It felt important somehow.'

Don feels himself soften. The tremor in his eye reducing to the occasional blink.

'He died shortly after we saw him, didn't he?'

'Yes he did. It was one of the biggest regrets of my life that I hardly saw him when we moved to England.'

'You were fond of that old man, weren't you Bella?'

'I loved him. And I think if I am really honest with myself, he was the only man who loved me for who I really was.'

Don felt the tic taking up again. He needed to end this call.

'Well I'm just checking that you are alright. Evie just seemed a bit concerned when I spoke to her. Money coming through okay?'

'Yes, thank you.'

He hears her hesitate before changing to another tack.

'You haven't mentioned anything about getting a divorce Don.'

'Divorce?'

'Don't let me spell it out like that corny song. Divorce. It's what usually happens when couples separate.'

'But I don't want a divorce.'

'But you wanted to leave me. Don't you want to marry Brenda?'

The thought unsettles him. He feels his eyelid behave like a camera shutter:on: off: on…

'I'm quite happy the way things are.'

Silence at the end of the phone, burdened by the weight of things not said.

'Unless of course you have met someone else.'

'No. Not yet.'

And hearing the clipped 't' at the end of 'yet' he wonders what will come next.

'But I have taken my wedding ring off.'

'Oh!'

'You?'

'Mine seems a permanent fixture… won't shift… arthritis I expect.'

He knows this sounds feeble.

'You could always have it cut off.'

'Maybe. But I don't want to do it right away.'

'Why not?'

He thinks carefully before replying.

'A sense of history perhaps. We've been married for a long time.'

'That's present tense. Aren't we past tense? Past perfect perhaps?'

'You can't just cut off thirty eight years.'

'You did.'

He shrugs. Time to give up.

'Well if that's all Bella.'

'It is. Thank you for calling and helping me with my memories. I feel much better now with some of the blanks filled in. But there is absolutely no need to check up on me again Don. Don't listen to Evie.'

He thumps the phone down on its cradle.

'Damn the woman! Damn and blast!'

'Who was that?'

Brenda on routine eavesdropping patrol stands at the door.

'Just Bella. Family matters. You know how it is?...'

'No Donald I don't.'

'I think I'll take the dogs out.'

'But it's pouring with rain.'

'I know, but they will enjoy their constitutional.'

'You'd better wrap up then.'

Outside he turns towards a glowering sky. He can feel the east wind pierce his skin through the waterproof jacket and the layers of woollen fleece underneath. He braces himself against its force, concentrating on one step at a time.

'A good blast,' she would have said, her fingers holding him lightly through his arm. 'Great for blowing the cobwebs away.'

Bella!

He puts his left hand into the pocket of his trousers and feels the little pinkie finger touch its neighbour. The gold band was still there. It wouldn't come off that easily.

Then a snapshot from his own collection of memories enters his head; his mother bending over his father's hand in hospital. The nurse had just told them that he had died. Annie asks for a bar of soap so she can take off Jack's ring. It had embedded itself over many years into a little crater of flesh round the joint. No amount of soap would shift it, so his father was buried with that symbol of commitment held fast to him.

The recollection touches Don. Tears begin to spill from the corners of his eyes. They sting his face as the wind whips round him.

She had taken her ring off. She wanted a divorce.

It's what couples do when they separate.

She was right. It made logical sense.

It didn't make any sense at all.

Reason told him that he now had a life he had craved for. A life Jack and Annie would have blessed for him. Each day plotted with no ambushes to catch him unawares. A routine he could implicitly trust. Certain words had begun to wrap themselves around him. Words like :'predictable', 'regular', 'comfortable.' Words that would bring with them a sense of peace. A sense of contentment going into the next phase of his life.

Until that ruddy phone call!

Don felt hot. Loosening his scarf around his neck, he shouts for the dogs.

'Monty! Rommel!'

Two black labradors appear. They shake themselves with the pleasure of his recognition.

'Good boys!'

And pats them ferociously. This action pleases all three. He starts to feel a little better. At the bungalow she would have a hot toddy waiting:his favourite single malt, sweetened with lemon and brown sugar. He turns and the dogs run homeward in front of him. Above his head in that great expanse of sky, he hears the 'thwack-flap' of the wings of two swans on their way to the fens. He stands for a moment till their sounds are absorbed in the wind.

'They mate for life!' he shouts to the dogs. 'Poor sods!'

SIX

LILY'S STORY

THE JOTTER.

October 19th 1920.

Lily has been taken away. Her howling in the night could not be curbed by the vigorous ministrations of Sister Jewell. I saw two heavy henchmen hold Lily down on her bed. They wrapped her in binding cloths and then lifted her up. I heard her protests as she was carried away along the corridors to the locked Nightingale ward at the end of this wing. How long she will remain there I cannot tell. I will not be permitted to visit her and can only hope that Mistress Niven can bring me news via her contacts in the laundry.

Poor Lily. She has had a sad life. Thankfully she knows nothing of my history and I wish to keep it so. If she ever heard of my misdeeds, I very much doubt if she would offer her hand in friendship. And her friendship is precious to me in this place.

She is but three and thirty, not much older than myself, but the ravages of time and despair are written heavily on her. Lily was brought up in the Gorbals district of Glasgow, a place of vile repute. Her mother died of tuberculosis and Lily was left as a young girl to look after her three brothers and two sisters, whilst her feckless father drank away what little money he earned. If ever the Temperance movement needed a convert, it was Jimmy Cochrane. She took in the washing of others to earn a few pennies but they were often hungry.

Eventually the older ones were taken away by the Nuns and put out to work.

Lily saw little of them but she struggled to keep her two youngest sisters away from the beggars and thieves that lived all around them.

She was only thirteen when a man molested her and she bore him a child. She called the baby Robert after her favourite brother but he too was taken from her. It is often Robert's name that she cries out for in the night.

When she later went with an older man, she miscarried several of his babies and one died shortly after he was born. This is what finally unhinged Lily.

She pined for her babies and took to minding others, keeping them for longer and longer periods of time. One day she wheeled away a pram from the Trongate and hid the baby boy who was inside it under the railway cuttings at the back of St. Enoch's station. She kept him there for three days wrapped in her shawl and fed him with her own breast milk meant for the infant she had so recently buried.

'My he was bonny Jean, just like my wee Robbie!'

A porter discovered them on his way home and took her to the polis.

Lily spent time like me in Duke Street prison, but her outbursts there were ungovernable and so she has been here for nigh on twelve years now.

Most of the time she bears her lot with good humour. She is a good worker and serves the needs of the kitchen and the laundry well. She also has a kindness and shows patience to the simple souls at the end of the ward.

Those are the women who sit and dribble and recognise no one. Lily brings them their food, talking away to them whilst they masticate the poor fare round their toothless mouths. They burble on at her but give Lily no thanks.

Occasionally one of her sisters will bring in her own little girl called Flora to see her aunt. When Lily returns to the ward after one of these visits she is radiant with happiness. I have taken to sewing Flora some dolly's clothes from the scraps of material left over from my work.

I give them to Lily and she presents them proudly to her niece. These little acts of thoughtfulness earn me much in Lily's esteem. She will bring me morsels of food from the kitchen and tempt me to savour some pleasure in the act of eating.

Mostly though I value her as a bulwark against the cruelty of others.

Lily has rightly earned their respect and induced their pity. I remain to most a mystery. I refuse to speak in the Scots dialect as it mocks my fine education.

I am also careful to give no confidences away. But I have acquired a position of merit attending to the daily sewing needs of Housekeeper Niven, a much cherished

*role amongst the inhabitants of the Asylum, so Lily
protects me from their spittle and their spite.*

*I am feeling altogether more vulnerable now she is locked
away and pray that her latest bout of what they call
hysteria will not last long. Mostly she stays away for four or
five days and then returns to me much drugged and dazed.*

*Gradually her good humour returns. I read to her in
the evenings and she fills me in with the gossip and so we
bide our time together in good spirits.*

*'Aw my, we twa are a fair pair, Jeannie; we'll mind
oorsels and let the others go hang!'*

'Lily, dear Lily, come back to me soon!'

~

LITTLE CEREMONIES AND
SMALL INDIGNITIES

November 15th

*Today Dr Scobie rose from his bed and planted a weeping
birch tree in the east garden. It was such a blustery
November day and he did well to withstand the rough
winds and rain. Sister Hermione Jewell stood by his side,
looking for all the world like a battling Boadicea. I saw
her steady the old man as he leant on his spade. This is
the only act of kindness that I have seen her perform. Lily,
who has mercifully been returned to me after her period of
solitary confinement, noted this as well when we compared
our version of events before returning to the Ward.*

The slender tree stands in a small rise, opposite a sturdy oak which has graced the outside of this building for many a year. On clement days I walk there when allowed, round the rose garden to the south of the grounds. Here I can view the distant city with its grey spires and see the river Clyde take a broad meander to the sea. It reminds me that there is a world outside and I am no longer part of it.

After the tree planting, a few of us that had helped in the kitchen were asked to sup tea and eat scones albeit some way apart from the guests who were especially invited for the occasion. I was glad to see that none of those from the locked wards were present. Their manacled bodies would not have been a fitting sight for all those honoured dignitaries to behold. Dr Scobie's speech was uplifting, extolling the audience to be compassionate to all God's creatures. Chaplain Sewell was less charitable, reminding all of the pervasive ways of the Devil and the need for it to be locked away from Goodness. I saw the good doctor frown at these words but they got a hearty applause from the harridan Jewell.

There is to be a programme of events to be held here and open to the public.

The sales of work will continue with emphasis on arts and crafts. Seemingly a new branch of medical science is to be offered to us, called Occupational Health. I shall bide my time to see what this entails. Dances are to be held every two months with musicians that play in the Barrowland Halls. The Glasgow Abstainers Union will open their sixty fourth concert here with a recital and Mr Anderson is to repeat his Magic Lantern Show at Christmas. Back due to popular demand so they say.

Members of the public were invited to use the boating lake as well as the croquet lawns and tennis courts in summer months, by kind invitation from the Board of Trustees. These same members of the public in attendance today seemed a little uneasy when this invitation was given.

I noted that they were all smiles at Dr Scobie and his entourage but few paid any attention to us beyond the odd furtive glance in our direction from time to time.

It was, however, a polite occasion. When Elsie Macpherson came to lead us back to work, I took the liberty to compliment Mrs Creel from the kitchen on her excellent baking skills. If only, I said to her, we could sample her delicious fare more often! Our daily diet of porridge for breakfast, mutton broth for dinner and bread and butter before bed, is monotonous to say the least.

Still food is not important to me.

When she did her final round of inspection at the end of the day, Sister Jewell was quick to criticise me for stepping beyond the bounds of social etiquette by speaking to a member of staff without permission.

I bear this reprimand in silence. Humility and humiliation are close cousins after all.

SEVEN

DON

Dr Donald Cavendish surveys his wardrobe with a sense of mounting alarm. Normally his everyday wear would involve few choices: his favourite green pair of corduroy trousers teamed up with a clean and pressed check shirt, and after a peek at the weather outside, the selection of a wool or a cotton sweater. But today was different. Today he had been invited back to the university for a graduation ceremony. One of his PhD students was collecting his award, so today he would have to wear a suit and a tie.

He had over the years amassed a collection of neckwear, for unlike his wife, Don rarely threw anything away. In the rack beside the neatly folded socks, he picks out the fading blue and azure stripes of his old grammar school tie, bought in the summer of 1958 by his proud mother Annie, straight after getting the news that he passed the eleven plus exam. The old tie hung modestly next to a collection of 'kippers' that Bella had selected for him. These were the 'bully boys' of the tie world, loud in their vulgarity and worn to please at parties in the seventies; never since then. His fingers pass over paisley patterns for work, silks kept for weddings, an old bandanna last sported by Tom when he dressed up as a pirate. At the end of the rack he alights on a black strip, his funeral tie.

Thoughts send him back to his mother again. He see her look of unspoken pride as she purchased his uniform for school, selecting a blazer several sizes too big for him.

'He's a growing lad, my son!'

Tucked underneath the black tie was a narrow knitted band made from a cotton weave. Don feels his face break into a grin as he catches another lingering scent from the past.

~

On the dance floor, a pint of beer in his hand and he is watching a young woman with auburn hair sway to the beat of a rock 'n' roll band. He dare not blink in case she disappears. He sees that several young men, much bolder than he could ever be, make their advances towards her. To all of them she gives a smile. To a few she takes up the offer of a dance. But after every number he notices the shake of her head as she turns away from any on- going connection with a partner.

She's at the bar now, laughing with some female friends as she sips a Babycham. He decides to take his chance.

'You'll want a cherry in that. I'll fetch you one.'

She turns to him. He catches an expression of surprise in those grey flecked eyes.

When he returns to her, she takes the toothpick from his hand and places the small red globe in amongst the bubbles.

'It's the same colour as your tie,' she says.

~

Don takes out the tie and places it round his neck. It responds to his touch and falls into an easy knot. Glancing at the narrow mirror at the back of the door, he looks for the young man who had once worn it. He is just about recognisable: the same steady gaze, now through bi-focal lenses, that stubborn cows-lick in his thinning hair that would never lie still, the same lop-sided smile that looked on joy and disappointment in much the same way. Yes he was still there, he told himself.

Still smiling, he glances down and feels the warm muzzle of a dog at his ankles.

Just time to check his e-mails before he goes.

Evie's latest is on the screen.

Dad just thought I'd let you know that I'm a bit concerned about Mum. Iona and Rosie are worried about her and I thought I should give you her new address. Don't tell her it was me who gave it to you. PLEASE!

We are all a bit scared about what she might do next.

You know her better than most what she's like, though I don't suppose you could stop her now. Josh sends his love.

He had a good birthday last week and is into things like. Thomas the Tank Engine so the toy microscope you sent him didn't quite hit the spot. He's only two Dad after all.

Hope you and Brenda are well,

Evie x

Don clicks off the message with the mouse then reaches for a pencil in one of the drawers in his desk- that great lump of mahogany and brass that Bella had 'liberated' from the dump.

It looked out of place now in this small, neat room and he had argued with Brenda about bringing it here. She wouldn't give it houseroom she had huffed. It wouldn't go with all that flat-packed Swedish stuff she had purchased before the move. But on that occasion he had stood his ground. Finding a pen and post-it he jots down Bella's new address and sticks it on the screen. He would transfer it to his address book when he returned.

His glance now falls on a collection of photographs on top of the desk. One of them catches his attention. It was probably the last one taken together as a family at Evie's wedding. Don takes down his glasses from the top of his thinning hair for a proper look. He sees Tom and himself, freshly scrubbed up in their morning suits, flanking the Cavendish line-up. The older man has a slight stoop to him; the younger is upright and smiling. The camera has caught Tom's ponytail in a flick of rebellion. Iona stands beside her father. They were closer then. Much closer. His first born child, now way into her thirties, holds her hands to attention down by her sides. Don can't help thinking she looked a bit out of place with her ample figure trussed up in that cranberry coloured outfit that Evie had chosen for her. Next comes the bride and groom, posing with all the confidence of a celebrity couple in a magazine. And there is his mother-in-law. Ailsa centre stage holding a large bouquet of flowers.

'No show without Punch!' Don murmurs.

A little apart from the group is Bella, arm in arm with Tom. Don can't see her face under that hat but he notices the glint of amber as her hair falls onto her shoulders.

Had he lost sight of her even then?

The scientist in him knows with certainty that he could have pinpointed that particular gene that gave Bella those stunning blue-grey eyes that were hidden under the brim of that particular bit of frippery that Julia had lent her for the day. But he is now aware with equal conviction that much of his wife, or was it ex wife would always be an enigma to him.

His reverie is interrupted by the appearance of Brenda at the door.

'I've had your suit cleaned and the waist band let out a couple of inches Donald. You'll want to look the part today,' she was saying, 'and I thought this might be appropriate for the occasion. It's one of Eric's but hardly worn.'

She holds out a tie to him, olive green with a pattern of purple faintly embossed on its surface; one of the Major's regimental ties, no doubt.

'That's very thoughtful of you. But I've already got one on.'

'What time will you be coming home?' she continues, 'only I thought if you were going into town you could perhaps pick up some dog food in one of those warehouse places on your way back. Much cheaper than round here.'

'Okay. I'll try and remember,' he says, 'but I'm meeting up with Hugo afterwards. We've arranged to have lunch in the pub.'

'Hugo?'

Don tries to ignore the tone, which often strays from curiosity to interrogation when people from his past are mentioned.

'Hugo Lindsey. Julia's partner. We used to go to the races at Southwell every now and again when the girls went shopping.'

'One of Bella's bohemian friends, I suppose?'

'You could say that.' Don forces his smile into lopsided action. 'I'll give you a call when I'm on my way back.'

~

He parks his car in the area marked 'Visitors only.' Then looking across the asphalt he picks out his old parking space now occupied by one of those large people-carrying vehicles. Catching sight of the name beside it, he recognises the name of its owner: Dr Colin Spencer. Colin? Could this be the same Colin, his protege, fresh down from Cambridge with a first class degree? Tongue-tied Colin who would blush to the top of his ears every time a woman came into the laboratory? Colin was evidently a man of substance now, with a parking bay dedicated to him.

'My word!' Don lets out in surprise, 'Colin's a family man.'

He reads the bumper sticker at the back of the car: 'Princess on Board,' it proclaimed.

Times had definitely changed.

He scans the scene around him searching for more evidence of change. Beside the post graduate block a group of 'hard hats' were consulting plans whilst a building crane began its ascent into the air. Something was up. Ahead of him he sees the buildings that he knew so well, the steel and chrome of Science City built in the nineteen sixties when the phrase 'the white heat of technology' was newly minted. The buildings were wearing well. However on close inspection he notes the brown paintwork round the doors beginning to chip and peel. The windows of the Chemistry building had a grimy look to them and a crack in one of the panes refracted a pale beam of winter sunlight which fell onto the concrete walkway.

A gathering of students huddled on the steps of 'Microbiology' smoking cigarettes. Don notices that there were more women in the group than there had been in his day. Then he and his friends had made for the Psychology block in their break. 'Psychology', as his pal Dai Lewis was constantly saying, 'maybe the hope of a science, but there are girls there, boys, totty by the dozen!'

Don smiles in recollection. Good old Dai! Where was he now?

Walking down the path leading to the main campus, he recalls his first fumblings with psychology. Evenings spent with Hannah Pearson in her room while she prepared essays on operant conditioning and they listened to the music of Miles Davis. It was Hannah who helped him achieve a modest proficiency in navigating the fastenings of female underwear and he had a lot to thank her for.

He took in a gulp of delight from the cold air around him. The memory of cupping those breasts of Hannah's helping him find his way through the latest crowd of freshers en route to the canteen. In those days you had to make your sexual moves quickly, before the curfew bell sounded and all the male students were banished from Florence Boot Hall. 'Poor Florence, never to have a man inside her after eight o'clock! Don't know what she is missing,' Dai had mourned.

Why had he never contacted his old friend after they had graduated? And Hannah? Those lovely breasts!

He shook his head. Another image passes before him. It stops him in his tracks.

Bella opening her bandages when she came out of hospital; the cavity in her chest criss-crossed with scars.

Turning to the stone facade of the Portland Building, he sees a face that is familiar.

'My word Doug, you've gone up in the world!'

'Oh the whistle and flute you mean Doc? We all wear them now. The place has gone all corporate since your day. It's all about public-private partnerships now, selling the brand so I am told. We have motivational meetings at breakfast, would you believe? All that 'rah-rah' stuff that lasses do in American football games. Must be something to do with the new Boss – a woman. She's some big shot economist from a Business School. I just do as I'm told now. Keep my head down. Only six months to go before I collect my pension.'

'Very wise Doug,' Don agrees, giving the old caretaker of his Lab. a firm handshake.

'Anyhow, you've scrubbed up nicely yourself Doc. Put a bit of weight on too, if I'm not mistaken. The missus must be looking after you well now you've been turned out to grass. How is she?

And the kids?'

'All fine,' Don replies quickly. 'I'm a grandfather now, a little boy and more on the way perhaps.'

'Can't beat it, can you? That's what it's all about. A good marriage and family life. Beats all the letters you have after your name.'

'Quite so.'

He allows Doug to usher him into the 'Guests' section of the main hall. Beside him sit an assembly of young middle-aged parents. It didn't seem that long ago that Annie and Jack looked down on their one and only son with a sense of bafflement at his Graduation Ceremony. His mother squeezed into the blue costume that she kept for best, his father trussed up in his one and only suit, looking as all working men do when they are out of their overalls and into the mufti of formal dress; awkward and out of place. And alongside them his young bride with a flush of good health on her cheeks. Inside her rounded belly lay Iona, curled up like a comma, just biding her time…

A flutter of applause. On to the stage came four men, elderly like himself, with balding heads and paunches, looking in their ermine cloaks and caps like extras in a Holbein painting at the court of King Henry the eighth. One, a Thomas More look-alike, he recognised as the Nobel prize winner Martin Hastings. Don had shared digs with Marty in his second year in a crumbling house off Lenton Boulevard. When they'd both graduated together, each with a first class degree, Marty had gone off to Cambridge for his doctorate to begin some pioneering work on the human genome project. Did Don want to join him there? He had been tempted. But Bella was working part time, they'd put down a deposit for their first house...

'Stick with what you've got lad,' Jack had said.

'The road not taken,' Bella said later.

He shrugs, and then catching the sight of his student Christos Kimitri, he gives a cheery wave of his hand.

More clapping, heralding the arrival of the Vice Chancellor Dr Charmian Temple. A slight figure in high heels walks onto the stage. Don can't tell her age from this distance but he knows by the way that she takes her ease amongst the men around her that she would never have been on one of those television makeover programmes to change her looks. She exuded, what was the word? Confidence. Confidence like an invisible aura around her, outlining every nip and tuck of that well tailored suit that she was wearing. Don knew that confidence was a quality that he never possessed himself. And if he didn't have it, it went without saying that he could never pass it on through his genes. Iona would have lost out as well.

Afterwards in the reception area, he drinks coffee and nibbles at the two shortbread biscuits offered to him. At the other end of the room canapés were being handed out to the invited glitterati in their gowns. Don lingers on the borderlands between celebrity and success, seeking out an eyebrow of recognition from his old flat mate. He sees Marty in deep conversation with some TV pundit. The other Hoods have gathered round Professor Charmian Temple; medieval bees round their honey-pot Queen.

He turns to the company of Christos and his colleagues, wondering how best to advise them. Some he knows would be scientific chancers, ready to hitch a ride to the big money in pharmaceutical companies. A few would jump ship and work in the City as Iona had done. Would any of them stick at their profession and see a Fellowship at the Welcome Trust as their ultimate reward for their endeavours? Christos had been offered a place at UCL where he could pursue his research into the genetic complexities of sickle cell disease. It would be nice to go back to Cyprus again and be with his family, he tells his tutor, but that would mean a tin-pot job in Larnica.

'And that's not where the action is, is it sir?'

Don nods his head in compliant agreement. He looks at his watch: twelve thirty. Time to leave, find Doug and get his coat, then join Hugo in the pub. He turns to go. The hand on his shoulder checks his progress. A female hand; the slender grip of Elspeth Fremantle holding him back.

'I thought it was you,' she says, in that clipped way of hers that makes him feel that he was being reprimanded. 'I would recognise that hovering stance anywhere as being my old friend and colleague Donald Cavendish. The look of a man not knowing quite where to put himself.'

Her voice softened: 'How are you Don?'

'Elspeth, once again, you've caught me out.'

She shakes her head. 'Not your scene, eh? Not mine either actually. I'd much rather be back in the Lab with my petri dishes than smoozing up to the little gods in here.'

'We back room boys and girls, more interested in the pursuit of knowledge than vainglory!'

He knows that this attempt at humour will fall flat but he could never resist teasing his old colleague.

He was right. It was lost on Elspeth, whose considerable genetic endowment did not include a sense of the ridiculous.

'For back room, read backbone, Don. That's where the real work is done. We are the ones who put our lights under a bushel, not on torches as these people do; modest pioneers as opposed to our more showy brethren. Anyhow, changing the subject, I've got myself on to this ethics committee on bio-genetic engineering and you are just the right chap to join me.'

Don makes a wry face.

'Aren't committees the places where those of us with the odd bushel to spare while away our time by wrangling with each other in perpetual obscurity?'

'Nonsense Don! You are a scientist with considerable expertise and experience. A man of principle, much needed now with all those carpetbaggers around here. And your knowledge of haematopoietic stem cells is what we need to contribute to the mix. I'll put in a good word for you, if you like.'

'Let me think about it Elspeth. I've moved house. It's not so easy now.'

'Of course,' she replies, detecting his reluctance and responding with her usual brand of kindly impatience. 'But I'll stay in touch nonetheless. By the way how is Bella? I think I saw her in town recently. She looked awfully thin. Is she okay?'

'I think so. It's complicated. We are not together now. The illness changed her a bit. She needed time on her own.'

'Oh! I see. Poor you!'

Back at the car park Don scribbles a note and sticks on to the windscreen of the people carrier: 'Congratulations Colin. Look after your princess while she'll let you.' Then loosening his tie, he takes his leave.

~

He finds Hugo in his favourite place, surrounded by the regulars at The Salutation Inn, and engaging in what he did best. Singing for his supper.

And succeeding by the looks of it, Don thinks, counting the pints that stretched beyond his elbow. He sees Hugo stand to greet him, his long body bending to hold out a hand of welcome.

'My dear fellow. Better late than never, eh? Though I have to say that these good people have kept me amused in your absence. What can I get you?'

He watches as Hugo indulges in his familiar dumb show, patting his pockets for the wallet they both knew would not be there.

'It's okay. I'll get them. Want a bite to eat?'

'Wouldn't say no to one of those delicious doorsteps of yours,' Hugo says, smiling at the landlady. 'Ham please with a hint of mustard spread, English mind, not that grainy French stuff for me.'

'Who's paying?'

Don sees the raised eyebrow of the landlady, and proffers a twenty pound note.

'And keep the change my dear. Don't say that my friends are not generous.'

'How do you do it?' Don lets out a 'whoo' of appreciation at Hugo's cheek as they manoeuvre their way to a table in the corner. 'As far as I know you've never done a proper day's job in your life, Hugo, and yet you want for nothing.'

'Do I detect a little of the green eyed monster in your line of questioning Professor Cavendish?'

'Leave out the Prof. But yes, maybe I am a little jealous.'

'Don't you know?'

'Tell me,' Don urges. He sees his friend give a wink to the young woman now serving behind the bar.

'Charm, dear boy. Charm always does the trick in my experience.'

'Well that's something I wasn't born with.'

'I don't know Don. You have that shy appeal that always goes down well with the ladies. You should play up to it more. Anyway I never fancied being a worker bee like my old man. He slaved away all his life, made a pile and then dropped dead in his forties, fortunately leaving most of all the honey to me so I wouldn't have to toil. Give me a drone's life any day. Besides Julia's got muck and like a good organic farmer, she believes in spreading it around. I get the odd spadeful every now and again.'

'But did you never want to make something of yourself?'

'Not really. Fame and fortune are fickle beasts to my way of thinking. So how about you? I was sorry to hear about the pair of you splitting up. She's a cracking girl Bella.'

'Thanks for rubbing it in. My fault probably. I've never been that good at understanding women. And as you know, Bella takes some understanding.'

'Have you ever tried? Seriously. Understanding women, that is. I've made it a hobby of mine to get on with the fillies. 'Keep them amused,' that's my motto. Julia often says: 'give me a man that can make me laugh… that can make me laugh in bed.' I always try to oblige.'

Hugo looks up; a still handsome man. Don observes the slight tremor in his right hand as he lifts his pint to a group of giggling women at the window. He also notices the fraying cuffs of Hugo's jacket. On his sleeves they would have seemed shabby but on his friend, well they just added to that raffish look that Hugo had cultivated over the years.

'I'll tell you something Don, there's a big difference between the sexes and it's not all between the thighs I can tell you. Look at those chaps by the bar and tell me what you see.'

Don stares at a collection of men: different ages, different sizes, different drinks. The young lads were drinking lager out of bottles. Don hated lager.

'What am I supposed to see?'

'They are all lined up, aren't they? That's what men do. They line up. They line up in bars. They line up in games and in a minute they'll all be lining up in the urinals. And do you know what they are doing when they line up?'

Don shakes his head. 'You'll have to tell me.'

'I will my son. All the while they are lined up they are comparing themselves with one another; who is top dog, who has the biggest dick, the swankiest car, the most money, the prettiest girl? Believe me. Look at them. They may be talking about the game on the telly last night but that's not what is really going on. They are testing each other. See that one there', he points to a balding man with a beer gut in the middle of the line up, 'he's just said that he's got a fifty six inch HD screen, whatever that is, twice already. Who the hell cares about that? But Andy Capp over there is impressed.'

Hugo gestures to a large man with a beanie hat drawn round his ears.

'He's asking if he's got SKY. He has. Thinking of getting 3D when it comes out. Andy is moving closer now; that's the alpha male in the middle, you mark my words.'

'But not all men are like that Hugo. You? Me?'

'You may not think so, but where have you just come from? If a prize giving is not a line up, I don't know what is. And what about all these qualifications you've got? That's one hell of a wank to show off to the rest of the world, isn't it?'

'For all the good it did me.'

Don tells Hugo about Martin Hastings.

'Illustrates my point exactly. You never took the time to do a spot of brown nosing Don. That was your trouble. But I bet that Marty friend of yours made sure he was in the Masons or Rotary or one of those daft male line ups with sporrans and trowels that see to it that they and their kind get on.'

'Probably. But that doesn't account for you.'

'You're the scientist Don. There are exceptions to every rule aren't they? And I was ever fond of putting myself in places like over there.' He points to the group of women by the window, their heads bent together in animated chatter.

'You see them? Women don't line up naturally, unless it is for a queue at the sales and even then they don't do that very well. No they get together in circles, like the ones over there. It must be a hangover from their gathering days. Whilst the men all line up for the woolly mammoth hunt, the women are there in their little rounded groups gathering the berries, bashing out the washing by the river, suckling the bairns, sitting round the stew pot; talking and listening to one another, remembering what each one said. These chaps will get up and leave in a minute and won't have a clue who they were with if you asked them in half an hour, but the girls? I bet they know all the kids' birthdays, where they spent their holidays, whose turn it is to have the in-laws for Christmas. Tell me, are you the one that sends out cards at Christmas Don?'

'No, that was always Bella's job.'

'Why is it that I am not surprised?'

'When is her birthday by the way?'

'April sometime. Twenty fifth I think.'

'Wow! No wonder you don't understand women. Do you even like them Don? Sorry. Rude of me. You had a peach in Bella.'

'I know. The trouble is she wants a divorce. And she's only thinking of changing her name.'

'Why shouldn't she? It was your bloody name that she took on when she married you. That's another thing men do. They pass their line down as well as across.'

Hugo sees Don's shoulders fall into a slump.

'Well that's the psychology lesson over for now, but mark

my words I know my stuff when it comes to the battle of the sexes. I tell you what Don. You look like you need cheering up. It's time we had a bit of fun. Another day at the gee-gees would go down well before Christmas, wouldn't it? Now there's a line up we would both enjoy!'

EIGHT

'IT'S A JOY TO BE HIDDEN...'

Standing at the stop Bella reflects that she has not been on a bus for over thirty years. The last time she climbed onto a double-decker there had been a conductress to take her fare; a bright metallic creature with peroxide hair and a voice that boomed: 'move along there please!' Were there still women like that? Now she realises with a growing sense of panic that the whole protocol of riding on a bus would have changed. She looks around her, searching for clues; an old lady with a shopping trolley and a pale youth with hands in his pockets, no one else to come to her aid.

She examines the old woman again and begins to study her profile. So this is what happens when you really got old; contours disappearing like an eroding coastline, a face losing all shape and texture. This lady had a jawline of a stork, a great gullet hanging down to her chest, the folds of her neck wobbling as she closed up her scarf against the wind. Is this what she could look forward to if she was lucky enough to survive? She lets out an involuntary laugh. The woman turns to her and Bella remembers the Klimt painting and feels ashamed.

'Old age ain't for cissies.'

Who said that?

On the bus she struggles to find the right change and is chastised by the driver. Now red in the face, she turns to find a seat, avoiding the front row, reserved she notes for the elderly and the disabled.

Ah well!

'Hey up my duck!'

The voice coming from a friendly face behind her.

'Not to worry love. Them drivers are all Polish now, you know. They can't get our lads to take the wheel for love nor money. First it was the Irish, then the Blacks and now this lot from the EU. Half the time you don't know what country you're living in.'

'Shirley! What are you doing here?'

'I could say the same for you love. I'm off to the hospital. Today is my day for the WRVS. Taking books and stuff round to all the wards.'

'Aren't you the proper Florence Nightingale?'

'No really duck. It passes the time now my old man's passed on. Mondays and Wednesdays are Barnados and Tuesdays I'm at the General. I'm often there at weekends too, that is if they are short of staff. How about you?'

Bella tells her. She is off to the Children's Centre to spend time with teenagers in trouble.

'And you call me Florence? I think you're a bloody saint to do what you do.'

'Not really,' Bella smiles, 'most of the kids I see had a rotten start in life. They don't do well in school and they make bad choices later on: girls getting pregnant, boys into gangs, drugs, petty crimes, you know what I mean, the papers are full of it. Though,' she adds, nursing her wounded hand, 'I have to say I find it a bit of a struggle sometimes, believing that I can do some good and help change their lives.'

'I know what you mean,' Shirley agrees, 'but if it wasn't for the likes of you, they'd probably end up in a reformatory or a loony bin. I've been reading such sad stories of people who got locked up in the past and it seems to me they threw away the key in times gone by. Shocking what they did to people in them days. One poor woman banged up for life because she lost her baby and took someone else's just to love. Just to love! Imagine! So you carry on my duck and do your best to keep them out of mischief. You can only do what you can do.'

'I'll try Shirley. Thanks.'

~

She walks into the large Victorian Building, carrying with her in every stride a sense of dread. The receptionist greets her kindly; only girls on her books for a while until she felt up to it again. She goes into her office and takes a few deep breaths. Presently she hears raised voices outside and opens her door.

'Madison! Good to see you! How has your week been?'

A raising of the shoulders from her young client, then the predictable:

'Dunno.'

Bella sighs.

'Okay. I wonder what sort of 'dunno' that could be today? I suspect it comes from the 'can't be bothered' school of 'dunnos' but I could be wrong. Do I have to go fishing again Madison? Go on, give us a clue.'

She scans the face of the fourteen year old, searching for a spark of animation that would connect them. Bella felt that she had earned a PhD in 'dunnos' and all the other phrases and shrugs that were part of the typical adolescent vocabulary. Until now she had loved being with her 'ASBO' kids, defending them against all the prejudices held by those of her age who had swallowed fears of gangs and digested beliefs that young people were a race apart.

'They are not! Most of them are great, if you would only take the time and the trouble to get to know them.'

Friends would often raise an eyebrow at this retort.

But today felt different. She feels irritated. Impatient. She wants to shake her young charge into eloquence.

She sees Madison eyeing her over. Her counsellor has changed a bit since they last met. No sloppy sweater today. A skirt and nice leather boots. And her hair had changed. Cropped over in a punk look.

'I like yer hair Bella. It's cool.'

'Thank you.'

'What have you done to your hand?'

'Oh that? It's nothing. Burnt it on a kettle. No big deal.'

'Can I go for a fag now?'

'No you can't. You know the rules Madison.'

'Oooer! Snap! Snap! What's got into you today? I don't have to come here if I don't want to you know?

'I know. I'm sorry. I haven't been sleeping well recently.'

'Why? What's up?'

'Lots. Oh never mind. Have your fag if you want to. Only you'll have to go outside. That means less time to hunt down the 'dunnos.'

Bella steadies herself. She's given too much away already, a 'no-no' in her profession. 'Come on Bella, she tells herself. Don't let one rotten apple...'

She watches and sees this young girl battle with her need to keep secrets to herself and her desire to share them with someone that she can trust.

'It's a joy to be hidden, but a disaster not to be found,' Bella thinks.

She would play the waiting game a few minutes longer.

'Actually this week has been alright. I've had a few shags since I saw you last.'

'Really?'

Bella forces herself to keep a straight face of enquiry. She knew she was being tested.

'Anyone I've heard of?'

'No. One of my mates. He's not much older than me. It was a laugh really.

Now she was on the alert. Inside Bella a whole barrage of questions were lining up; questions that would determine whether her young client was in danger. She knew full well that many of the youngsters that she saw had underage sex. If it was with a friend and they had consented, then there was little that she could do, except perhaps to look for other ways to boost self esteem. Hints about protection against pregnancy or disease were sometimes useful. Bella could still be shocked at the amount of ignorance that was still around about sex. But this girl sitting in front of her right now, this child, she reminds herself, was vulnerable. Madison had been the victim of sexual abuse by her step father and possibly others besides.

'Madison, you know what I am going to say.'

'It's okay Bella. He's seventeen. We hang out at his place. We do other things as well like playing video games and watching DVD's and stuff. His mother doesn't mind. It's cool.'

'Are you sure? You would tell me if…'

'Yeah Yeah. Honestly.'

Bella regarded her young client with affection. Madison had an eating disorder. She worried everyone around her and she knew it. Therapy had been another way of feeding her and it had fallen to Bella to pick up the spoon. It had been a long process. At first the girl had gobbled up all the attention given to her. Then, true to plan, she would sick up all the good work they had done together in cries of angry rejection: 'you don't mean that, you don't care, you're crap making up all those nice things you say about me.' Bella had needed patience at these times, lots of patience before a slender foothold of trust had been built up between them.

Today she notices that Madison was dressed in her favourite pink puffer jacket. She was all piercings and cheek; fingernails newly painted in bright rainbow colours, but the varnish couldn't disguise the tallow stains on her fingers. Madison lived for her fags.

'Do you ever have a shag Bella, at your age?'

She avoided giving an answer. But it did help open up a conversation about sex.

'I guess people have always shagged,' she replies, wincing at the word. 'If it wasn't for shagging you and I wouldn't be here. But I have to say Madison, that word is hard for me to say. My age perhaps, but it suggests to me something done without much affection or feeling. Like those other words I find difficult: 'fucking' for instance. I suppose you must think that I am really Jurassic but I prefer words like 'making love', they sound to me like two people involved with one another and caring about what they are doing.'

'Making lurve,' Madison parodies back to her. 'You are going all cheesy on me now Bella.'

'Am I? Only I don't know how to put this to you and be on the same wavelength, but I wonder if you want your boyfriends to take time to really get to know you and like you, even love you before... well ... before you have a shag. Does that make sense to you Madison, or am I from another planet?'

'Fucking Venus, Bella!'

They laughed together.

Why 'Madison?' Bella thinks. It's an avenue in New York, a million miles away from this street-wise kid from Hyson Green. Where were all the 'Susan's' she was at school with? And the 'Patricia's?' Those rather simpering girls called 'Anne?' She never saw a 'Mandy' or a 'Tracey' now yet there were a locust plague of them a few years ago. Now the names were all pop stars or footballers wives or places like 'Chelsea.'

But where had 'Madison' come from?

'So you kept yourself safe when you were having sex?'

'Yeah. I've been on the pill for months. You know that Bella.'

Now Bella fights against all the sermons going on inside her head, longing to preach to this young survivor of social care to take more care.

She knew that there was a part of her that could stand outside of herself at times like this: compassionate, yet uninvolved. It was almost as if the thinking part of her had climbed into a helicopter and was hovering overhead, scanning the process going on below in search for shapes and themes that might give some clues into what was really going on between them. Occasionally little cargoes of insight would make their landing from above and help in the delivery of a course of action that would tilt the direction of life forward, away from the stuckness or despair of the present. This happened a few weeks ago after Madison had gone on a bender of drink and drugs and trashed her room.

'I wonder why you did all that Madison? It doesn't sound to me like you get much out of that whole thing.'

'She fucking well threw me out.'

'Your foster mother was angry with you.'

'Called in the Social. I had to spend the night in that hole.'

'Rivendell hostel? You were sent there before after one of your outbursts, weren't you?'

But am I missing something here? I thought you liked your foster mother. You were happy staying a her place?'

'I suppose...'

'So why trash and make her angry?'

'Dunno.'

That word again!

'Let me try this out for size Madison. Everywhere you go you always test the people you stay with. Something inside you says: 'How far can I go with this one and she'll still have me back?' You did that with me the first time we met. Swore like a trooper all through the session and didn't turn up the following week. Yet I was still there. And so was your foster mum if I'm not mistaken. She took you back from the hostel after you'd cooled down. That's more than your real mother did, isn't it Madison, when she threw you out.'

A shrug of the shoulders, then: 'Yeah.'

That had been a serious session, touching on themes of loss and abandonment. It had ended with the recognition that her young client was terrified of bringing about what she most feared, being left on her own again. Since that time she could see that Madison had worked hard to salvage and restore relationships that she cared about.

Holding her in that cradle of insight had helped her to change. Could Bella do that again?

But she felt distracted today. And tired. Her hand throbbed under its bandage. A great sense of weariness took its claim on her frail body. That word 'shag' had got to her.

Did she ever shag?

She allowed her mind to wander back.

Of course she had shagged. Don and she shagging each

other silly when they were young. But that was after the advent of the pill: A.P. in the lifeline of sex. Before then Pill there was no shagging, only the joys and frustrations of 'heavy-petting'- what a phrase! Imagine explaining to Madison what went on in bus shelters and behind bike sheds in prehistoric times when she had been young. Those frantic fumblings with zips and fasteners: all those love bites in her neck and having to wear high collared sweaters so her mother wouldn't see them. But no touching below the waist in those days my girl, no trespassing into the southern jungles of her body.

I was a good girl Madison.

A frightened one more like!

But there were times when it was lovely. Like coming back to Nottingham once on the bus from Leeds. Sitting in the back seat, just the two of them and touching Don the way he liked, her hand inside his jeans. Watching his face explode in an ecstasy of pleasure as she felt the sticky cum in her fingers. That wasn't a shag was it? That was something special, a real moment of intimacy between them. Would Madison ever treasure such time of innocent pleasure?

Don't be silly! She didn't need to. Sex was available to her as all the Alco pops that she drank at the weekends to get high and make her feel alive.

She comes back to the present and lands her thoughts beside her client.

'I miss my Nan Bella. She was a bit like you. She would have told me all about sex and stuff.'

'Would she? She sounds alright your Nan.'

'She was. She's dead now. Did you have a Nan Bella?'

'I never knew either of mine. My Mother's mum died in childbirth and I never found out what happened to my Dad's mother. She remained a mystery till the end.'

'My Nan used to say that men were like gas stoves. You

just flicked them on and up they shot. POW! But girls she said were electric. They took their time to warm up but lasted much longer she said.'

'She would have made a good sex therapist, your Nan.'

'Is that what you do?'

'Did. Not now. Too old I expect.'

'Gross! Who did you fancy when you were young then?'

She was surprised that Madison used the gentle word 'fancy.' It had travelled well through the generations. She could answer that question, surely?'

'Well Madison, I remember seeing a film called 'Butch Cassidy and the Sundance Kid.' My two favourite men of all time were in it: Paul Newman and Robert Redford. There's a scene in the movie, after they've robbed a bank, somewhere in Bolivia I think, and they are riding a bicycle with someone called Katherine Ross. She is on the handlebars being wheeled around by these two gorgeous hunks and all the while someone is singing:'Raindrops keep falling on my head.' If I had been Katherine Ross, I'd have shagged them both!'

'Good for you Bella.'

They laughed together, then:

'Madison?'

'Uh huh?'

'Is this still working? You and me? Counselling together?'

'I don't know what you mean?'

'All these weeks. Have they meant something to you?'

'Dunno.'

'What else would you be doing if you weren't coming here?'

'Boring stuff. School an that.'

'And this isn't boring?'

'Not all the time.'

'Thanks. I suppose that I am being damned with faint praise.'

'Faint what?'

'Never mind. Can we do some boring stuff now before you go back to your class?'

'If we have to.'

Ten minutes rehearsal for the week ahead. How could she stop her from being excluded again? Were there other ways of managing her anger instead of sounding off every time someone pissed her off? What about those girl gangs at school? It was a tough world that Madison inhabited and Bella felt for her at times.

But did those same gangs ever walk down her street? And what would happen if Madison was one of them?'

She watches her client go out and light a cigarette, waiting for the taxi to take her back to school. Bella wonders to herself if one day she would ever get it right as a counsellor as she felt she had never got it right as a mother. As she begins to write up her notes, the phone in her handbag takes up a ringing tone. Her daughter Evie was making a call.

'Hi Mum, are you okay?'

'Yes I'm fine Evie, just writing up notes after a session at the Children's Centre.'

'Oh, so you're with your waifs and strays are you?'

'Just finished. How's Josh?'

'He's fine. Well he's not actually. He's a pain in the bum. Back teeth coming through I think. I didn't get a wink of sleep last night.'

'I'm sorry.'

She bites her lip, fighting back a suggested remedy. Grandmother's suggestions were never in favour with her youngest daughter.

'Anyway, have you had this card from Iona?'

'About their wedding? Yes.'

'Hardly a wedding, Mum. What do you think?'

What could she say?

What would Evie like to hear?

'Well it may not be a wedding in the conventional sense. But they both want a ceremony to formalise their relationship. A way of telling the world that they are committed to each other.'

'Huh!'

'I take it that you don't approve.'

'It doesn't matter what I think. When has Iona ever taken any notice of me?'

'But she wants you to be there. Rosie too.'

'So you've discussed it, the three of you?'

Bella senses a trap in waiting.

'Well yes, in a way,' she adds lamely, 'they took me out for lunch on Saturday and told me all about it. They really are very keen that you should come Evie.'

'But they don't want Josh or James.'

'Well that's just typical of my big sister.'

Bella sighs. 'It's her big day. Can't we just go along with it?'

'And what will Daddy say? And Tom?'

Bella hesitates. Choosing her words carefully. 'Oh they won't mind. And Tom is busy with his new life.'

Then unlocks what she really feels.

'Look Evie, don't be churlish. Let's wish them well. You know how happy your sister has been since Rosie has been around.'

She thinks she can detect a small change in tone at the other end of the phone.

'And I suppose you are in this in a big way?'

'No they just want me to be there and perhaps say a poem for them.'

'God knows what Gran would have thought. What's the poem?'

'A Shakespeare sonnet or that lovely poem by Elizabeth Barrett Browning:'How do I love thee, let me count the ways.'

'Oh, cringe-worthy! That bit is disgusting!'

'Mmmmmmm…'

'You don't agree?'

'No.'

'Well I'm with Dad on this.'

'You are entitled to your own opinion. But remember Iona would be very upset if you weren't there.'

'Anyway, whatever. It's not why I rang. I'm pregnant again.'

'That's great news…'

'And they think it might be twins!'

~

Coming back on the bus was easier this time. She has the right change. Maybe in time she'd be entitled to a bus pass. Past Clumber Avenue and she knows that she is headed in the right direction. And thankfully the pavement seems empty as she rounds the corner of her own street.

Bella walks briskly feeling her legs chaff themselves into warmth. She dares not turn her head in any direction other than forward. Inside her pocket her bandaged hand tightens into a clench. She swallows hard, forcing some moisture into her dry mouth. Quickening her pace now, willing her knee to stave off its trembling. The wind picks up speed as she gains on number 36. And was that then first flurry of snow beginning to drop on her littered path?

NINE

THE WEDDING

It was a day to remember. An event the sociologists would record: Diverse ceremonies of the Twenty First Century. Iona and Rosie in matching white trouser suits, both clutching identical bouquets of roses. They stand together and smile: arm in arm, posing for photographs that were framed by the grey facade of the registry office.

Inside, guests sit quietly in a circle. No rows. No segregation of family and friends. Someone that Bella recognises from Iona's schooldays begins to sing: 'The first time ever I saw your face…' She closes her eyes. The words hold her in simple rapture. They spoke to the frailty of love and the innocence of sensual pleasure. Iona and Rosie shyly exchange the vows that they had made up together, giving the ceremony a real sense of spontaneity. Bella warms to the experience. Such a contrast to her own stiff-backed wedding and the pomp and circumstance of Evie's. When she gets up to deliver her own poem, it felt right; something from the heart.

ON YOUR JOURNEY INTO MARRIAGE

As you begin your journey into marriage
Take with you solid suitcases of trust
Pack garments of hope
For they will warm you in cold times
Put in cloths of passion
For they will bind you in joy
Find room for the fabrics of friendship
For they will sustain you in times of strife
Leave space for soft scarves of tenderness
For they will soothe you from life's bruises
Don't forget some toys from childhood
For a good marriage will help you to play
Take stout shoes of common sense
For they will help you tread sensibly in this world of chaos
A first aid for conflict is essential
Bandages for binding up wounds of hurt
Leave enough space for the self in your packing
For you will grow separately as well as together
And close your case with the keys of commitment
Entrusting them to each others safekeeping
Create your own marriage map
Others have walked their paths
Your footsteps are your own
And all of our blessings go with you.

The party at the Boathouse was also a success; delicious home cooked food and champagne. No long speeches but many toasts, with songs and stories in between. What was it being in the company of women that felt so different? Bella was not used to it never having been a Brownie or a Guide, but once or twice in her student days she had joined the marauding gangs of the factory girls of Boots for nights out on the town. Nights with her hair piled high in a beehive style. Her little paisley dress with the Peter Pan collar, its length coming high above her thigh. 'Don't bend down for Heaven's sake in that pussy pelmet of yours,' they had joked. These times had been fun, if a little risqué. But today it felt like being round a campfire and she did not feel out of place.

Later as Evie drives her back home, she says, 'you know Mum, I wish you had recited a poem like that on my wedding day.'

Bella is touched and a little embarrassed.

'Do you love? I'm sorry, but yours was a rather grand affair. My homespun little ditty would have seemed out of place, don't you think? Anyway, your Grandmother was in charge, wasn't she? Just as she was at my wedding.'

'Why did you let her take charge Mum, if you didn't enjoy it?'

'Oh I don't know Evie. It just seemed easier. She was a great one for the big occasion, wasn't she? Maybe it was because she had such a hard life in her early years and it made her happy to organise us all. Her own wedding was very low key. My father had a twenty four hour pass on compassionate leave from the Navy and when he went back to his ship he was off on the Atlantic convoys. She didn't see him again for nearly two years. By the time he came home he had a wife and a daughter he had never clapped eyes on. 'Besides,' she added ruefully, 'your Dad and I were never keen on weddings. If we'd had our way we would have probably eloped.'

'So instead you had a miserable day you didn't want!'

'Not miserable exactly, just a bit strange. I went along with it all. I remember at the time thinking I was in an old B move that we used to have to support the main feature. You know the one that gets second billing and is always in black and white? I couldn't wait to get off that ridiculous dress she got for me and wash all that lacquer out of my hair. It was terrible stuff, Evie, the smell of dance halls in the sixties, that was 'pompadour' lacquer. It was just good to be myself again.'

'Didn't you want your father to give you away?'

'No love. When he walked out on us that was IT as far as I was concerned. Anyway your Gran would never have allowed him to be there. They had a terrible marriage.'

Evie is quiet for a few minutes.

'There's a lot you don't talk about, isn't there Mum? I sometimes felt when I was a child that there was a sadness from way back that still clung to you.'

'Really Evie, mostly I was very happy.'

Bella is aware that her voice has become breezy. Too breezy. Her Mary Poppins voice. 'Spit Spot!' in its tone. She must change that and be serious with her younger daughter.

'But yes, I did have a terrible time of it when you were born. Post natal depression they call it now. Horrible. It seemed to last for ever. I wouldn't wish it on anybody. But then thankfully Tom came along and it was all different.'

'Tom. Your pride and joy!'

'Well,' she adds quickly, too quickly, 'we were proud of you all.'

But Evie is not fooled. Bella sees her daughter shrug.

I've got it wrong again, she thinks. Damn. And it was such a wonderful day up till now.

TEN

TOM.

26th November.

My darling Tom,
    Still no news from you. I wonder if I sent the last letter to the right post box number? I know I should join the modern world and get a computer so I could dash off e-mails to you like your sisters. But that's not me. The last of the letter writers, that's your mother for you, like the last of the Mohicans!

    Somehow thoughts don't flow when I face a screen, so you'll have to do with the old fashioned 'snail mail' and keep the ailing Post Office in business.

I loved the photos that you sent to Evie. She had them printed off for me and I have them printed up in my new study, well not so much a study as a cubby-hole in the kitchen. The Yukon looks wonderful and the views of Mount Logan are awe-inspiring. It would be great to visit you sometime. Perhaps when you take up your lecturing job in British Columbia next year I could come and get in touch with some of my Scottish relatives who migrated to Canada many moons ago. My great Aunt Meg moved there in her later years and I fancy that my Auntie Margaret, her niece, went out to join her and stayed on in Manitoba when Aunt Meg died.

Life here is sadly much more prosaic. I wish I could say I was settling into my new life on my own, but it all feels rather transitional at the moment. Don't get me wrong. I love my little house, even though everyone tells me I was mad to buy it, but somehow the city of my imagination doesn't quite fit the reality of how it really is. I suppose I am mindful of the old adage: be careful what you wish for!

I've been trying to find a new image for myself. One that suits my age.

'Hooray!' I hear you cheer. Julia took me shopping with my credit card. Fatal!

We cruised round some of the posh boutiques in the Flying Horse Arcade in Nottingham and for a while I felt as if I was one of those bulimic girls that I see in counselling. I would buy an outfit in a big sugar rush of delight and later when I got home, I would be sick at all the money I spent, so I took all the clothes back feeling rather ashamed of myself. Iona and Rosie had me at an image consultant last Saturday. I can't say it was a great success. I felt like a trapped bird in the well-manicured grasp of someone called Gaynor who looked like something out of Harpers Bazaar (not that you would have heard of Harpers Bazaar). Still it was quite an experience.

Julia and I will make a few forays into the auctions when I've done all the decorating. I've kept a spare room in your honour, if and when you ever return, and bought a bookcase from Swallow's Rest to house some of your reading from the past. I had a little smile to myself, and also a little weep if the truth be told, when I came across your copy of ' My Family and other Animals '. Inside you had written a note to yourself. I quote: 'This book belongs to Thomas John Cavendish who wishes he could live with the family in this book and have a mother that would let me keep newts in my bedroom. When I grow up I am going to have a zoo like Gerald Durrell. I would like him to be my father instead of the one I've got who is always too busy and never has any time to go exploring for wildlife. TJC September 1985.

Well sorry about the newts Tom, but we didn't live far away from the nature reserve, did we? I seem to remember that the house was full of jam jars of frogspawn in the spring and birds that you rescued from the clutches of Elvis.

I haven't got much of a garden here and that suits me fine. I can spend time sitting in it and not feel guilty about all the jobs that need doing. Your father was never one that took to a spade, was he? Elvis, however, is not so happy. He scratches around the tubs and misses that old plum tree we had in the front garden. He is sitting on my knee right now and I am feeling very guilty on his behalf.

Dad has moved into Brenda's bungalow in Sleaford. And you will never guess what! He has taken up bird watching! Your Dad, the dyed-in-the-wool academic whose idea of the great outdoors was a brief walk round the university park once a year when the azaleas were in bloom. Whatever next! I hear all the news from Evie who keeps in touch with him and feeds me little gobbets of gossip every now and again. He seems happy enough she says. It certainly wouldn't do if we were both miserable.

Now the difficult part for me to write about. I know you took the news of our separation hard Tom. I think you saw your parents at this stage of their lives like one of those vitamin adverts on the telly- you know the ones I mean- on a cruise, gazing adoringly at one another as the sun sets over the horizon.

How do you tell your children about your marital problems? 'Too much information mum,' I hear you say. But I must say something, partly because my mother never told me anything about why my father left us. For years I even thought it was my fault. Did I upset him for not eating up my dinners?

Was he cross with me because I was hopeless at maths?

From my point of view I think your father and I changed in ways that didn't help each other in growing older together. We were married very young remember and for many years believe me we were happy. But when your sisters left home I think we just rubbed along. It happens. They even have a name for it now: 'empty nest syndrome' it is called. When I think of all those years that I have spent counselling others and I couldn't even semaphore to my own husband that we were in trouble. The crunch came when you Gran died and then I got ill. I don't think your father knew what to do. I became a patient to him, not a wife.

So when he finished work there was a yawning gulf between us. We both felt it keenly. It was at my instigation *that he joined the local conservation society, something to get him out of the house I suppose. And there was Brenda with all her enthusiasm for the life outdoors and her passion for baking. Seemingly he's put on a stone and a half since he's been living with her. Is she fattening him up for his first heart attack, I wonder? Still I mustn't snipe. And you must keep in touch with him; I know he loves you very much and is very proud of what you have achieved.*

I'm still working at the Children's Centre one day a week, but I'm having doubts as to whether to carry on. I didn't tell Evie or Iona but my car was vandalised by a bunch of boys right outside my door a while ago. One lad seemed straight out of 'Lord of the Flies'. It's shaken me up I can tell you.

But don't worry Tom. I'm fine now.

I'm sending some photographs of Iona's and Rosie's wedding. It was a lovely day and you would have so enjoyed it had you been here and the only honorary man on the guest list. Unlike Evie's very formal affair, we dispensed with all that religious nonsense and had fun. They both made up their own vows and then we had a picnic at the Boathouse. I even made up a poem for the occasion. Pity about Dad but Iona didn't want him to be there and it would have been very awkward not inviting Brenda. I think Evie has sent him some snaps though so he has some memento of the day.

How will you spend Christmas? I'm hoping to put a duvet over the whole experience. That may sound maudlin but it's not meant to be. I'm going to Iona's the Sunday before

Christmas and then I'll pop over to Plumtree and give the family their presents. Josh is getting a big boy now and in many ways he reminds me of you. I took him round the gravel pits a while ago with his wellies and his fishing net and I felt I was going back twenty years. He has that same screwed up look of concentration when he is busy like you always had. It's lovely!

Heigh ho! I think I've rambled on enough.

So in the meantime, take good care my son. Wrap up and keep yourself warm from the harsh winds of the Rockies. (I'm beginning to sound like Ailsa, aren't I?) And I am looking forward to hearing all your news when and if you can bear to find that old fashioned thing called pen and paper.

Much love,
Mum x

ELEVEN

THE CHAPEL

Sunday November 28th November

This morning I was persuaded by Lily to join her in a visit to the chapel in the grounds of the asylum. She tells me that there are children coming to sing from one of the local schools and wonders if her niece Flora will be one of the choristers.

I am hesitant to accompany her, fearing recognition from the outside world but I am told that the building is of a pleasing Arts and Crafts design, built by a famous architect. So it will be an aesthetic experience if nothing else for I fear that I have lost all faith in the presence of an almighty creator.

I however make a vow to Lily before I consent to accompany her that if Chaplain Sewell gives one of his 'Hell and Damnation' sermons, I would quit the house of worship, no matter what.

I did not expect the little building to be so crowded when we got there. The front seats were occupied by ladies from the West Wing of the asylum. These patients, Mistress Niven informs me, pay for their care and consider their stay in this place as a 'rest cure' for their nerves. She says that she often has to order embroidery threads and tapestries for their gentle pastimes in the pretty rooms they occupy during their stay. No doubt Dr Scobie spends much time in their company as Elsie Macpherson informs me that in certain quarters it has become quite fashionable to be treated by a new branch of medicine called psychiatry.

What a contrast to those of us who occupy the East Wing! We are labelled as being paupers and lunatics and rarely get to meet our fellow inmates from a different class of Society. The difference between us is stark. These ladies are all got up beautiful attire, whereas we are clothed in the discarded leavings of those who donate their unwanted raiment for charitable collections around the city.

We could indeed be living on opposite sides of the world, although I believe many of us may be suffering from the same maladies of mental illness.

So Lily and I sit at the back in our ill assorted outfits. The boots I am wearing are of differing sizes and only one has laces. Lily is still in her rough calico nightgown worn underneath a greatcoat that she took from one of the men in the George Vth Ward. We thus make a comical pair!

Looking down on us from the stained glass windows are the stern faces of St. Luke and St. Paul. They flank a depiction of Christ in the middle. He seems to be the only one in this place that offers some benediction as he lays hands on a mother and child and a poor man by their side. I wonder if he would offer such a blessing to me if he knew what I had done?

'Suffer little children to come unto me,' he is reputed to have said.

I warm to the word 'suffer.' My bairns have suffered under my care and I wonder what may befall them in the future, and the fate of those that come after.

Yet such thoughts often lead me into Mr Bunyan's 'Slough of Despond' and I long to be back at my chores and busy my hands again, forcing my mind to be free from the past.

The boys and girls dressed in their Sunday best give us a passable rendition of 'All things Bright and Beautiful' and a few other jolly hymns intended to lift the spirits and cheer up a dull day. Sadly Flora was not amongst them but Lily is heartened by their cheerful faces. A sentimental soul is Lily.

I sometimes envy her in her kindly innocence.

We come out of the chapel before Chaplain Sewell takes up his position of unctuous piety at the door, before shaking hands with the ladies in the front rows.

Out into the greyness of a late autumn day.

'No sun, no moon, no morn , no noon- no proper time of day- November'

TWELVE

THE ONE THAT GOT AWAY.

'Hi Bella. How are things?'

'Julia! Fine. You've caught me blacking that old kitchen range we bought at the reclamation centre. I'm covered in grime.'

'Why in the name of old Harry you couldn't have bought one in that new Aga shop, like we sensible mortals would have done, is a mystery to me.'

'I like a challenge. Besides I needed to work something out of my system.'

'How come?'

'I've had this really pompous letter from Don accusing me of being a neglectful mother to Evie.'

'What did he say?'

'Hang on a minute. Let me find it and read it to you before I throw it in the fire.'

Bella puts down her cloth and attempts to scrub her blackened hands. The letter lies open on the counter by the sink, stained with coffee grounds.

'You still there?'

'Yup. Shoot!'

'Well it starts Okayish. He's writing because I told him not to ring again. I just can't bear to hear his voice at the moment. Then he goes on about Iona's wedding – you know we didn't ask him, and then, what do you think about this?'

...what really concerns me is the news of Evie's pregnancy. Has she told you she is expecting twins? I really do believe she needs to be informed about the circumstances of her own birth Bella. I know you will say that lightning rarely strikes twice but being forewarned can mean that both she and her medical advisors can be forearmed. Will you tell her, or will that lot fall to me? I sometimes feel very guilty about Evie. You were so ill after she was born and I was very involved with Iona then. I get the feeling that Evie felt very left out. Thank goodness for your mother being around because without her I might even venture to say our daughter could have been rather severely neglected. I know she was never an easy child but she's turned out to be a good wife and mother to James and Josh. We should be proud of her Bella...

A moment's pause, then Bella hears her friend speak.

'Well don't you think he might have a point, about Evie's birth I mean? It was all very 'hush-hush' at the time, if my memory serves me well.'

'No!' Bella says, surprised by the ferocity of her feelings. 'I don't want to go there again. And lightning won't strike twice. It won't! Besides she tells me James is paying for them to go private. She'll have the best treatment money can buy.'

'Maybe... you know best darling... but if it was me...'

'Well it isn't! Then he has the cheek to tell me he has been invited over to Plumtree at Christmas. And SHE will be there too. The pair of them!'

'What are you doing for Christmas Bella?'

She hears the cadence of concern in Julia's tone.

'I've no idea. I'm certainly not writing any cards this year. Can't be bothered explaining why there will be just 'love Bella' instead of the usual greeting. How about you?'

'Hugo wants to go skiing and thinks we can get a last minute deal. He can wear himself out on the slopes and I'll catch up with him in the evening. My knees aren't up to it any more.'

'Sounds fun.'

'You can always come with us if you like. Hugo would enjoy your company.'

The thought playing gooseberry makes Bella wince.

'That's very sweet of you Julia. But I wouldn't want to cramp your style.'

'You are my best friend Bella.'

'I know and you are mine. By the way, how long have we known one another?'

'I'll have to put my thinking cap on. 1957 was it? We were ten. I remember your first day at school. Skinny little thing you were, all freckles and a mass of red hair. Speaking in a dialect none of us could understand. We used to say to you: 'say something in Scotch,' and then pretend you were some foreign and exotic creature.'

'You were told to look after me and you threw my school bag out of the window of the bus on the way home. Ailsa was furious.'

'Yes, your mother was good at getting angry. Quite a character your old mum. Then we failed the eleven plus. No new bikes for us!'

'But we got our own back on the 'grammar grubs' in the end, didn't we Julia? And became stars at the Secondary

Modern school. I liked that school. We did well there. I wish in many ways we could have stayed on. It was fun.'

'And didn't we give that old Keyworth crowd the elbow when we caught them up after we passed that exam? Remember Kit Norton's face when we pitched up at the Grammar school in the third year? A whole band of us with memories like elephants. We weren't going to forget how they wouldn't speak to us with their posh blazers and swanky new satchels.'

'The duffel coat brigade we called ourselves.'

'None of us became prefects, did we? It was our badge of honour.'

Bella laughs at the memory of their mutinous adolescence. How much had that early branding of failure scarred them both. The iniquity of an educational system that separated children into sheep and goats at the tender age of eleven had always angered her. For Bella in particular it had added another seam of shame into her family geology. Ailsa had not been able to hold her head up high in the little village of Plumtree where they then lived.

At first George Anstruther had taken an interest in her homework, giving her his time and patience as she struggled with maths. But that didn't last long. He left the family before she passed the exam which got her into the grammar school and somehow at that time her success didn't seem important. She and Ailsa had by then escaped from the prurient eyes of the village into a council flat on the other side of respectability. But failure had fuelled in her a determination to do well, even if just to spite him. Her English teacher in the sixth form had spotted this and got through the layers of make up to say: 'Bella Anstruther, that chip on your shoulder does not suit you. You have the makings of a fine mind if you would only direct it towards something constructive.' From then on Bella had worked hard and proved her right.

But for Julia it had been different. Her family were socialists. Wealthy people too. This paradox did not strike Bella until she was well into adulthood. Her father was a writer and her mother an artist. Julia's failure was regarded as cocking a snook against the class system. When they were teenagers Bella was often invited to join the family in attending Trade Union meetings where speakers railed against the class system and the 'inequalities of Society', always with a capital 'S'. This always seemed rather abstract to Bella. She would hear Julia's father boom 'Hear hear!' from the back of the hall and then imagine him going back to his large house in Edwalton, pouring a stiff drink of whisky from his crystal decanter and then bashing out pamphlets preaching Revolution with a capital 'R'. This is what the Fabians would have been like Bella thought and some aspects of nineteenth century history began to make sense.

She on the other hand came back from those meetings on a trolley bus to the ironically named Meadows estate. Back to a flat on the tenth floor where she lived in a wasteland of concrete. She would dodge the drug users in the lifts that seldom worked and pinch her nose to block out the smell of urine and cigarette butts on the stairs. She never asked Julia or her parents to see her home. Somehow the sight of so much lived-in socialism may have spoilt their high-blown illusions. But she would never dream of telling her friend this. She didn't want to lose her.

'We didn't turn out so badly, did we? I went off to Art School and you, clever clogs, went on to Uni. and married your very own Brain Box!'

'Talking of art Julia, can I afford that latest abstract of yours, the one with the black and red squiggles. I think Rosie and Iona would love it as a wedding present.'

'My homage to the Russian school. Yes of course you can have it.'

'I'll pick it up when I take the Christmas presents over to Evie's next week. I'm spending Hogmany with them by the way, babysitting so they can go to a dinner dance. By that time Don and the She-devil will be well gone.'

~

The picture was heavy and difficult to carry on and off two buses. Bella is tired when she crossed the river to West Bridgeford. 'Bread and lard' island it had been called when she was a child, a place of petty snobberies and pretensions.' Aw fur coat and nae knickers,' Grandfer would have said. But it was a nice place to live and Iona and Rosie had chosen wisely in their new home. A good solid semi, built in the thirties, with a long back garden where Rosie grew her vegetables.

When she walks through the door, she takes a deep breath. On the wall, beside the telephone table she sees a poem, her poem, framed for display. Someone had written it out in a beautiful hand of calligraphy.

'Meet my mother, the poet.'

Bella blushes in confusion.

'If I'd known it was going on public display, I would have spent more time on it, Iona.'

She takes in the gathering of her daughter's friends. Many had been at the wedding. She recognises Sam and once again remembered her in the Boathouse striking up a parody of an old song, giving it a lesbian twist: 'Nothing could be finer than to be in your vagina in the morning...' She had not known where to put herself. But Bella liked the good natured Sam. She liked most of her daughter's friends.

Iona is saying, 'she says everyone has a poem in them. Remember the builders, mum?'

'Oh not that again please.'

'But its a great tale.'

Bella sits back with her glass of wine as Iona begins to recount the story to her friends.

'Mum employed these lads from the Children's Centre to do some work on the kitchen and got fed up with the the blare of pop music all day long. So one day, National Poetry day, wasn't it mum, she switched off the radio and made a bargain with them. Cups of tea would appear every hour if they would listen to a poem on Radio Four.'

Iona mimics the look that they had given her at the sound of this suggestion- a shrug, index finger pointed to the forehead- mad!

'At ten o'clock Bella appeared with the mugs. On the radio Michael Malone was reading Keats' "Ode to a Nightingale. The guys drank their tea in embarrassed silence. Then one of them said: 'what was that all about?'

'So she explained the theme of the poem to them, patiently. Keats was dying. He had thoughts of suicide but the beauty of the birdsong had persuaded him that living was more important. Have I got it right Mum?'

'The gist of it, yes.'

'The lads then went back to their plastering. At eleven it was cakes and coffee. 'The Rhyme of the Ancient Mariner' got an airing. This time there was more curiosity on display; more boldness in the banter: 'I understand that one, a good story. Did you say that bloke Coleridge was on drugs when he wrote it? I wish I could turn out stuff like that when I've had a spliff.'

'And so the day progressed with hourly punctuations. Poetry and plastering. Plastering then poetry. Kipling's 'If' and then Jenny Joseph's 'When I am an old woman I shall wear purple.'

'I can see you in that one Mrs C. When are you going to learn to spit?'

'At three o'clock she was so absorbed in rubbing down an old Welsh dresser in the living room that she forgot to put the radio on. Two faces appeared at the door. 'Time for a poem?' they said. And they supped their tea in quiet concentration to the sounds of 'The Highwayman' clip clopping to the old inn door.' When they'd finished doing the house, mum bought them copies of 'Poems on the Underground.'

'I hope they read them,' Bella says wistfully.

'I'm sure they would have,' Sam says pouring Bella another another glass of wine. 'Great story Mrs C.'

It was a lovely lunch. Bella listens as they talk about plans for the Christmas break. The group were renting an old stone cottage in Derbyshire. Log fires, long walks in the Dales.'

'Sounds lovely.'

'Why don't you come Mum?'

'That's very sweet of you all but I've made other plans.'

'What plans?'

'Oh, you know...' Bella replies vaguely.

'By the way,' Iona says, 'I've had an e-mail from Tom. He's found himself a girlfriend. A nurse. I think she's French Canadian. Eloise, is it Rosie? He's going to stay at her place over the holidays. He says he will write and tell you all about her when he has the time.'

'Cheek!'

But her heart sings. Her boy was happy!

'We've bought you this. You can open it now if you like. I know you don't believe in delayed gratification.'

Inside the expensively wrapped parcel was a Missoni shawl. She had gone on and on about wanting this designer creation ever since her trip to Rome. Don had said: 'Ridiculous! All that money for something you can get for next to nothing in one of your Charity shops.' But that wasn't the point. This was beautiful! Hand spun silk in a pattern that took her breath away. She is unable to find words of thanks, but wraps the exquisite cloth round her shoulders in a gesture of loving appreciation.

~

The pre-Christmas bash at her other daughter's was a very different affair. For a start, James would not hear of his mother-in-law getting on a bus. He would come to her small terraced house in his BMW car. A series two or three Josh had told her but it could have been twenty three for all she knew or cared. All she had to do was to play the role of the rather helpless parent and they were both happy. Bella was fond of James and forgave his occasional outbursts of pomposity. He made her daughter happy and he loved his son. What more could she ask?

She hadn't, however bargained for the crowd that is there when she arrives. James was entertaining clients. They had got the caterers in. Evie wasn't up to cooking for large numbers of guests these days. Bella seeks out her grandson and together they go upstairs where they knew Thomas the Tank Engine would be waiting to play. This is where she feels at home. Through the floor they can hear the sounds of jocularity below. 'Mein host' was noisy and affable and the guests were enjoying themselves. She was on her third reading of the story about Pingu the penguin when the door opens and Evie's flushed face looks in.

'There's someone downstairs who seems to think that he knows you, mum. Can you come?'

'Must I?'

'He's very insistent. Please.'

On the way downstairs she stops by the bathroom and puts on new lipstick. It helps frame her public mask and gives her some confidence for facing the crowd. She loosens her new shawl and holds Josh's had tightly as they descend.

' This is Rick Taverner. He got very interested in you when he found out your maiden name, mother.'

A tall burly man stands up and holds out his hand. For seconds she is puzzled. The man in front of her has the well fed look of a Chairman of the Board. Or perhaps a Tory MP, she thinks. Ruddy faced, thickening jowls, a well cut suit flattening what she can make out as an ever expanding waistline. Only something about his eyes holds some clues of recognition.

Irony and amusement take her back.

'It can't be Freddie, can it?'

'In one. And if I'm not mistaken I'm looking at the lovely Isabella Anstruther.'

They laugh. Josh tugs at her skirt. 'Bamba, let's go and play!'

But she holds his gaze.

Age is a cruel thing, she thinks. Something makes her remember a visit to Robert Burns' house in Dumfries many years ago. Over the fireplace in that rather dark and dreary room two portraits come into her mind: one of the young bard, beautiful at thirty six just before he died, the other is Jeannie Armour, Jeannie of 'I dream of Jeannie with the light brown hair' fame. Only no light brown hair. Jeannie at eighty six, old, crabbed and fat. She had outlived her lover by fifty years. It had been quite shocking to see them both together like that; youth and age in horrible juxtaposition. Now she knew why people envied Marilyn Munroe or the late Princess Diana. They would never grow old and look like Jeannie Burns.

And at this minute there was not much left of the gorgeous Freddie Taverner that she had known as a young woman.

'I can't lie and say that you haven't changed a bit.'

'Ditto. What happened to that long lovely red hair.'

'You are old Father William...' she begins to recite.

~

She is nineteen. Her first year at university. She is moving to the slow, rasping voice of Long John Baldry. And he comes into her vision. 'A walking cliché,' she would say to her friend Pam when they walked back to their hall of residence. 'Tall, dark and handsome, just like George Chikiras in West Side Story.' He is asking her to dance. She closes her eyes as they glide together in a slow smooch.

That summer it is all Freddie Taverner. Paddling by the sea in Mabelthorpe, galloping skip jives on the dance floors to the sound of Chuck Berry, and once, unhitching a boat on the Trent at midnight, drifting down the river and finding their little craft stuck in weeds, falling asleep under that willow with soft waves lapping their dreams.

It had been love, it had been lust; it had been lovely!

'Whatever happened to you? I looked out for you at the Freshers Ball and you were nowhere to be seen.'

'I know. Sorry. Got a job offer in September. Sports Coach, travelling all over the place. Never did finish my degree. Did that for years until I bought my own business. James does all the auditing of the accounts.'

'Well fancy that!'

'Do you still sing? I remember when you took me to a club and you sang all that Bob Dylan stuff with a couple of friends of yours. You had a good voice Bella.'

'Well thank you kind sir. No, now it's just in the bath or with this young man here.'

Josh tugs at her skirt were becoming more insistent. This would be a good time to end this encounter.

'Hey we should get together sometime and play some Moody Blues.'

'I'd like that. By the way when did you drop 'Freddie' and become 'Rick?''

'Public image. Daft I know but important in my line of work.'

'Pity. I was fond of 'Freddie'. It suited you.'

'So was I. Perhaps you might like to see him again?'

'Maybe...'

She is quiet on the way home in the sleek black car with a rich smell of leather coming off the seats. James starts to quiz her about her past. She was a dark horse wasn't she? How come she knew Rick Taverner and why had their paths not crossed before? He was a rich man now, one of his best clients. Bella says little. Freddie was the one that got away as far as she was concerned and she wasn't sure about meeting him again.

Then suddenly, unexpectedly Madison pops into her head.

'Did you ever shag him Bella?'

'No Madison'. She smiles a smile of regret. 'But I wish I had. Under that willow tree a long, long time ago.'

PART TWO

WINTER

ONE

CHRISTMAS

The Jotter.

December 15th 1920.

Winter has laid a cruel hand on us all. My fingers can hardly hold this pencil; they chaff and itch with the pain of chilblains.

There has been a coal strike all over Glasgow and we have not had fuel to warm us for over eleven days. Hoar frost clings to the inside of the walls in our ward. At night by the light of such candles that we are allowed to burn, I marvel at the intricate webs that the frost creates on the dark surfaces. Filigree fingers of white seem to spread and reach down to gather up the bodies that shiver in the beds beneath. I have managed to bring some of the kapok stuffing for the pillows I am making and put it between the thin blankets that are our only covering. An extra layer of warmth to keep my body from becoming a frozen block.

I also strive to keep Irene Parker from becoming stiff but she is so weak that I am minded to think that her blood has stopped flowing round her limbs. The tea that she sups from time to time would not sustain the smallest creature on this earth.

The temperature is too low for my fingers to thread a needle.

And the scars on my wrists stand out blue against the whiteness of my arms.

I will join Lily in the kitchen. Some of the men in the George Vth ward have roused themselves to scavenge for logs and bits of broken branches that are to be found in the grounds surrounding us. I can see them from the window, wrapped in their greatcoats, bent over timber and sawing it up to keep the kitchen range alive. One man tells me that this activity takes him back to the frozen fields of the Somme in 1916. I see that he has cut up strips of sheets from his bed linen and wrapped them round his legs like puttees, to keep out the icy winds.

And the influenza is spreading amongst us. I hear that the medical wards are full of those who cough and splutter. Many are dying. When Lily hears that a soldier has gone to his Maker she brings in his coat and we use it to wrap around Irene. But yesterday the rattle in her lungs told us that she has not long to sojourn in this world.

18ᵗʰ December.

Mr Anderson brought his Magic Lantern Show last evening. He set it up in the dining hall and I was pleased to note that the curtains I made served to black out the room and heighten the experience. He began his talk about how his various 'slippers' as he called them worked, and took apart his triple lantern to illustrate the versatility of the machine. There were sighs of admiration from the audience as we saw volcanoes erupt and fireworks appear to brighten up the sky. And there was an amusing sequence where a butcher ran chasing a dog that had stolen a joint of meat; the slides running together like a man in pursuit of his quarry. Much laughter went around the room and I found that a chuckle was trying to rise within me. A rare event in my life now. Needless to say I caught the wayward noise before it escaped from my throat.

Then he showed us some slides of ships. In a series he called 'The Pride of the Clyde' we were treated to the launching of a passenger vessel called the "Aronda". We saw crowds of people standing by the dock waving their arms in cheer and I wondered if Tam had been amongst them.

I strained to look but the machine blurred and faded the images and moved on to other ones. We saw the ship slipping into the water and later her decks were heaving with troops on their way to India to serve in the Great War. Bombay, Karachi, Marseilles, Suez were ports that she served; places I had seen on the map of the world in the classroom. Was my cousin Alf one of the herd on board that ship? He had served in India as one of the Seaforth Highlanders in that terrible conflict.

There was a hush in the hall when Mr Anderson showed these scenes. I saw a few ex soldiers and sailors who had ended up in this place shuffle their feet in their disquiet of recollection.

Finally we were treated to an encore. The good man illustrated some special effects by rotating and sliding sections into his main plates.

We all marvelled at the pictures that he produced. One sequence stays with me. A sleeping soldier lies peacefully on his bed and then suddenly a series of rats appear to leap out of his mouth. Gasps of disbelief amongst us as this vile but fascinating tableau unfolds and much applause at the end of it. Mr Anderson says that 'The Rat Catcher' always goes down well especially with children, but I saw a few of the men tremble in their movements as they made their way to their wards for further incarceration.

As a distraction I thought of my own two bairns and strained to hear their laughter.

No more of that. Not now!

Not ever!

Some men stayed behind to help the good man dismantle his apparatus. I heard him say that perhaps his days were numbered as the moving pictures were putting him out of business. I have not much notion of these happenings but evidently according to Mistress Niven, new buildings were appearing all over the city in order to show silent films with musical accompaniments. And very popular they are appearing to be, she says.

Before he left, I ventured to ask Mr Anderson if it was the Alexander Stephen and Sons Company of Govan that had built the "Aronda". He told me it was and I said that I knew someone who had helped build that ship. 'Who was that?' he asked, and I replied straight away, 'Tom Anstruther, my husband,' without thinking first.

'Anstruther, now where have I heard that name before?'

In my foolish babble I fear I have given myself away. I turned on my heels and left him standing, my heart racing *into my mouth as I ran along the dark corridors into the emptiness of the sky.*

25ᵗʰ December

Lily brings me a cootie dumpling that she has stolen from the kitchen. She tells me that the smells from the raisins as I open the cloth are like the scents of Heaven. I take her word for it and eat it to please her.

But it is sawdust and ashes in my mouth. I have knitted some gloves for Lily from the unravellings of jumpers too darned and patched for further use. On them I have sewn her name so they should not be stolen from her.

And with two clothes pegs I have made more dollies for her niece Flora with clothes to match. On their bonnets I have used up the rest of the wool for pom-poms; pink and white little balls with flecks of green. Lily kisses me on both cheeks with gratitude.

I made myself scarce when Chaplain Sewell made his rounds today, finding some sewing to while away the time as he was conducting the Christmas Day service. Seemingly the new science called occupational therapy is no more than sewing for women and basket making for men.

Where is the science in that? I wonder what these poor soldiers who fought in the war will make of this task; their fumbling fingers working to shape the unruly hazel twigs?

Janitor Armstrong tells me that the coal strike may be over by the new year. He is feeding batches of The Hospital Gazette into the furnace to keep a modicum of heat for bare necessities.

A letter has arrived from my sister Meg. It has the post mark of Clydebank on it. Tam and she and my children have moved there as he has a position as a welder in John Brown Shipyards. They have taken a room and kitchen in Yoker. It is pleasantly appointed she says.

My son George is doing well at school and can read much of the text of the bible that he was given. My sister says in her faltering hand with much poor handwriting that he might take after me in his scholarship. I hope this is so. George has stopped asking after his mother. I am glad of that.

Margaret, she tells me, is musical like her father. Tam found an old piano which was being thrown out of a public house. He has taken it home and the blind man in the tenement has tuned it for them. Little Meg loves to play it and my sister hopes that she will have enough money from her cleaning jobs to pay for musical lessons later on. Both of my bairns now call my sister MOTHER.

29th December

Irene Parkes was buried today. It may seem strange to say this and I would not share my thoughts with Lily, but I envy her in her ending.

'Nae mair o' life's struggles,' my mother would have said. I know not whether she will rise or fall in the afterlife but Hell is at least a warm place Irene.

Take some comfort in that. There were none of her relatives present so Maggie, Lily and I joined a small gathering to make our goodbyes. I notice that her coffin was a mean crate, roughly hewn with no flowers upon it. She will lie in an unmarked grave, as will all of us I suspect when our time comes around.

Chaplain Sewell barely bothers to commend her soul to the Almighty before hastening back to the kitchen where Mrs Creel is waiting with a tumbler of whiskey for him.

2ⁿᵈ January 1921

Another New Year arrives with little to commend it but the blessing that the coal strike has ended. We will return slowly to normal.

Today Janitor Armstrong has filled the boiler with its first batch of black gold and has brought some nuggets to light our stove in the ward. When I undressed this evening I noticed my thin arms and ribs sticking out from my poor body.

I never thought I would look forward to mutton stew but at its mention my lips move in a gesture of anticipation. My thoughts go back to the tasty dumplings my mother made for us all and I feel my stomach tumble into itself with the memory of their sweet providence. In my dreams tonight please let me hear my father sing in thanksgiving and his wife, our mother, who was once so bonny, give out one of her rare smiles of tender warmth.

~

Christmas day arrives with a biting wind and sharp showers from the north.

'Merry Christmas Elvis!'

Bella comes downstairs and looks about her . No bunting, no tree and not a card on display. She sees the stack of mail that lies unopened by the fireside chair. After examining the postmarks she opens the ones from faraway places. Aunt Meg in Manitoba was coping well after a recent heart attack.

Friends now settled in New Zealand were enjoying all that space. An old colleague of Don's who had retired to France asking them to stay, any time they liked. 'Them: 'they': Dear Don and Bella.'

Ouch!

A large envelope with unfamiliar handwriting catches her eye. Inside an expensive card with a famous landscape that she recognised and a greeting:' What a stroke of luck meeting up with you the other day. Hope we can see each other again in the New Year. Love F.'

'Love F.' Mmmmmmn. She can hear her heart quicken its beat.

Then the one she had been waiting to open. A letter from her son. Tears came; sadness and pride flowing into the folds of her dressing gown. She studies the photograph that had been placed inside the letter. Tom posing awkwardly in the snow, squinting shyly up at the lens. At his side, a small dark-haired woman looks up at him as he holds her in a tight embrace around her shoulder. So this was Eloise!

Phone calls interrupt her reverie. A chorus of laughter from the cottage in Dovedale.

'It's not too late to join us Mum!'

And then the strained voice of Evie who had woken up in the morning and been sick. Don and Brenda had arrived the night before.

'With their two dogs mum. They are running around the kitchen as I speak. Two bloody great labradors! And she's never lifted a finger to help. They just expect to be waited on hand and foot. James says he'll take Dad to the pub later on but that leaves me with HER.'

Evie's voice had risen to a wail.'And you can tell she doesn't like children. She's ignoring Josh, who has been up since five by the way. She's just sitting in the living room doing her bloody crossword, leaving me to do it all! You won't change your mind, Mum and come over, please…'

'No I'm sorry love. I've made other plans. I'm meeting up with my friend Shirley today. How is Josh? Did he like all the new engines for his train set?'

'Listen for yourself.'

The voice of her young grandson brings a smile to her face. No Bamba can't come over today, but she would have him all to herself next week. She listens on to his prattle and feels herself weaken. Should she swallow her pride? Out of curiosity she opens the envelope postmarked 'Sleaford.' Inside it, a card with robins and glitter, one of the cheap sort, part of a set bought from somewhere like Woolworths no doubt. After the cloying rhyme she read then printed greeting: ' Best wishes for Christmas and New Year from Brenda and Donald.'

'No sorry, love, tell Mummy I can't come over today. Big hugs. Bye!'

She walks into the kitchen and lights one of the gas rings on the range. Holding the cheap card over the flame, she laughs as she sees the embers of insincerity float high into the warming air and come down again as fine black soot.

Methinks a large breakfast is called for. A fry up with a tot of brandy in my coffee to set me up for the day. She hears Elvis purr with approval as crumbs of sausage and crispy bacon fall from her plate to the saucer below.

Walking down from number 36, she notices a few people out and about. One or two brave fathers and sons testing out new bikes or roller blades. Some youths hanging out by the corner of the street. Several shops were open for those who would run out of milk or stale bread for the ham sandwiches at tea time.

Christmas! Were there any happy times that she could remember? She strives to get in touch with that sense of rosy anticipation on Christmas mornings when she was a small child. The times when a pillowcase was at the end of her bed and she heard the stumblings of her father's steps coming up the stairs. She had known who Santa was at an early age. She could smell the drink on him in her sleep. When he left the room, tripping over something in his wake, she would light her bedside lamp and hug away the secret hours till morning with the latest Enid Blyton, sucking the juices from the thick orange always to be found at the bottom of her pillowcase. The big present she would save until breakfast so he could see how surprised she was when she opened it up in front of him. Then the rare sight in the Anstruther household, her father's face folded in genuine pleasure.

Smiling to herself, she quickened her pace through the empty streets, saying to a passing lamp post: 'That's how I learnt to fake pleasure from an early age to please others, especially men.'

But when George left home, Christmas rituals were bleak affairs. Often there would be no presents as her mother slept her way through the day in order to avoid facing it. So Bella was left to entertain herself. Mercifully when television came into their lives, she would join another lonely little girl from Kansas, watching 'The Wizard of Oz' till she knew each scene by heart.

'Somewhere over the rainbow...'

Oh my, you are feeling sorry for yourself. Come on, remember the good times when your own kids were young.

But was she then ever really at the heart of things? Ailsa, after years of depression, suddenly woke up like Rumplestiltskin and took command of the family. Bella can see her mother now, notebook in her hand, writing down the names of those who had sent parcels which took all morning to unwrap, ready for the Boxing Day thank-you letters chore. After lunch they would be herded into teams for charades. As the children grew older they sought to outwit their grandmother in their choice of words to act out, inventing saucy phrases to shock her. She was never shocked. On her last Christmas before she died Iona had suggested 'coitus interruptus.' Nothing daunted, the old lady mustered the family to perform a series of elaborate mimes. The exaggerated motions of putting on coats served up the sound of the first phrase.

Then followed a group embrace before she began the silent imitation of tearing up newspapers, ending again with a group hug. Only when it came to the time when they had to act out the whole word, did she begin to look perplexed.

'Well, what does it mean?' she confronted Iona. 'How will we act out the whole word?'

Tom had scuttled off to feed his guinea pigs, and then Don, bless him, reminded his mother-in-law that the Queen's broadcast was due. 'Any minute now!'

Bella chuckles and smiles to a passing cyclist.

'Merry Christmas. Have a good one lady!'

'Have a good one!'

What would that be like?

She makes her way into the old city. High Pavement, Middle Pavement, Low Pavement, names bearing the testament to history and their places in the hierarchy of social life. Now these old streets harboured the swank of new money. Sushi bars, fitness centres, a Lizard Lounge, whatever that was, nestling amongst offices of lawyers and architects and software consultants. Towards the lower end of the town the cobbled streets took on a seamier look. Here were the sex shops with their blackened windows. Tattoo parlours. Charity outlets. An all-night cafe and a martial arts academy for those who felt brave enough to walk these streets after dark. Approaching Hockley, she sees the ample frame of Shirley and waves a greeting.

'Hi Shirley! I made it!

Inside the run-down Hall of the Salvation Army a warm fug of cigarette smoke hits them. She inhales the fume with gratitude. The bare space was decked with gaudy decorations and a large Christmas tree donated by the local Lions Club. Its few lights winked on and off in spasmodic greeting. Bella notes as well as the old lags she had expected to see, there were young people too. They all seemed intent on carrying out the familiar rituals of packing thin strips of paper with tobacco and lighting up to keep warm or be comforted by the nicotine or whatever else was inside their spliffs.

'Big Issue boys and girls,' Shirley says and smiles at one in happy recognition.

'Hey up Doug! Good to see you.'

'You too duck. Fancy a game of cards later on?'

Bella stands by her new friend, looking and feeling self conscious. What was she doing here? She had only volunteered to help in a moment of weakness one day when Shirley found out she was to be on her own on Christmas Day.

'Come with me love and make yourself useful. You'll enjoy yourself, I promise you.'

She notices an upright piano in the corner of the hall and remembers Ailsa vamping out 'You are my Sunshine' in Swallow's Rest. Then a brisk young woman asks her if she would help peel vegetables in the kitchen. She follows her gratefully in to a makeshift canteen where she finds others busy at their chores. Picking up a peeler, she starts to work. Soon the repetition of the task takes on its own rhythm she finds quite soothing. Maybe this was a fitting place to be at Christmas, amongst the lonely and the dispossessed.

A stable and a stall. In the company of those who have lost their way. Like me.

TWO

A STABLE AND A STALL

It wasn't until later on in the afternoon when she had washed up the last of the congealed gravy off the plates that she notices the young man. He had been following her around, gathering up the leftovers and handing out sweet mugs of tea along with the gifts of warm socks, torches and twists of tobacco.

'You don't remember me Bella, do you?'

She stares into the growth of a week old beard and struggles for a name, a memory, a story that would give some clue to his identity.

'Of course not. Why should you? You must have seen hundreds like me. And it was a long time ago, before I became a gentleman of the streets so to speak.'

Now she regards him carefully, intent on muscling her brain into retrieval mode.

'It's the beard,' she says lamely.

'Barry.'

'Barry?'

'Barry! I think it was seven years ago since we last met. I was referred to you at the Centre. I kept running away from my foster home. Trying to find my dad who turned out to be in jail after all that.'

Then she had him. Talk of the jail was the trigger. She now could see that truculent fourteen year old who dealt with his fears by frequent flights to London. Bella never knew if he would turn up to sessions with her, so chaotic was his life at that time. And here he was, under that facial furze, a good looking young man with intelligent blue eyes.

She smiles in happy recognition.

'We used to spend time writing to your dad.'

'You corrected my spellings.'

'Oh God, I didn't, did I?'

'Yes you did. But I didn't mind. I was the world's worst speller. Still am.'

'Weren't you good at music?'

A filament thread of memory comes to her rescue. She hadn't quite lost it yet.

'Didn't you play the guitar? You loved the old rock stars if I remember rightly.'

'Yeah!'

His face beams in gratitude.

'You bought me old Eric Clapton LP's you picked up in Charity shops. Derek and the Dominoes and The Cream.'

'Well I never! Fancy you remembering that.'

'I remember lots. Its good to see you Bella. I missed you when our time was up.'

'I'm sorry Barry, that's just the way it was.'

Time was always up with the youngsters that she saw. A long waiting list with other boys like him to see and other girls like Madison.

'Hang on a minute Barry. Just let me finish taking

round these mugs of tea and Christmas cake. Can you find somewhere a little more private so we can carry on talking?'

He takes two chairs from the dusty stage and places them against the radiator. When she joins him he starts to light up a thin white pencil stub of tobacco.

She says: 'I'll find you some more. I think I know where there is a secret stash.'

'Thanks Bella. Want one?'

'I'd love one!'

She inhales deeply and allows the blue ringed circle of smoke to rise into the air feeling a warm rush of pleasure flow through her body.

'Why can something which tastes so good be so bad for you?'

'What makes you say that?'

'I've had cancer.'

There! She had said the word. Cancer. Casually saying 'cancer' in a matter of fact voice. No hedging, no euphemisms to disguise the shame of the sound. Out it had tumbled without restraint.

'I'm sorry to hear that.' His voice low with concern.

'Don't be Barry. I think I'm okay now. People survive after breast cancer. Anyway I expected something like that to strike me at some time in my life.'

'Why Bella? What makes you say that?'

'As a punishment. If I was a religious person I might even say it was a punishment for my sins. Are you a religious person Barry?'

She sees him knit his brow in a furrow of a frown.

'Not specially. Why a punishment Bella?'

She laughs, but it is tears that he sees pooling at the corner of her eyes. He watches her carefully as she takes another gulp of the cigarette.

She is older than he remembers. Thinner. Careworn. There are lines around those blue grey eyes of hers. But now as then there is an innocence about her. A warmth. He would like to bury his face into her body but fears that she might just break.

'It has been a long time since I have smoked.'

'Why punish yourself Bella?' he persists.

'I'm not sure I should tell you. Me counsellor. You client. Remember?'

'But you're not my counsellor now. It feels like you are an old friend. Someone I've missed and caught up with again.'

'Really?'

'Really. I often wondered about you when we had our times together. What were you really like? And I had these pictures in my mind. You lived in this perfect house, were the perfect mum, led the perfect life. I wanted a piece of that perfection.'

'Then I'll have to shatter your illusions Barry and I'm not sure that would be fair.'

'I'm not fourteen any more Bella.'

She looks down at his calloused hands as he rolls up another lump of tobacco in a slice of paper, carefully easing the fibrous threads into the shape of a tiny tube.

'Go on Bella. I'm listening.'

'Well you are right in one respect Barry. I am a mum. I've got three children, all grown up now. But but I did have four.'

'How come?'

'I had twins. My daughter Evie was one of a twin, only she doesn't know that she had a sister.'

He hands her the roll-up. She shakes her head.

' You have it Barry. Iona my first child was perfect you see. She was born at home and everything went to plan – such a beautiful baby. My husband Don called her Snowhite because she had jet black hair and a smooth white skin. Then we named her after the place that she was conceived, but you don't want to know about that – too much information my kids would say. So when I was pregnant again I thought it would be the same. But it wasn't.'

He sees her look up at him and then around the hall. Raised voices at the billiard table catch her attention for a moment. Then she drop her head.

'Why wasn't it?'

'I could tell something was wrong when the labour went on for hours. The midwife getting flustered and Don insisting that an emergency doctor be called. By that time I was well past it. I just wanted it all to be over. The doctor came and eventually Evie was born. She wasn't a pretty sight. Bruised all over and with the brand of forceps on her forehead. But she was healthy and strong. And then I could hear Don saying something like, 'There's another one!'

'I didn't feel a thing when it came out but I remember hearing whispers at the end of the bed. By that time Evie was crying and the midwife had put her to my breast. Then the doctor hands me this bloodied shawl. There are big clots of purple on it and inside,' she pauses, taking a breath and reaching out for his hand, 'this thing with a huge head,' her voice now faltering now, 'like one of those monsters that you see in Dr. Who.'

'Put her to the other breast,' the midwife is saying, 'she's a poorly little thing. It will give her some comfort. But I couldn't do it Barry. I couldn't even look at her. I remember shouting for her to be taken away, saying that she wasn't mine, then I felt this spurt of milk come into my right breast.'

'Was that the one that had cancer?'

'The one that should have fed my other baby.'

Now both her hands were clutching his in a tightened grip.

'What happened to her Bella?

'At first I didn't know. At the time I really just wanted to get rid of it. If only someone would wrap it up in The Manchester Guardian and take it away with the afterbirth like they did when Iona was born. Isn't that an awful thing to say?'

She looks up at him and starts to shake. Those amazing grey eyes wide open and seeming to see right through him.

He takes off his fleece and wraps it around her. It reeks of smoke and smells of the city, but he knows it is warm.

'They did take her away. First to an intensive care unit at the hospital and then later to a Home where they look after babies and children with defects. I think it was run by the nuns. I never saw her again. I got ill you see, Barry. Depression. I couldn't feel a thing for months. The world just went on around me. That's when my mother came to live with us and look after the children. Then eight months later I was pregnant with my son Tom. And he was the perfect baby. I just poured all the love I had left inside me into him.'

'And your other little girl? The one in the Home with the nuns?'

'They told me she died just before Evie's first birthday. Iona had just started school and Tom was moving inside me – and still I didn't want to know. I never talked about her. I never gave her a name. Would you believe that? That's your perfect mother for you Barry. I'm sorry.'

'So you felt you needed to be punished?'

'Yes I did.'

'But that's so unfair.'

She reaches up and with her fingers begins to soften the creases on his brow.

'That's very sweet of you to be so concerned. Thank you Barry. But I think I would call it justice.'

Someone begins to play the piano. One of the older men starts to sing: Oh Danny boy, Oh Danny boy I love you so…'

The hall quietens, first out of respect, then in appreciation. The man has a good voice. He carries the tune well.

Another man starts to tell a story. Then a joke risked in the company of strangers.

She hears the melancholy notes of a harmonica ascend a scale and feels a sense of calmness return to her.

~

'You okay Bella?' I saw you were being looked after by one of the Big Issue lads. He seemed to be very fond of you.'

'Yes I think he was, despite, well yes, a lovely young man.'

'But hardly the Christmas you expected love. A bit of a busman's holiday for you eh?'

'Yes, I suppose so Shirley. But actually it was very special. I can't explain but somehow I feel a little lighter.'

They are sitting in the Old Angel Inn. Crowds of young people have gathered in the early evening to escape from their families, the washing up, the quarrels over presents, the joy of jigsaws and charades... and they were spending money, more money than Barry would earn in a year selling his magazines.

'What is a cootie dumpling Bella? You are Scottish, you might know?'

She raises an eyebrow in surprise.

'A clootie dumpling? Where did that come from? It's a steam pudding I think that's been wrapped up in a cloth; a Scots expression I haven't heard for years. My mother used to make them when I was a child. They were lovely and tasty. And people ate them at Christmas.'

'I thought as much.'

'What made you ask?'

'Oh just something I have been reading. Such a sad story love, I won't go into it now, but there is a part in it where a woman called Lily gives a clootie dumpling to her friend at Christmas time and she says the smells of it were like the scents of Heaven.'

'What a lovely phrase!'

She leaves Shirley on Stoney Street and begins her walk home, not heading the warnings of her friend. She would be okay. She had a mobile phone. It was such a lovely night. She needed time to think. Threading her way back through the city she imagines Barry crouching in a doorway. She wonders what he will do with the twenty pound note she gave him. Would it go on drink? Drugs? Did it matter? His choice. Who led the perfect life anyway?

But what made her choose to tell him her secret. She reflects that in all her time in and out of therapy over the years she had told no one about that part of her life. Months spent on the tortuous relationship with her mother, years in endless analysis about her missing father. Yet there was no one she really trusted to open up to and reveal that stain of shame that had clung to her for decades.

Until now.

At Christmas time in a Homeless shelter with a boy she scarcely knew.

The house is cold when she gets in. On the way into the kitchen for a nightcap, she notices that Elvis has not touched his gourmet meal that she bought for him especially for the day. 'Too rich for your digestive system was it my friend? Let's hope you are keeping my side of the bed warm.'

But when she climbs into bed Elvis is not there. All night long she reaches out for him in her sleep and feels only the emptiness of the air around her.

THREE

DR. SCOBIE.

January 5th 1021

I FIRST MEET THE GREAT MAN!

'Mrs Anstruther? I believe I am talking to Mrs Jean
Anstruther.'

He catches me at my sewing; bending over and
unpicking an unyielding thread from the petticoats of a
woman's skirt.

'I prefer to be known by my maiden name if you don't
mind.'

Then I add the word: 'Sir,' so as not to sound
impertinent.

I look up and find him flustered, opening up a large
buff file and scanning the pages within it for clues.

'Its Logan. It's Miss Jean Logan, Dr Scobie.'

He looks surprised, then relieved. Long drooping moustaches, flecking rust with grey, rise and fall. They frame a gentle mouth.

'So you know my name, Mistress, I mean Miss Logan.'

'Everyone has heard of you Dr. Scobie. You have been ill have you not? I can quote from the Hospital Gazette: 'Dr Archibald Scobie has endured a lengthy sickness with quiet forbearance and fortitude.' Is that not so?'

I see the moustaches dance at their edges as he smiles.

'You have been well informed dear lady.'

'I make it my business to be acquainted with the running of this,' I pause for a while before I say, 'asylum.'

'Indeed,' he replies, clearing his throat. I note that his expression is now much more guarded.

' Asylum it is indeed.'

He clears his throat again and then takes a breath.

'Miss Logan, how came you to be here?'

'I was sent here Dr.Scobie. I thought you would have known that.'

'You were sent here from Duke Street prison where I believe you were held for nearly nine whole months.'

He is no fool this man, for all his 'indeeds'. He has read all that there is in that big buff file. I tell myself to tread carefully in my interactions with him.

'And why do you think you spent time there, in one of the most notorious places in our city?'

I reply again as evenly as I can.

'I was sent to that place as well, sir.'

Another throaty growl and an 'ahem' before he pursues his point.

'You were sent there for a crime that you committed Miss Logan. Some might say it was a hanging crime and

you are lucky that your life has been spared. I note that
you did not not deny any of the facts put before you at
your trial.'

I suffer the blow that he has dealt me and give him
an answer.

'I don't deny it now. But I have no wish to rake over
the coals of my misfortune that have brought me here. To
this, eh, asylum.'

'I see,' he says and ponders on me with those pale blue
eyes of his. They seem to look right through me. They take
in my braided hair, now turned the colour of snow over
these past few months; they glance down to my grey dress
and my apron, borrowed from the linen room, they note
my slippers, two sizes too big for my slender feet. Only the
brooch belongs to me and he can't see through that.

'I believe that you have also refused to see your
husband when he tried to make visits to see you. And
your bairns as well. A boy and a girl I believe.

George and Margaret. How old will they be now?'

He makes another dumbshow of consulting my notes.

'Six and four years of age and missing their mother I
shouldn't wonder.'

'They have a good mother in my sister Meg, sir. I have
no worries on their account.'

There is a pause in the interrogation. I continue with
my sewing. Mistress Niven has given me some close work
today. My eyes hurt and the spectacles I have been given
are too weak for the purpose.

'Dr. Scobie, what is it that you want from me? You have,
after all my whole life folded in front of you.'

'I wish to help you Madam, but I need to know the
best way of going about it.'

'You are seeking for a diagnosis for my condition with a view to finding a cure, if there is one?'

'Indeed. Precisely so.'

'So can I ask have you come to any conclusions thus far?'

'Not yet. Forgive me, Miss Logan, you are an intelligent woman. I see that I can be direct with you. I am not yet sure if I am dealing with someone who is suffering from a profound sense of melancholia or who has perhaps a delusional insanity that needs to be treated more directly. Mental illness is not an exact science. It is a youthful branch of medical enquiry and I have to tell you that straightening out a deformed mind is much much more complex than mending a broken limb.'

I am silenced by these words but mind myself to keep my composure.

I see him fidget with his pen, unscrewing the top off and placing it on his left knee which seems to cause him pain. Up and down he rolls the gold clasp; up and down those expensive Harris Tweed trousers. I catch it gleam through his fingers. He doesn't know what to say next. Poor Dr Scobie with all those letters after his name and his recent training at the John Hopkins University in the United States of America.

'I am sorry if I appear something of a mystery doctor but I am not unduly concerned what label you may attach to my malady. I have been called many things that we would both regard as being singularly unpleasant. All I ask now is to be safe here in this place for I am truly in need of sanctuary.

Just a stable and a stall where I can rest my head against the cruelties of this world.'

He screws the top back on his pen and puts it away in his top breast pocket, alongside a neatly folded white handkerchief. I may even have embroidered that pattern that shyly peeks from its corners.

When he speaks again his voice is gentler than before.

'I understand your wishes dear lady and I won't take up any more of your time this day for I can see that you are busily occupied. We will meet again shortly in my office. I will ask the good Sister Jewell to make a more formal appointment.'

'I shall look forward to that Dr Scobie. And I hope you progress well in your convalescence.'

'Thank you Miss Logan.'

And so he takes his leave. He bows his head to me in polite recognition, then turns to gather up his papers. I see that he has a slight limp in his left leg and his measured steps falter occasionally as his polished brogues make their way up the corridor into the distant sunlight. When I return to the linen room I find that my body is shaking. Mistress Niven sees my distress and allows me time before I pick up my needle again. This dear lady never intrudes upon me and I am grateful for her silence.

I never want to hear that name of Duke Street again. I can still feel the spittle on my face, gobbed from the mouths of the common women; thieves and miscreants clamouring to insult me as I came through those high walls for my months of living hell. There are no depths to the shame that I suffered there.

Haud on Jeannie and haud things DOWN!

FOUR

LOST

Bella wakes with a start. Reaching out she feels the empty space with its tufts of orange and white in the hollow. So it wasn't a dream. Elvis wasn't there.

She dresses quickly, working her way into a fury. Opening cupboards, looking around all his familiar haunts. And when she had done, she starts all over again, heart racing, body lathering itself into a sweat. Opening the back door, she calls beyond the bare yard.

'Elvis! Elvis! Elv…' her voice rising in desperation.

She studies the contours of his favourite cushion, the one she had left him on the previous day. It was still perfectly formed in his curled up shape. But when she puts her hand on it she finds that it is cold.

Then it dawns of her that although she had lived here for over two months she still didn't really know any of the neighbours. She nodded at Mrs Chakrabatti, from number 34, in passing and smiled at her teenage sons when they walked in from school. Nice young men; studious and quietly spoken, destined to be doctors or lawyers maybe she thought. She avoided the man at thirty eight. Mr O'Dowd had wanted to be friendly when she moved in, too friendly Bella thought, for someone in her position. The Polish family across the road had asked her if they could do anything for her when the removal men had done their job, but she declined politely. Anonymity was what she craved for then. And the rest of the street was a blur. Young people mostly, with careers in the city no doubt. The older ones kept themselves to themselves, perhaps sensing that their neighbourhood was in transition and their artisan houses were being taken over by those who had no sense of their history. Come to think about it, neither had she. She had just toured haphazardly round the old parts of the town with the romantic notion in her head that she wanted to live somewhere completely different from 'Swallow's Rest'. The 'For Sale' sign outside number thirty six prompted her to put in an offer, without weighing up the pros and cons as Don would have done. The offer was accepted and so she made an exit from her old house and her marriage in a matter of weeks.

She knew Elvis would have to come with her. He belonged to her; he was the bridge from her old life to the new. He had not been the most tolerant cat they had during their married life, but he had been special.

'Damn it, he is special. Stop talking to yourself in the past tense.'

One day, was it twelve or thirteen years ago, Tom had walked into the house with a stray cat he found mewling around the lake. No one had the heart to turn it out Three days later Mog, as she became known, produced a litter of six kittens. Elvis was the runt. A puny ginger and white ball of fluff. He had to fight for the teat and scramble with his siblings for warmth and protection. When the rest of the kittens found new homes, they were left with Elvis. This cat was a contrary animal, refusing his basket and preferring the laps of those who did not like felines. He didn't mix with other cats. He followed Tom around like a puppy. He let birds live. He regarded most people with disdain.

'That animal has a old soul in him,' Ailsa would say. And when she spent her dying months with the family, the two old souls kept each other company. Elvis was a friend; awkward, idiosyncratic but always there.

Don was fond of repeating: 'Dogs have owners but cats have staff!'

He couldn't desert her now! Surely not!

So Bella decides to take the plunge and begins to knock on doors. Mrs Chakrabatti had not seen Elvis but she would send Sanjay and Vik on their bikes to scout the neighbourhood when they came home from school. Perhaps he had strayed into the allotments? Mr O'Dowd was at his sisters in Kent, number forty told her, and wouldn't be back until the New Year but she would keep her eyes peeled. The Smologas often saw Elvis across the road to their side of the street and make for the green area in the corner. But not today or yesterday. It was Christmas Day after all... And then there was the Sikh couple, and Mr and Mrs Kaur who ran the shop with her brother who helped out at the weekends. They didn't know anything about cats, but were sorry she was upset. Would she like to come inside for some refreshment?

It occurs to Bella as she is making her rounds that her street was a very cosmopolitan place. Over half the people she spoke to were migrants. Mr O'Dowd had come from County Clare in the sixties. The Chakrabattis were part of the wave that fled from the tyranny of Idi Amin in Uganda. The Kaurs spoke proudly of their past home in Northern India. The Polish family were the most recent settlers since the advent of Britain joining the European Union.

Everyone seemed to get on. She remembered her first few months in a strange country when she moved from Scotland, feeling at first out of place but then soon feeling at home. Others around her laughed at her accent and then just shrugged and accepted her. Has that happened to the Smolagas and the Prasads and other she had met today?

'I hope so.'

Feeling tired, she goes home and finds a photograph of Elvis. One taken in the garden of 'Swallows Rest', lying in a wheelbarrow on a pile of compost ready to spread over the vegetable patch. She takes it to the Post Office and makes copies of the print then puts up signs round the neighbourhood: LOST a ginger tom cat called Elvis, much loved family pet. If found please phone... She debates about offering a reward but decides against it.

Then she begins to get the phone calls. The first one was in the middle of the night and it scares her. A drunk, doing an impression of 'Love me Tender' and asking her if she had any knickers on. Others follow. A bunch of lads say they were phoning from the box opposite her house. They tell her they had skinned a cat and put it on a pole. She was shaking with fear and fury when they slammed down the phone to the sound of raucous laughter. One or two callers tells her they had sightings as far away as Loughborough and at breakfast a few days later a strange voice with menace in its tone says he was holding her cat and wanted a thousand pounds reward for its release.

She takes down the notices and begins a process of mourning that she found satisfying, willing herself to imagine that her old companion had gone out for a pee and curled himself at the base of an oak tree. He was surrounded by leaves to keep him warm when he died, quite painlessly in his sleep. In her mind she picks him up and lays him to rest under his favourite place under the plum tree in 'Swallows Rest', burying him with his favourite cushion. Although she did not believe in God, she went out and bought a bottle of cheap champagne from the Off Licence and said her own prayer in his memory. Draining the last of the bubbles, she feels a cathartic sense of release.

Later she phones Evie and tells her the news. Her daughter was not as upset as she would have liked her to be. 'He was only a cat Mum, for Heaven's sake. You are not going to turn into one of those dotty women that rescue donkeys, are you?'

'I know love. But he was part of our family when we were all together.'

Evie's tone is now more thoughtful. 'I thought you said you were beginning to move on.'

'I am, just indulge me a little now, will you?'

Her daughter's voice is gentle now. 'Okay. Listen Mum. You wouldn't like to come over a little earlier than you planned. I'm actually finding life a bit difficult at present.'

'Of course just say the word. When?'

'Tomorrow?'

She enjoys her ride to the little village where she once lived and where Evie lives now. It takes her out of the city to the small hills or Wolds as they were called here that rise and fall gently to the south. Gentle country she thinks, pleasant pastureland, with strips of development fingering their way into the flatlands of Leicestershire and beyond.

When she arrives at Evie's she sees her daughter looking tired. Anxious to mask her fears Bella begins to bombard her daughter with questions. They were met with weary but patient replies. Yes, she had seen the doctor recently, sure her hospital place was booked, things were fine but she wasn't sleeping, she was still being sick in the mornings and they might have to do a caesarian.

Bella was alerted. 'Why what do you mean? A caesarian?'

'Well the consultant says that the twin born second may not have enough oxygen if stage two of labour is protracted with a normal birth. It's best to be on the safe side, he says and quite honestly I'd rather not do all that hard work again if I can help it. Don't fuss Mum please!'

'I see.' Bella feels rebuked.

Now would be the time to tell her, she thinks. Before Don steps in. She checks her tone of voice, her body language, the expression on her face and begins rehearsing an opening statement.

'Evie...'

'Anyway Mum, they look great. Do you want to see them? I've got the scan.'

'Really?'

Evie hands her a small black and white strip of negative film. In it she begins to detect small outlines. A swirl of cloud and shadow, and the distinct shape of two little tadpoles with large rounded heads formed into a mandala-like circle. Yin and Yang snug in their ocean deep within her daughter's belly.

She gasps in surprise. 'They are so real Evie. Oh if only they had such things like that in my day.'

'And can you see the arms and the legs?'

'What's that, there?'

'Where?'

Bella points to two places that lay in a fuzzy shadow.

'That's their hearts Mum. We can't tell what sex they are. But we know it is two eggs not one. They are not going to be identical.'

'Well I never!' Bella sighs in relief. 'Have you got the dates yet?'

'Middle of March. The sixteenth or thereabouts. You haven't booked a holiday have you?'

'Of course not. I'll be there. That is if you need me of course.'

'Oh I'll need you. We will all need you. And this young man will want his Bamba.'

Josh had woken up from his afternoon nap, floppy, tearful and a little too tetchy for his grandmother's liking.

'How about we go and feed the ducks Josh? Give Mummy a bit of a rest.'

She carries that picture of the mandala in her head as the small boy tugs against her in the winter cold. Should she have been brave enough to persist in talking to Evie about her own birth? She tussles with her choices and decides to take the cowardly option.

'Bamba! Want to go home. Want to see 'C Beebies!'

She looks down at him. With his red wellies and bobble hat to match he was entering that difficult phase in toddler life when his behaviour could not be predicted from moment to moment.

'You know Josh if my mummy was here she'd say you were being a big tumfy now. Let's walk on for a bit and see if we can see the horses in the field. Bamba has brought some sugar lumps for them.'

'I want C Beebies! I want C Beebies!' He was working his way into one of his tantrums, his pint sized body quivering with rage.

Oh Lord, give me strength!

'And I want a little boy who is going to do what he is told and go and feed the horses.'

Then comes the wail, the throwing of his body backwards and forwards, his fists pummelling into her legs. Purple cries of anger begin to punctuate the air.

Bella watches the performance with fascination. Then she begins to sing:

'Anything you can do I can do better. I can do anything better than you.' She lets go of his hand and starts to rock about, contorting her face into a grimace and stamping her feet. 'Ney ney ney ney ney!,' her voice ringing up and down a scale, 'I want to feed the horses! I want to feed the horses! I want!'

That did it. He stops and stares at her, then looks round to see if anyone is watching, his small mouth opening like a beak in a mixture of surprise and admiration.

She stops. He takes her hand meekly. She passes him a lump of sugar and he sucks on it greedily.

'Now don't tell your mother you were eating sugar. It's bad for your teeth.'

She teaches him how to position his tiny hand flat and places the sugar at the centre of his palm. 'Keep it steady now Josh, we don't want the horses to think that one of your fingers is a sugar lump.'

The big brown Bey bends down and sweeps his long tongue over the boy's hand and onto his sleeve before making a crunchy noise and swallowing up the sweetness in a 'neigh' of gratitude.

'He's tickly, Bamba. More! Again!'

James comes in from the golf course with the fresh smell of goodwill and the remnants of the nineteenth hole on his breath. He will run to fat in later years Bella thinks. Already he has the look of a well fed auctioneer.

He picks up his son and swings him about his head.

'My goodness, aren't we pleased to see Bamba. Grandpa wasn't much fun under the thumb of 'Brisk -and- bracing,' was she?'

'He wasn't that bad,' Evie says quickly rising to the defence of her father.

'He wasn't that good either. Be honest, Evie. Whatever does Don see in her?'

'She's kind. She likes dogs.'

'Hitler liked dogs so I'm told.'

'Anyhow, they've gone now. I just think Dad was embarrassed. I don't think he knew how to behave with us Mum. It felt a bit weird them sleeping together in your bed.'

Bella starts in mock horror. 'I hope you are going to put me somewhere else. I'll sleep in the spare bunk bed in Josh's room if you like.'

But James had not finished. 'Anyway Bella you are very welcome if you want to come to the dinner dance with us on Hogmanay. We can always get someone else to babysit.'

'Who at this late hour?' Evie hedges.

'One of the girls in The Close would do it, especially if we made it worth their while.'

'No it's fine,' Bella interrupts. 'I'm really looking forward to a quiet night in with Josh.'

'You know who will be there, don't you?' James is handing her a large scotch by the fireside.

'Tell me. I have no idea.'

'Rick Tavener.'

'Really,' she replies, trying her best to affect a languid tone of disinterest.

Evie curls her lips in distaste. 'I expect he will bring one of his trophy women.'

'Maybe my love, but he was asking a lot of questions about my mother-in-law when we played a round of golf the other day.'

'And I hope you were suitably circumspect son-in-law.'

Bella could see that she was being baited for the hook. 'Tell me about these trophy women' she adds, looking to Evie for an answer.

'Well whenever Rick Taverner is at some important 'Do' where he has to look good, he always brings some blonde, years younger than himself. It's hardly ever the same one. Bit pathetic I think. He must get them from an agency: 'Rent a bimbo', that sort of thing.'

'Isn't he married then?'

'Was a couple of times, so I've been told.'

'Quite the Lothario,' Bella says, scathingly. 'So if I came I'd only cramp his style. Remind him how old he really is. I'll leave him to you both, and his latest dalliance, thank you very much.'

But she wonders about him. He lingers in her thoughts. She spends that night in the cramped little single bed wondering about him.

Freddie now transformed into Rick.

There was not much that worth watching on New Years Eve when she finally put Josh to bed. No Jimmy Shand. No White Heather Club or Kenneth McKellar in his full regalia of kilt and sporran warbling on about 'his ain folk.' Times had changed. She remembered Ailsa telling her stories of tenement life in Glasgow at Hogmany. Small kitchens heaving with friends and family; singing and shortbread and on the stroke of midnight, a dark haired neighbour stepping into the room with a lump of coal to put on the fire.

'Lang may yer lumb reek wi' o'er folks coal.'

A good Scottish sentiment that! Hospitality and parsimony wrapped up in one phrase. And then the strains of 'Auld Lang Syne.' She taught Josh the first verse before he went to bed and they crossed their hands and pumped their elbows up and down in due solemnity.

When Big Ben sounded the final toll of the old year, she takes a glass of James' single malt onto the patio outside. It was a clear night. Stars stood out in white relief. Bella feels humbled by their presence. Fireworks race across the sky from some way away. Tollerton airfield perhaps? She raises a glass and whispers to the big universe all around her: 'Ring out the old, ring in the new Whatever it might be.' Then a shiver of foreboding takes her back inside.

FIVE

ON THE COUCH

THE JOTTER

JANUARY 8TH 1920

When the call comes again to see Dr. Scobie, I am ironing the hospital sheets.

An arduous task which causes my back to ache. It was Elsie Macpherson who took me to the great man's office. When I arrived he was standing by the door and welcomed me with a shy smile. I noted the dark shadows around his eyes and the yellow pallor on his kindly face and wondered to myself how effective his convalescence had really been.

'I hope that you may be returning to good health Dr. Scobie,' I say.

'It must be hard for a doctor to take care of himself and abide by his own medical ministrations.'

'Indeed Mistress, er Miss Logan. Indeed. Thank you for your concerns. Step this way if you please.'

Oh my, what a room! I will describe it to Lily when I am finished here.

Everywhere the smell of burnished wood and leather. I take in the grand old desk with a mass of papers scattered on its surface. There is a photograph of a young woman neatly framed at the edge of it. Would this be his daughter Grace that Elsie has told me about on our journey through the winding corridors to his sanctum?

Bookcases line the walls, filled with hide bound volumes of what I suppose to be medical tracts. Two large commodious chairs sit on either side of his desk.

In the middle of the room, standing on a patterned Persian rug, there is a sedan couch. It is the only furniture that looks as if a woman's hand has been upon it for a tartan cloth is folded underneath its corners, giving the seat a hue of gaiety.

Sumptuous cushions of red and green silk sit at intervals along its smooth back.

Someone has plumped up these cushions; they perch in anticipation.

Dr. Scobie bids me to sit on the Royal Stuart plaid and I do so, feeling somewhat apprehensive by this invitation. I see that he sits behind his desk and takes out a gold watch from his waistcoat. I await his next utterance with a fluttering of nerves rising and falling within me.

'Miss Logan,' he begins, 'I have brought you here to commence a series of treatment sessions that I hope will have some remedial benefit.

They certainly have ameliorated some of the symptoms of those shambling wrecks of humanity that you may have seen wandering round the asylum; those poor men who lost their minds during the travails of the Great War.'

I see him shake his head and so I follow his lead by looking grave myself.

'You may have heard of a new branch of science called psychoanalysis. Pioneered by a distinguished doctor called Sigmund Freud?'

I nod, obligingly. I have never heard of this person but it wouldn't do to show my ignorance to this clever man.

'Well Dr. Freud and others, and I include myself as one of his brethren, believe that our minds are very deep and complex. May I take the liberty to use an analogy that you may well understand? I am sure you were privy to the news of the dreadful fate of the Titanic ship, reckoned to be unsinkable, but which sadly floundered on an iceberg on her maiden voyage to America. When I say that our minds are rather like icebergs, Miss Logan, I know you will be able to hold such a picture in your imagination.'

I nod my head again in agreement. I was aware of the fate of that beautiful vessel that had succumbed to the underwater treachery of an iceberg, but what had this got to do with the workings of the mind? I sense that Dr. Scobie has trouble getting to the heart of things so I must be patient and follow his circumlocution.

'Well, ahem, the conscious mind inhabits only the tip of the iceberg, the part that you see out of the water; that is our rational self, says Dr. Freud.

But what lies beneath dear lady is a large and powerful mass of mystery.

Here resides our unconscious self. So far no one has fathomed out what primitive forces inhabit that region, but the psychoanalysts say that if we begin to explore it we may come to understand a little better what drives us to do the things that we do in our conscious lives.'

I could see that he was getting carried away with his

own rhetoric and though I had a wish to ground him with clarification I keep silent.

'There are diamonds of joy and devils of destruction inhabiting these areas of our minds, believe me.'

At this point I feel I had to intervene. 'Pray sir, how do you propose to access these places you say lie so deep? Will it require a surgical procedure? A sharpened knife perhaps?'

I see him smile and smooth his flowing moustaches with his fine, pale hand.

'No my dear, we will merely talk to begin with. This is our initial pathway to the high road of the unconscious. Later we may try some hypnosis to find a way into your dreams but for the moment let us just converse. Allow me to request that you sit more comfortably on this couch. You may indeed arrange these pretty cushions about your head so you can be more at ease.'

I sense a trap in waiting. The doctor wants my nightly dreams!

He requires me to confide in him. I cannot trust this process. I cannot trust anyone.

So I reply: 'I am very comfortable where I am sir, Dr. Scobie. Pray continue to talk and I will answer your questions with diligence.'

'It is not diligence that I require Miss Logan. It is honesty, spontaneity, your free associative thoughts... we may need a little time for them to flow but nevertheless I would like to make a start by exploring your childhood with you in order to see if we can make any links to your present condition. Let me start by sharing what I know about you.'

I see him take his spectacles from a small case on his desk. He opens my buff file and reads for a moment before putting it down again. Now he folds his arms across his chest and leans back on his cracked leather chair.

'I know something of you history. You were born into poverty, were you not?

Brought up in a room and kitchen in the slums of the city with eight or was it nine brothers and sisters? Your mother wore herself out with the constant trammels of childbirth. No way out from the mire for her and many of her class, sad to say.

And yet you were an intelligent child, spotted by the minister of the kirk and your teachers as one who showed great promise. You rose up from your background and became a teacher yourself. From all accounts you were thought of highly at your school on Scotland Road.'

He consults the buff file again, taking time to find reference to my teaching days. 'Miss Logan has a fine mind and manages her pupils with admirable strictness,' those were the words that Mr Mayhew, the headmaster, wrote about you, I believe. And yet it seems that you return to your origins when you marry Thomas Anstruther, a welder in the Fairfield shipyards. I confess I read that news with a tinge of disappointment for you may have had a sense of your mother's history repeating itself in your own experience as your family multiplied over the years.

That is of course until something within you snapped and we begin a chain of events that brought you eventually here. But let us not speak of that now.

First tell me about your early years, Miss Logan. Share with me your first memory if you please.'

I am taken aback. Is nothing of me withheld from his scrutiny? I must seek to stall him, to recover my wits.

I catch him take out his expensive fountain pen from his top pocket and poise it over a sheet of clean white paper. He is going to write things down.

The man wants a story that will fit his new-found

conversion to, what did he call it? Psycho? Psycho-
something? I did not catch the whole word in my head.
But by the manner in which he describes my early life, he
wants to hear a sad story. He requires 'The Little Match
Girl' in its pathos. I therefore must fashion my tale to the
melodramas like the 'Penny Dreadfuls' my mother read
and kept hidden in a box under her bed.

So I strain at my imagination to run away with itself,
half closing my eyes in the search of suitable things to
share. Then I begin:

'My first memory was the room I grew up in, sir, in
the bed wherein I was born.'

'In the bed where you were born Jeannie, Miss Logan,
pray child go on...'

'I am in bed, Dr Scobie. I am with my mother and my
new sister Meg.

It is in a bed with a mattress of straw. My mother is
feeding the baby and I can smell the milk upon her. It is a
sweet smell but stale as well, as it clings to her unwashed body.'

'How old are you child? Jean, Jeannie?'

'I am not sure sir. I must be a little over a year as that
is when my sister was born.'

'Remarkable recall, remarkable.' I hear him scratching
the expensive gold nib over the paper. 'Continue if you will.'

I can tell that he is pleased with what I have given
him so far. I trawl down deeper and catch more images
through the nets of recollection.

'I feel the rough army blanket drawn up about us. I am
cold and I too clamour for the warmth of my mother's breast.'

'Clamour!' I see his moustaches quiver with delight.
'That is an excellent word. You are clamouring for attention
from your mother but your sibling has usurped you from
your rightful place. Is that not right, little Jeannie?'

'If you say so, sir.'

'Indeed! What do you remember next?'

'My mother puts me from the bed, Dr. Scobie. I land on the floor.'

'You are ousted from her bed at so early an age.'

I hear him 'tut' under his breath and shake his head in sympathetic delight.

'There are splinters on the floor, sir. We have not yet got the linoleum covering that we had in later years, and I cannot crawl for fear of skelfs in my skin.

So I sit and hold my dolly though she be but an old wooden spoon my father fashioned for me.'

'I suppose then that your dolly then becomes your attachment figure and your friend. I see that now. Does it distress you to admit it, my dear?'

I now feel that I must feign some emotion. I pick up one of the cushions and clutch it to my breast as I would to a real doll. Peering through my eyelids I can see that the good doctor is impressed.

'Poor lonely child seeking her mother's love and abandoned by her at such an early age. On a cold floor with splinters on her knees.'

I blink my eyes and manage to find a few tears that course their journey down my cheek.

'Tell me about the room- a tenement, wasn't it, in the district of Govan?'

'Yes that's right sir. Govan. Where the great ships go down to the sea. My father worked on those ships.'

But he did not seem interested in my father or the ships. Only in my mother and details of our deprivation seemed to excite him. I give him a guided tour of our room with its sparse furnishings and gloomy vista over the middens in the back green of the building. I see that he is *moved by my description for his grey eyes begin to water themselves.*

'Your mother lost a child, did she not? Can you bear to tell me of that event?'

Well Mr Charles Dickens would have been proud of my rendition of Agnes's death by the cruel hand of diphtheria. It made the final moments of the death of Little Nell in 'The Old Curiosity Shop' joyful in comparison. I linger on her yellow waxen face with a cloud of golden curls around her head, arms folded to Heaven in that little shoe box that served as a coffin.

Dr Scobie has now taken the handkerchief from his top pocket.

He blows his nose before speaking again. ' And your mother, I believe took took to her bed after that tragedy, Jean, suffering from a melancholia which lasted for the rest of her life.'

'Yes she did.'

I answer this question with a modest simplicity which although I say it myself becomes me well.

'Thank you Jeannie. Thank you most kindly. I think that will be all for our time together today.'

He has had enough!

I see him rise from his chair. He takes out the gold watch and advances towards me holding on to its chain. I see him swing it like a pendulum in front of my eyes. He stares at me thus for a few moments, then says, 'I'm going to count from ten slowly backwards. When I say 'one' you will come to your present state and tell me what you see in this room. Then our session will be over for now. '

I nod and stare as if I am lost in thought. I hear him count the numbers slowly and at 'two' I oblige him by blinking.

'Was that satisfactory sir?'

'More that satisfactory Miss Logan. Now tell me in your present voice what do you see around you?'

I take my time with this. My eyes fall onto his desk. 'I could not help but notice a pretty young woman amidst your papers sir.'

I see the old man's chest swell. 'That would be my daughter Grace. She is also an intelligent young woman – a medical student now herself. Studying at the university of Edinburgh.'

'Oh sir, if only I had been born in a different place, into a family such as your own, what may I have become?'

I lower my eyelashes and sigh.

'Indeed! Indeed! ' The doctor says and claps me on the shoulder whilst leading me to the door. ' Till the next time, Miss Logan.'

'I shall look forward to that sir.'

Along the dark corridor, away from him now, my mind unravelling, my educated voice deserting me, leaving only a slaver of drivel spilling out from my mouth.

DAMN! DAMN AND BLAST! DAMN AND DAMNATION!

My loosening thoughts running...

I must not lose my head. Loose ma heid

I canna gie mysel away, even for his pity

How could he? How dare he? For aw his clever ways, fine suits, fine study, fine daughter called Grace, who is at the university of Edinburgh studying to be a doctor, and doing fine by all accounts.

DAMN HER! DAMN HIM!

No! I must not hold on to these thoughts. Mercy on us. Mercy on me.

God have mercy. Christ show mercy Forgive me Jesus for I have sinned.

Sing it Jeannie . Sing it to yersel. 'Jesus loves me this I know'

What does HE know? What does he ken of poverty? Poverty, doctor?

Poverty is reeking of rot and stale piss and the bones of broth that have been stewing for days, a ham bone, fat streaming from the knuckle, we bairns fighting for its juicy drops.

Bairns with snottery noses and rickety legs, wi' nae shoes on wur feet. But chilblains, doctor as big as the golf balls you play with wi' these pals of yourn on yer Sunday rounds.

Gentle Jesus meek and mild. Look upon this little child. Suffer its simplicity…

And sharing a blanket, top to tail. Snores and farts and scabby knees that catch the skin.

And hearing THEM in the bed rutting and moaning and her underneath crying oot: 'No, not another bairn on the way. I couldna bear it.'

Suffering. Suffer little children to come unto me.

ME! And Meg and Agnes who died. Agnes with her cloud of golden curls, then Alec and George and Aggie who lived and then? WHO? Me, Meg, Agnes nai mair, Alec George, little Aggie forever spoilt by us all, then Iain, aye her boy.

Iain her favourite out of us all. And the wee twin girls, her girls not mine, who finally wore her to her grave.

'They'll be the death of me!'

And she was right.

And me? Nae place for me in aw this. Just fetch and carry, scrub and sew and grow up hauding yer tongue for fear it will fly away with you, fur fear it will gei you away.

Damn you Dr Scobie! Damn you for your kindness and leave me ALONE!

SIX

TROUGHS AND PEAKS

Bee is shaking him. Wakes him up. Has he been snoring again?

'What the …?'

'The phone Donald! It's the bloody phone ringing again. Bound to be one of your lot.'

'Oh Lord! What time is it?'

The phone keeps ringing and now the dogs have joined in.

'Monty! Rommel!' she barks at them.

Daft animals dogs! They pad into the bedroom with their tongues lolling out. There will be no shifting them from his side of the bed when he get back.

'Dogs!'

'Don?'

'What? Who's speaking?'

'It's me Don. I've just had this terrible dream. I've got to talk to you. I've got to know what happened to our baby.'

He look down at my watch.

'Such a dream. The stuff of fairy tales Don. A nightmare.'

'Christ Bella, it's three on the morning!'

'Is it?' But there were these two little ones in a sort of forest all by themselves. Like Hansel and Gretel. And this man with an axe. He looked a bit like you Don, same smile... same trusting eyes...'

'Bella, have you been drinking?'

A pause at the other end of the line. He hears her take a breath. When she speaks again her voice is cold.

'No I haven't. I'm sorry. I shouldn't have bothered you. I should have known.'

'I'm coming over,' he stumbles. 'Hold on and for Heavens sake don't go phoning up anyone else at this time of night.'

Bee comes into the room, an ample figure in her checked dressing gown. He can tell what she is thinking by the look on her face. He sees an expression of reproach with a tinge of scorn. She hands him a flask of coffee. Eric's flask, the one he used for fishing trips: EMB is monogrammed on the silver rim.

'I've put some brandy in the coffee,' she is saying, 'don't drink it until you get past all the speed traps on the A1.'

He catches her expression again as she goes back to bed.

Now he is sweeping ice off the windscreen. He wonders what I has let himself in for. He punches a postcode into the satellite navigational system. Maybe he will ring Evie on the way. On second thoughts she would only worry. When he talked with her yesterday she had rattled on, something about the babies lungs opening and closing soon in silent rehearsal for coming into the world. Did he hear the fanciful words of his wife in that phrase. Bella again off on some poetic riff.

At least the traffic was quiet. The world belonging to the lorry drivers at this time of day; creatures of the dawn she used to call them. And where was Iona? Away in London her sister had said, sitting on some Government Quango she thought.

She'll have a report to write soon and then perhaps a trip to New York on some fact finding mission. Well he supposed at least she was using that brain of hers. But if she'd stuck to science she could have been a Professor by now.

'Oh Dad,' he can hear her saying, 'You'll never understand me.'

Tried to love, but missed somewhere along the way.

But what he wanted to say was: 'I did my best.' Would she ever understand that?

He knew that his parents understood. Dad's chest pressing out with pride on prize giving days at school. 'No one can ever say that my lad never did his best.'

Four thirty. He's would have been marking up papers at this time of day. Lugging them into that big bag to go round his son's shoulders ready for themselves off.

'Wear your blazer lad. Let them toffee nosed people up Acomb Avenue know that my son is as good as any one of theirs.'

'Better!'

Yes they understood.

So what will he say when he gets there? When he finally crawls through those little back streets that could be in Bombay or Warsaw, with their Star of Bangalore launderettes and Polish deli's. Don begins to filter out the raw edges of painful memory. He would opt for a simple account if only she would listen. 'Bella we gave it our best shot; three kids and a little one that didn't make it. She was born with a malformation by some accident of nature and nature eventually took its course.'

But he knew he wouldn't use these words. It was in his nature to equivocate, to always look for an alternative explanation. It's what scientists do don't they? On the one hand ... then on the other... It was a trait that made him an excellent researcher but it probably cost him his Chair. He remembered that when he was at work he was known as 'Dr. Detail' by those who liked him, those that didn't had that other name: 'Dr Dither', so it wasn't surprising was it, when that paper was published in 'Nature' that another name was at the bottom of it, not his. He in fact was the one who found that the Huntingdon Chorea gene was located on the short arm of chromosome four, he just had those few possible mutations to consider before he was certain. And then someone else had to jump the gun.

Ah well! There we are. Glory and failure: two sides of the proverbial coin.

Heads or tails?

Heads.

Dad's mantra: 'stick to what you know and don't take any necessary risks.'

True Dad, you lived by that. And so you didn't sell your shop to the developers when you got that offer. You didn't make a killing, did you? You chose to stay and then you had to close up when all your customers went to the supermarket up the road.

So much for Heads!

Tails?

Different as chalk and cheese Dad, you and your brother Jem, the bookie. And what would he have said? 'You can can have all the best form you want, be best pals with the jockey, but in the end you've got to take a chance, son. You can't go through life betting each way...'

But I was ever too timid for tails Uncle Jem.

Nature? Or nurture?

He begins one of his perennial debates inside his head. It gets him to the boundaries of his known world in the city. A few people are up and about in the unfamiliar streets: a man in a turban is walking a dog, a mother and her small son on their way to the shops; all that is visible of the mother in her long black burka is the hand that clings to the infant by her side. Then the voice of the Sat. Nav. tells him he has reached his destination.

~

Bella rushes round the house in an effort to tidy up. The two day's stack of dishes in the sink are lathered and rinsed and put away. Curtains drawn, bolts unlocked, chains unleashed from the front door.

Had she ever locked the door at Swallow's Rest?'

She opens up the cupboard underneath the stairs. Digging out the vacuum cleaner she goes to work. First over the bare wooden boards in the kitchen, into the living room with its carpet of sea grass twine. Upstairs? Would he go upstairs? She gives a few cursory sweeps round the bedroom. She cleans the bathroom sink and puts the top back on the toothpaste; her toothpaste, the tube pressed and bumped in many places unlike his... neatly rolled from the bottom. Catching sight of her now familiar face in the mirror, she sees herself unprepared. A comb, a slash of lipstick, some perfume behind her ears...

Has she got any fresh coffee? Croissants in the freezer?

Opening the door she glances at the collection of throwaway crap thrown from passers by. Today a burger carton smeared with the remnants of tomato sauce. An empty cigarette packet. A can of lager crushed and dented, and a single glove with wool unravelling from the index finger tip.

~

'Don', she smiles, 'I'm glad to see you.'
She gives him a hug and he can smell her. That same

musky citrus scent: sandalwood and oranges and some other ingredient that only belonged to her body. He is confused and becomes embarrassed when he feels the hydraulic lift of his penis begin to stretch out his trousers. It is the first spontaneous erection that he has had for months.

He grasps her shoulder, holding her body away from his.

'You look tired Bella. And you've lost a bit of weight.'

'Thanks,' she replies. 'There are some who would say that I was now slim or slender, but I guess in your eyes, the word would be scrawny.'

'Not at all,' he says, anxious not to step into the ring again, 'you're just that bit thinner.'

'Which is more than I can say about you. You've been fattened up Don.'

'Bee is a good cook.'

'Evidently so. Whereas I was rubbish?'

He sees he cannot win this particular round.

'She likes baking.'

How can he explain that life with Brenda was just so much easier? He'd put weight on, so what? There were no troughs in his life now; on the other hand... he strives to dismiss the little voice from within that enquires about the peaks. Peaks he tells it are hard. He no longer has the energy for the climb.

She hands him a cup of coffee and they go into the kitchen. It is a small room but pleasant and it catches the morning light. He notices all her recent acquisitions. There is not a trace of him here. Only one of his late mother's embroidered cushions on the chair by the old fashioned kitchen range tells him that they once had a history together.

'No word of Elvis?'

'None!'

'I'm sorry.'

'No need to be. I'm over that now. He had a good life. You have dogs I hear?'

'Yes two black labradors. Monty and Rommel. Bee's father was a Desert Rat.'

'I see. And you take them out for walks in all that 'huntin-shootin-fishin'- gear, waxed jacket and all. What happened to you Don? You used to be Mr Marks and Spencer. Brenda's doing again I suppose?'

'Mmmm. It suits me fine. I expect it's the sort of stuff her late husband would have worn.'

'Ah, the galloping Major! And you don't mind being his clone?'

He swallows down the bile of irritation rising in his mouth as she takes him into the living room. It is tiny but bright; a Julia original on the wall, rugs on the floor, pictures of their children around the room. Then he sees an expensive bouquet of flowers beside a recent photograph of Bella posing with a large bulky man in Evie's living room. Confidence oozes out of that smile and that expensive well-tailored suit.

She sees him look and says: 'Ah, you've spotted Freddie. I dare say Evie has told you all about him, quite a coincidence really meeting up with him after all these years. He's taking me to a Tribute band at The Royal next week.'

She is speaking quickly now in a rather off hand way, he thinks. Don is curious to know more, but he is also aware that he doesn't want to know anything at all.

'Bella,' he begins, suddenly wanting to get down to business. 'You said something about having dreams. You rang me up in the middle of the night. It sounded urgent. I have come a long way.'

Listening to himself he knows he sounds peevish. But HE is taking her out. He is getting to know her again. His wife! He might well see her naked soon. Those large hands cradling that brandy glass in the photograph could well travel all over her body. They may even cup the tip of that lovely left mound of a breast that once he felt belonged to him. And would this Freddie look at the space where the other one had been? The one he couldn't bear to see. Who knows? He may even see to it that she gets it filled with another breast to match, the best silicone that money could buy. He wouldn't put it past him.

'I'm sorry but I can't help but worry about you Bella.'

'Then put me out of my misery Don. Tell me what happened to our other baby.'

What explanation would she want? The one the scientist would give her, or the one from that still aching husband?'

'Well,' he starts, clearing his throat, 'she was very poorly as the doctor told you. We didn't want to upset you by telling you more than was absolutely necessary. And Evie was just perfect, wasn't she?'

'Don't patronise me. I'm a grown up woman.'

So it will have to be the scientist that will have to speak. He takes a deep breath.

'Freya was born with hydrocephalus…'

'Freya? You named her then.'

'Yes. As I said she was…'

'She was born with hydrocephalus on the brain. I was listening.'

'That's an accumulation of cerebrospinal fluid in the ventricles of the brain that leads to an enlargement and swelling of the head: water on the brain in everyday language.'

'I've heard of it. I'm not thick.'

'I know, sorry. But because her brain was still being formed it had probably become distorted in some way. It would never have developed normally , unless…'

'Unless?'

'Unless perhaps, and this is a big perhaps, we had been in a hospital which had a really up to date paediatric department and they could have put a tiny shunt in her heard to drain off all the fluids. But we didn't know that beforehand. We didn't even know we were having twins for God's sake!'

She is quiet for a moment, taking it all in. He notes the freckles on her face as her cheeks become paler.

Then she says: 'Was it my fault Don?'

'What?'

'Am I to blame for her illness and her death?'

'No Bella it was no ones fault. You mustn't think like that. It was just an accident of nature. And I guess the forceps didn't help either.'

'Why?'

'Don't you remember? It was because she was so hard to deliver. He head was so big. The doctor did his best, but no doubt those forceps contributed to all that other brain damage she had. She had spinal defects as well. She wasn't a pretty sight.'

'I could have grown to love her.'

'You wouldn't even look at her properly.'

'I know.'

She starts to weep. He sees her lose all control and through the gulps he tries to comfort her, proffering the handkerchief that Bee had put in his pocket before he left home.

'But you held her Don.'

'Yes I did. You were exhausted and Evie was having her first feed, so I held her for a while. She looked like some little goddess in miniature, so I gave her the name Freya.'

'Freya. Freya. It's a nice name. Then what happened to her?'

'The doctor took her to hospital. She was in a respirator for a long time. Then they moved her to another unit until she was strong enough to go into a Home. The Nuns at St. Josephs looked after her from then on. Until she died.'

'Nuns! I thought so. My baby was cared for by Nuns!'

'Your mother's idea Bella. It was a good choice. They tended to her very well. She was severely disabled you know. She could never have walked and she could hardly communicate except by crying. She was as Ailsa called her 'a poor wee soul'. And she was right.'

'Did you ever go and see her, I mean in the Home?'

'Yes, once or twice, but your mother visited her every week till she died. She even arranged a little funeral for her at the convent.'

'A funeral. Did you go?'

'No. You know how I feel about religion. But she's got a little plaque with her name on it somewhere. You can go and see it if you like. Ailsa was content that our little girl would rest in peace.'

'Rest in peace!'

She is agitated now, moving around her small living room, adjusting photographs on the mantelpiece.

'How can anyone rest in peace!'

'Bella,' he says as tenderly as he can, his hands open in supplication. 'You've not been well. You can't carry guilt around you for this sad event in our lives. You'll get ill again.'

'Can't I?'

She looks at him and then he does what he has wanted to do for so long. He reaches out and holds her, feeling her stiff little body soften into the contours of his chest.

Later, over bowls of soup they talk about Tom. She catches him by surprise.

'Don, don't you ever wish we had taken the risk and done something adventurous when we were young? Like those couples that emigrated to America or Australia as part of the ' brain drain' as they called it in the sixties? They took the plunge and we stayed put.'

'What brought this on?' he asks her. 'We had a young family Bella, we both had careers. Your mother...'

'I know I'm just as much to blame.' She adds impatiently. 'But weren't you ever restless for something else?'

He reflects on what she has said for a moment.

'Possibly, maybe. I don't really know. What makes you ask that?'

'Oh just something Tom said in his last letter. It struck a chord. Something about the thrill of being in the wild. It made me think that we had never done anything like that. We'd perhaps missed out in some way. You should go and see him soon Don. Catch up with his ambitions before it is too late. It's too late for me to love my baby, I've got to learn to live with that but it's not too late for you to keep loving your son.'

All this talk makes him feel unsettled and he thinks of some excuse to go home. He begins to take his leave, muttering something about picking up food for the dogs on the way home. Sensing his ambivalence she finds his keys, handing them to him with one hand upturned like an offering.

When he sets off he deliberately makes a detour to pass some old haunts from the past. 'Swallows Rest' didn't look that different. Someone had painted the front gate a deeper shade of green. But the garden looked as well tended as Bella had left it. The old rope swing on the plum tree was still there. Perhaps some other little boy would enjoy it? The gravel pits in the Nature park down the road from their old dwelling were full of Canada geese spending their winter in the relative warmth of the English climate. Maybe he would follow them back to see his son in the Spring.

Turning east, the flat earth holds no surprises but the sky gets bigger with every mile. And somewhere on that horizon at four o'clock this afternoon, a stout woman in green Wellington boots will be a small dot walking her dogs before tea.

~

'Shall I come and pick you up?'

'No!'

She didn't want him here. Not in her little house. Not yet anyway.'

'Can't I meet you in town?'

'Usual place then?'

'What?'

'Don't tell me you've forgotten Bella. Our usual spot. By the left lion in the Market Square. We can go for a drink before the show starts.'

He was there before her. Elegant in a blue Burberry coat, collar turned up against the biting January wind, a red cashmere scarf knotted casually round his neck as the current fashion dictated. He puckers his lips on both of her cheeks and she catches the smell of expensive after-shave: the tang of manly perfume lingering on the closely cropped stubble. Forty years ago their welcoming embrace had been a bear hug and a full-on-the-lips kiss. She wonders what that would feel like now, pushing away the fleeting thought that perhaps after all these years he may not even have his own teeth.

Sipping gin and tonic in the plush theatre bar, Bella watches her old lover order more drinks for the interval. What she sees looks distinguished: a tall man gone to flesh like an over ripe peach, but still handsome maybe. Sure of himself, certainly and so different from the diffident Don. She sees him produce a twenty pound note and then announce to the barman that his name was 'Aarons,' with a double A.

'Aarons? I didn't know you had a Jewish connection?'

'I don't,' he replies with a shrug. 'Just an old trick a client once taught me when ordering interval drinks. It's best to have a name at the beginning or the end of the alphabet so you can go straight to the booze, no messing at half time. So I tend to be 'Aarons' or 'Zimmerman' as the mood takes me.'

She laughs. 'Well I guess that's one way to steal a march on others. No wonder you have got on in life.'

It was easy being with him again she is surprised to learn; no awkward silences between them, no searching for the right words to say. He dominates the conversation telling her stories that although sound amusing, she suspects have been told many times before. She looks round and sees an audience that is reflected in Freddie and herself: ageing baby boomers brought up in that cod -liver -oil age just after the war and now out for a good time to enjoy a mid-life renaissance. Men in denim jeans and open necked shirts, their hair either shaved to now fashionable baldness or grown long and tied back. The women were harder to categorise. Some wore the bright clothes of the seasoned festival goer in rainbow stripes or tie-dyed caftans. Others, she surmises were definitely the rock chicks of their generation in leathers and permanently dyed blonde hair. She was glad that she had dressed more modestly and was much more difficult to place.

On stage, the line-up of the bands reflected the audience, only more so. Most had lines deeply etched into their faces, carved out perhaps with the excesses of drink and drugs; lives lived badly for most and proud of it. And then the simple chords of an old Chuck Berry number jangled into life and a jolt of pleasure rushed through her. A few brave souls were on their feet, singing, stomping; willing these old rock beasts of the jungle to do their stuff. Joints that would no doubt stiffen up tomorrow performing in magnificent fluid action now: they were young again.

What was it about the music of one's youth that held such potent magic? Each generation transported back in time by a riff, a phrase, a tremelo of sound. Bella saw her mother dance by herself, arms outstretched for the absent George, her feet in perfect step to the rhythm of the foxtrot and Al Bowly singing: 'The very thought of you and I forget to do...'

And here she was, the child that had grown old, sitting with a man she scarcely knew, with her eyes closed, back on the dance floor in a twist or a jive or better still a smooch with Wayne Fontana and the Mindbenders... lovely. She could never respond to what followed after the sixties and seventies had passed: punk set her teeth on edge and at the sound of 'Guns and Roses' blasting from Tom's bedroom she would rush out into the garden, her hands clasped firmly over her ears.

Perhaps that was how it was meant to be. Music helping to define us when we were young. So we should never trespass into the tastes or the times of other generations. It wouldn't be right.

'I really enjoyed that Freddie. It was good to see the oldies having fun again.'

'Less of the old if you please, young lady.'

Now he was flamboyantly ordering a bottle of champagne from the bar, in his own name this time, she notes.

'Beaded bubbles winking at the brim,' she says, holding the glass up in delight. 'All I need now is a cherry and I can pretend that it's Babycham again.'

'Very poetic. Have you just made that up?'

'I wish. No it's Keats. 'Ode to a nightingale' It's a poem about savouring life before dying.'

'Cheerful stuff!'

'Maybe. But it wouldn't be a bad way to go. Singing your heart out on stage.'

She starts to tell him of the time that she and Don had seen Lonnie Donegan a few years ago in some backwoods town up north when he was making a comeback.

'I went round to get a couple of beers from the bar and saw this van arriving. A whole lot of 'roadies' got out and then this little man. Somebody pushed him and his toupee got dislodged. I remember thinking that his hair looked like dandelion thistle when you blew on it to tell the time. A puff of wind could have blown him away. One o'clock, two o'clock, three o'clock, poufffff...'

'But when he got onto the stage, all dapper in his Italian suit, the first bars of 'Rock Iron Line' blew him into action and blew us all away. Amazing! After a few numbers he suddenly stopped and said to the audience: 'I'm good, aren't I? I can still do it!' It wasn't a boast. I think he was really saying it to himself. He couldn't quite believe that he still had it in him. And then a few weeks later we found out that he had died on stage. I hope it was in the middle of that old Leadbelly number. I'd like to think he went out on a high.'

'Bella, why are you telling me all this.' It was Freddie's turn to listen and he seemed unsure what to say.

'Oh I don't know, something about that poem I suppose. Sorry Freddie I didn't want to spoil the evening. But you should know there was a time in my life not too long ago when I felt I could have died and not to the sounds of skiffle.'

'I know.'

'How do you know?'

'James told me.'

'And you still wanted to see me?'

'You bet! Shall we do it again?'

'Please, but it can't always be just for old times sake, can it?'

'Why not?'

'Because I think I've done living in the past. If we do meet up again it's got to be about now. You and me, knocking on sixty's door and not pretending that we are teenagers any more. And to be quite honest Freddie I hardly know you. I'm not sure I even knew you when we had our fling.'

'But it was a good fling, wasn't it?'

'A fling is a fling. It's not real life.'

She notices that he is fidgeting with his watch. Fastening and unfastening the gold clasp on his wrist. He is outside his comfort zone she thinks. What now?

'I don't honestly know what to say Bella. All I know is that I like you. I got a great buzz meeting up with you again. I felt that I knew you somehow. And I like your family. It feels good being part of it. I never see mine. My fault I know. But let's say I enjoy being Freddie again and I enjoy being with you. Will that do for now?'

She looks at him steadily.

'I'll settle for that at the moment, Freddie. So now, can you take me home?'

SEVEN

THE SCARF

' Julia, I could have kicked myself! Everything was going fabulously well and then I came out with 'take me home,' before I realised what I'd said. I panicked of course, muttered something like, 'Sorry I can't do this', and then ran off and got a taxi. Whatever will he think of me?'

'Sounds like a classic prick tease Bella. Why? What on earth were you scared of?'

'I don't know.'

And then Bella feels she has to confess. 'If the truth be told, I was afraid of what I might be letting myself in for. I haven't had sex since the operation.'

'Since your mastectomy? But Bella that was nearly two years ago. Long before you and Don split up.'

'I know.'

They are sitting drinking coffee and eating Swiss chocolate biscuits in Julia's recently modelled kitchen: all bleached white and chrome, Julia could never bear to be out of fashion in anything. It was a clean and sunny room but rather antiseptic

Bella thought, lacking the warmth of her own place. She didn't mind being stuck in the past with her stripped pine and peasant look. When she looks across the marble worktop, she sees that her best friend is open-mouthed. Julia for once is lost for words.

'God! No wonder he went off with the 'brisk-and-bracing'! I bet he was longing for a bit of 'how's your father' by the time he met her.'

'Julia, don't be crude!'

She wanted to change the tone. She wanted to be serious.

'Look I haven't told anyone else about this and I don't want you to go blabbing off to Hugo or any of our friends, promise me, please. It wasn't easy Julia. I couldn't bear for Don to look at me. I just never felt whole again after I came out of hospital.'

'And you didn't talk about it! You the therapist who preaches to everyone the importance of communication with your partner?'

'I know. I hold my hands up. I am a hypocrite. But it was hard. And Don was so considerate. He didn't want to force himself on me he said. But actually I think that was an excuse. What I think he would have said if we had talked was that he didn't fancy me any more. And I could never have dealt with that. So sex just never happened. After a while he started to work later and later into the night and sleeping in the spare room so as not to disturb me, he said. I think I chose to believe the lie because it seemed kinder to us in a way.'

'And you never missed it? Sex I mean.'

'Course I did. I still do.'

Sex! Sex and loving; loving and sex woven into the heart of their marriage. She could even now feel the familiar touch on her breast as Don reached out, often tentatively at first, awaiting her response. Then in answer, she would feel that rise in expectation radiating from somewhere deep within.

And after that, their bodies taking charge, independent of will, unbidden by any command. Hands reaching out, pleasure in the folding of their fingers, skin on skin. His lips on hers, a gentle roughness of his tongue as it sought out the smooth curves of the cave inside her mouth.

Then the slow tension beginning to rise, stronger and stronger to the climax; out of themselves and into their own separate spheres of fulfilment. Then down again to that 'after time' before sleep. That was the time that was most precious to her; it held the meaning of lying together, of 'knowing' in the true biblical sense. A time of true intimacy. At such times she would read poetry to him and he often would play some of his favourite music. And their closeness was palpable.

'Of course I've missed it.'

She tries to quell the choking tears waiting to be spilled in lost regret.

'But I didn't want him to see me as a freak. I still feel a bit of a freak, so how can I start all over again with a stranger? Bad enough with the flab and wrinkles of age, let alone without a breast.'

Julia is quiet for a moment.

'That's why you gave up your sex therapy practice, wasn't it? I wondered at the time.'

'Yes. I'm not that much of a hypocrite. I've never been one to give advice and not be prepared to follow it myself.'

Julia lets out a sigh. 'I don't know Bella, but the phrase 'physician heal thyself' comes to mind.'

'Easier said than done. So where does this leave me with Freddie?'

'Well...' Bella can almost see the cogs of her friend's mind whirl in confusion. She starts to light up another of her scented cigarettes, and blows a puff of smoke into the air. 'From what you tell me, he's probably had it off with lots of those trophy women that Evie talks about. Perhaps he doesn't want sex from you.'

'Well thank you very much! And that is supposed to make me feel better?'

Suddenly they both laugh. Julia pours more coffee.

A bizarre incident comes into Bella's mind and she shares it. 'Julia do you remember that time when Tom was collecting every animal he could lay his hands on? Don and I bought him a rabbit for his birthday and we put it in a hutch in the garden. The next morning Don comes inside with a strange look on his face and whispers to me so Tom couldn't hear: 'You know that rabbit we bought yesterday from the pet shop, how many legs had it got?' 'Four,' I say, 'why do you ask?' 'Well it's only got three now, I should take it back if I were you.' We collapsed with laughter, it seemed so funny at the time but when we came to look, he was right. A fox must have come in the night and bitten one of the animal's legs through the wire on the rabbit run. The poor thing seemed fine with no lasting effects and lived to a ripe old age, hopping around like Jake the Peg.'

'There you are. You can love something even if it's incomplete. And some men,' she adds mischievously, 'get off on things like that.'

'Julia, don't go there. PLEASE!'

She feels a little better as she walks home. You could never leave Julia without seeming a little lighter. But her anxiety returns when she thinks of that time with Don, each locked in their conspiracy of silence.

Sex with Don was never the athletic experience that she suspected Julia went in for with her partners. At best it had been like a dance; each one knowing the steps of the other so well over the years: how to hold, how to move, when to lead, when best to follow. Sometimes their act of loving had the predictability of an old fashioned waltz: one-two-three, one-two, three... and when they were young it was all the Saturday Night Fever of disco and jive. Yet it was that 'after-time' that she missed so much now, the giggles, the stories, the sharing of secrets; the time when their child- selves were not afraid to come out to play.

When she gets home she feels some energy return to her. This afternoon she would work. She begins to run in the black leaded paste into the rusty surfaces of her kitchen range. On the radio an old show tune from 'South Pacific' was taking up its honeyed strains. She starts to sing along with the words, carefully easing the black goo into the thirsty metal surface.

'...see a stranger across a crowded room, and somehow you know, you know even then...'

Romantic tosh? Or was there something profound in those lyrics?

Theories about the various emotional glues that held couples together had always held a special fascination for Bella. In her student days of marital counselling, she was fond of quoting from an ancient book written by a man called Henry Dicks. She imagined Henry, he would never have been Harry or even Hal, in his study looking like Grandfer in his plus fours and curly stemmed pipe, constructing those long convoluted sentences of his with his Parker fountain pen.

'Henry says there are many layers in the whole process of falling in love.'

Julia butts into her thoughts: 'Go on! Amaze me!"

'Well there are some that are easily understood. Like choosing a partner from the same tribe or the same class for instance. Families can play a large part in this selection.'

'Birds of a feather?'

'Exactly. Most marriages that are arranged are based on that principle. It is still after all a trading transaction for many societies where wealth and power are used for bargaining chips in the buying and selling of sons and daughters.'

'Thank the Lord I wasn't born in one of those countries and had to settle for someone my old man found for me. I'd have led him a merry dance.'

'But you still chose men out of your own top drawer of society, Julia. John was an M.P. wasn't he? And Terence an artist like you and if I'm right wasn't Michael something in the City before he dropped out and took up writing?'

'But what about Hugo? He's certainly got no money.'

'His parents had though, didn't they? And what about all that private education that he plays down all the time? No! You've never got off with any lorry driver, Julia. Not a Wayne or a Gary for you! And that's another thing Henry says, we tend to choose people we have something in common with.'

'You like opera, I like jazz and we both enjoy going to the pub... that sort of thing?'

'Yes. I always thought that your mum and dad were a wonderful example to illustrate that point. They shared the same passions and fought the good fight till they died, didn't they?'

'The dear old red flag waving on their death beds! But some people don't do that do they? They shack up with someone of a different race or religion and it seems to work, doesn't it?'

' I know but it is harder for them to succeed, especially when they have kids. Then they will need an extra dollop of Henry's 'third level of marital fit.'

'God Bella, you make it sound like a disease.'

'Well in a way it is. He describes it as a compulsion. The power of the unconscious tugging away at us, pulling us to another without being aware of it. Romeo meets Juliet, Heathcliffe hits on Cathy, Rhett Butler collides with Scarlett...'

'And doesn't give a damn!'

'For good or ill there is no turning back.'

'How come?'

'Well Henry says,'

'Oh Henry says.' Bella can hear the mimicking tones of Julia in her ear.

'Yes, Henry says that each us of grows up with a piece of ourselves that is lost or missing or even yet to be discovered; a bit of our personality for instance, that we've had to forsake in order to be accepted by our families. And one of our needs in choosing a partner is to find that lost part of us in another person and try to reclaim it again as our own.'

'You've lost me there kid! Sounds a bit like a jigsaw puzzle.'

'You could say that. Thus the theory goes that when we meet someone who holds that promise of fulfilment we are immediately attracted to him or her.'

'Spooky!'

'Perhaps. But look at Don and me, Julia. There was loads of me missing in my early life. A father for a start and with that a real sense of security. I used to love coming to your house with your two parents and your brothers all around you.'

'We fought like cats and dogs all the time Bella.'

'But that didn't matter. You stayed together and your mother and father adored each other. I could tell. That's one of the reasons I loved them so much.'

'You never said.'

'But I felt it. I craved for the things you had and I didn't. And it wasn't all about money. And then I met Don. He was quiet, not at all like me then, and unassuming. And so dependable. Never late on a date and always there when I needed him. Until...'

Don, with his two parents, Annie and Jack who stayed together until they died. They might have seemed a little dull at times but they built a good nest above that corner shop and their one and only son was secure within its lining. Annie didn't like raised voices, so Don could never get angry at home. He would sulk instead and get his own way by quiet and stubborn persistence. Passive aggression I think they call it now. The Cavendish family were creatures of habit: holidays in Bridlington in Wakes week, routines well cemented into the structure of their lives. Bella used to tease her young husband whenever they visited Leeds. She would sing to him a parody of an old song on their way up the motorway.

… 'Today's Tuesday. Today's Tuesday,
Annie's shepherds pie, Sunday roast beef,
Jack likes fish and chips
Is everybody happy?
You bet your life we are!

Annie's motto had always been: 'there's a place for everything and everything in its place.'

Bella would see Don smile in happy recognition when he reached into the drawer of his parents old dresser in the corner of the living room. The scissors would be there, next to a roll of sellotape, the address book and a bound collection of his mother's favourite recipes. How maddening it would have been for him coming home at night and seeing Bella in one of her full-throttle days, spring cleaning and changing furniture around for a change.

Maddening yes, but exciting too. He used to confess in the early days of their courtship that he longed for some disruption as a child. When he met Bella he told his friends that he had never known anyone like her; she was expressive, she was creative, she was impulsive. She sang in a band, she read poetry in bed, she walked to Aldermaston and got arrested on a CND march. He loved her for that and all her crazy ways. Their friends said that their relationships was an attraction of opposites but Bella knew that she could somehow find a quiet sense of repose in the arms of this young man. And he felt he was discovering his own sense of excitement and risk by being part of her life.

Her arms ached. Beads of sweat fell on her face and turned to black pearls on the now shining surface of the stove. What time was it? She must remember to eat. She couldn't get ill again. Don's words tore into her thoughts.

'You have lost a lot of weight.'

But Julia's voice in her head was stronger today.

'So how come you two didn't last then, like your Derby and Joan in-laws? Sounds like old Henry's theories came a bit unstuck with you two.'

'That's just it, Julia. We got stuck. The things is, in a good marriage partners are supposed to regain the parts that they have lost. Little cargoes of confidence should go backwards and forwards to each other in invisible ferry boats of trade. So I should have helped Don into his more expressive self. Then he could rant at the world when he felt angry and sing in the shower when he felt good about himself. Instead he let me do it all for him. I got a double whammy of emotions. Let me give you a for instance. Do you remember me telling you about the time when I lost my rag with a salesman who sold Don a faulty lens for his camera? He took me into the shop and bottled out of complaining himself, leaving me to do all the talking. In the middle of it all, I suddenly thought to myself: why am I doing this? I don't know what I am talking about! I know bugger all about photography and what's more I don't really care. And do you know what he said when we left the shop, incidentally with a much better lens that than one he bought in the first place?'

'I can guess.'

'I think you rather went over the top there Bella', in that oh so calm voice that he used with his students when they'd got something wrong in their calculations. 'I think you went'... I could have brained him!'

After that she recalled, little cruelties set in between them. He would accuse her of showing off and deride her choice flamboyant choice of clothing in front of others. She in turn became less curious about his work. During dinner parties in the early days of their marriage she could encourage him to talk about his genetic discoveries. She would even go so far as to arrange for visual aids to be on hand for his explanations: salt pots, salad servers, serviettes all at his disposal in the service of understanding science.

She hears Don clear his throat as if preparing for a lecture.

'To solve the structure of DNA, four ideas have to come together. That the phosphate backbone was on the outside (salad servers at his disposal), bases on the inside, (a saucer moved to his left hand) that the module was a double helix, (here Bella was stumped) and it had a specific base in pairing.'

She gave up! When she saw the guests suppress their first yawns, she took over. Had anyone seen the new play at the Playhouse? Gradually, imperceptibly at first each became less interested in what the other had to say. Their differences became bones of contention; not pride. When they looked into the mirror of their relationship many years later they found themselves being reflected back: two distinct people, their separate quirks remaining intact. So they looked away from each other for experiences that would make them feel whole again: Don plunging himself more and more into work and spending his spare time coaching Iona for Cambridge and Bella using friends to develop her interests. She had at times contemplated having an affair; there had after all been plenty of offers over the years. But somehow she lacked the courage. And she was never any good at lying, remembering what betrayal does to people. The thought of her father pulling her back from many a brink.

But she did carry regrets that she had not tried harder in their marriage. Maybe she could have helped Don find that sparkle that would have got him noticed more. She knew the story about the research for the double helix off by heart and saw parallels in Don with the role that Rosalind Franklin had played in that momentous discovery. They didn't have the ego of a Watson or a Crick! No Nobel prize for them. In later years he had become, she recognised, something of a glorified laboratory assistant. Bella saw others with less talent and commitment to research outstrip him in the hurdles of promotion. His work on the protein deposits and their effect on the progress of Huntington's chorea did not have that sexy zing that was fashionable at the time. She had no doubt that someone would pip him to publication. And they did! Some scientists were like that in her experience: egotistical, ruthless and vain. When Don retired his new and much younger professor praised him for his long service to the Department leaving a worthy legacy for others to follow.

'Too right!' Bella had fumed, her smile frozen to a rictus. But Don bore the faint praise with a good natured shrug of modesty. Good old Don! What would happen to his anger now when she was no longer there to spit it out for him? Would Brenda take it on?

She put down her cloth. She must speak to him.

'Don Cavendish speaking. Hello.'
'Don!'
'Bella! What a surprise. What can I do for you?'
'Nothing really... I just wanted to say... sorry.'

'Sorry for what? Look, are you okay?'

'I'm fine. A bit down. But fine. And I mean what I say, Don. I've been doing a lot of thinking recently. I could have been a bit more understanding, sympathetic even over that business of your early retirement.'

'I guess everyone has their sell-by date.'

'Even marriages?'

A lengthy pause. She can sense an undigested silence between them.

'Do you want me to come over again?'

'No honestly, there is nothing wrong. As a matter of fact I've spent my day being very productive. I've been restoring my kitchen range. I bought it from that reclamation yard we used to visit for stuff we put around the garden at Swallow's Rest and then had it converted for modern use. It reminds me of the one your mother had in her kitchen. I'm now covered from head to of in black leading but its looking lovely. Only there is no one here to admire it but me. That's all I wanted to say. Sorry to have disturbed you.'

She puts the phone down, noticing that her black-flecked hands were shaking.

Why didn't we make it Don? Why couldn't I have done better?

Running a hot bath, she is aware of a sickening feeling inside her. She envied couples who did better; those partners who even after many years of being together smiled with patience or pride when one told a story the other must have heard a hundred times. The ones who still rose for the day carrying a curiosity about the other and asked at the end of it: 'how was your day?' She didn't know many like that. Some, like Julia, just moved on to other relationships when they got bored. Others got busier and busier as a distracting defence against any intimacy between them. However, one pair that she knew seemed to have found the answer. When they retired they bought a camper van and spent their time travelling to places they had never been before. They sold their house, bought a flat and got rid of a lifetime of clutter. And seemed younger, lighter, looking to one another for new adventures to keep them alive.

'Lucky them,' she says as she towels herself dry, her envy deepening and hardening to malice.

She dresses herself in her familiar shapeless working clothes as she draws the curtains together. No one in the street, but the distant thrum of traffic and the 'ting-ting' of the trams tell her there was never going to be any real silence in her new home.

She makes another cup of tea and settles down to review some of the writing she has done over recent months: sketches and scribbles, often done in waiting rooms, waiting…

One fragment of a poem catches her attention.

The Scarf

The first present you gave me was a scarf
Wrap up you said
Or you'll catch your death
So…
Well mufflered in my marriage years
I kept my warmth inside me
Now bare-necked
I chase each passing breeze
Till…
Turning to where should be home
I feel the wind bite
And feel I might
Just
Catch a cold
Oh my, she says out loud to no one but her own shadow

EIGHT

FAITHFULNESS

THE JOTTER

16TH JANUARY 1921.

I hold in my head a scene that passed in my life today; a cameo that I will call 'Faithfulness.'

I am returning from a walk that I have taken on the boating lake. Its waters are all frozen over and a few brave souls are skating on its glassy surface. I stride briskly to keep the circulation flowing around my slender frame when I see the outline of a woman approaching me. I can make out that she is crying for her eyes are reddened and the snotters that stream from nose I fear will turn to ice on the chilly air.

'Are ye aw richt hen?' I say to her in the vernacular for I can see by her poor clothing that she is a working woman.

'Nae, lassie,' she says to me. 'I mun leave him again in a terrible state.'

'You have been on a visit to someone in here?'

'I have, and every week for the last fourteen years. And he's nae better still.'

'What ails him?' I reply and hope my voice shows some concern.

'I dinna ken. He ran at me wi' his knife one day and I got feart. The next day he was as nice as pie, but the awfie moods got too much fur him and fur me to manage, so they took him away to this place, wi' the clouts aboot him so he couldna move.'

'So where does he bide?'

'In the Sebastapool Ward wi' all the other loonies.'

A tremor of fear passes through me, quickening my numbed state.

I have sometimes seen the wrecks of humanity that go through that locked door of this ward. Very few come out again and even fewer have visitors.

'But don't get me wrong hen, he's a lovely man. And as gentle as a wee pet lamb. It's yon sickness that falls upon him from time to time, that's what it is.

It's nae his fault, whatever anyone may say.'

'And you come to tend him still?'

'I'll do so till I canna do it nae mair.'

'Does he know you after all this time?'

'Och aye, my lassie. But not that you would notice if you saw us together.

But I know he's my Iain and somewhere, I dinna ken where, he knows I'm his Peggie. We've been marrit for over fifty years and there's been nae other man fur me.'

I admit to myself that I am touched by this devotion. There are small heartbeats of hope in this place, fluttering in the bosoms of good people like this old woman. I *fleetingly wonder if I have done the right thing by not allowing Tam to visit me here.*

I find a clean handkerchief in the pocket of the patched coat I am wearing and press it to her.

'Bless you my lassie,' she says as she turns to continue her long walk to the gates of the outside world. 'Whatever you may have done that's got you here, I mun see that you are a good girl, so you are.'

NINE

CUPID'S ARROWS

The voice of James on the answer phone cuts into her thoughts.

'Bella where are you? If you get this message tonight, can you give me a ring?' I've just seen our friend Rick and he seemed a bit concerned about you. I don't want to worry Evie if I can help it and she's out line dancing for a few hours with her chums. Thanks Ciao.'

'Hi James. Got your message.'

'That was quick. Hang on a minute will you? Josh has only just got to sleep and he never wants me if he wakes up again.'

She hears him clomp his way into the kitchen. In the background a sports programme on the television is blaring out a frenetic commentary.

'Rightio. Listen are you okay? Your pal Rick or Freddie as you call him seems all at sea.'

'Yes, I'm fine James. Just made a bit of a fool of myself when we went out last week. It all ended rather badly I'm afraid.'

'Sounds like it from what he told me. Look its not my

role to play Cupid, but can you get in touch with him? He thinks he's put his foot in it somehow. I know he can be a bit of a swagger at times but he's a good sort. I told him you'd been through a bit of a rough patch recently. He really is most anxious to make amends.'

'James, I never saw you as a marriage counsellor. You'll be doing my job next.'

'Oh Lord no! I'll leave all that 'touchy-feely' stuff to you. But I wanted to let you know the score without involving Evie. She's got enough on her plate at the moment.'

'Is everything alright?' Bella's tone showing concern.

'Fine. Nothing to worry about. The babies are great but when Evie saw the midwife the other day she was just a bit worried about her blood pressure. Did she show you the shots of Bill and Ben?'

'Yes she did. They are perfect James. You are a lucky man. And listen you can give me Freddie's address. I might drop him line, and I don't want to involve you any more than needs be, if that's okay.'

'Fine with me. Got a pen? You know,' his voice becoming serious again, 'Evie may be a bit funny at times, but she thinks the world of you. We all do. It's just that she's not very good at saying it. Don't ask me why.'

'I know. And thanks James. Tell me if there is anything I can do, won't you?'

'Sure will Bella. Bye.'

~

She takes time to get herself dressed and ready this evening. A long bath with a few sprinkles of essential oils, first floating on the water and then settling in to her body, into the pores of her skin whilst the aromatic fumes fill the air around her with the smell of spring. When she pats herself dry, she is anxious not to remove the lingering sheen that still clings to her.

Then she takes courage. She forces herself to look into the long mirror that she always covered with a towel.

No Botticelli! Definitely not 'The Birth of Venus' emerging from the water on that beautiful shell. On the other hand neither is she 'Whistler's Mother', not yet a while.

The eyes still have it. And the face? She peers closer. Beyond the lines, beneath the shadows; the face is an interesting one. It has lived an interesting life. She feels her skin, once dappled with the fine tracery of freckles. It was still smooth to the touch. Her hair had grown back and acquired some of its old lustre, the new style framing her face and giving it an elfin look that suited her.

Then her eyes fell below her shoulders. One small mound of flesh stood proud on her left side, its pink nipple beginning to engorge as her body cools down. Alongside it, a flat white surface scored with criss -cross scars intersecting at the centre. The lines had lost much of their angry red bruising but the fading purple marks still bore the reminders of a hasty amputation. She breathes in deeply. And as she does so she sees her ribs rise and fall beneath the stretched skin. She covers her hand over the battle-scarred surface and forces herself to look further down. Some folding of the flesh in the middle she notes, but still a neat waist, slender hips and long legs: dancers legs Don had called them in his courting days. When she raises her arms, she sees that they are still flaked with freckles: 'sun kisses', the voice of Ailsa sang. 'My aren't you the lucky one to be loved by the sun!'

Goose pimples gathering on the surface of her skin tell her it is time to get dressed. Which she does with great care, putting on new tights and black underwear, selected for her by Julia. She holds on to the wriggling jelly moulding and places in the cavity left by her right breast. A soft grey cashmere sweater bought in the January sales, falls gently over the disguise. Underneath, her faithful standby, the purple suede skirt drops obediently into place. As she zips up her boots, she hears the voice of her mother again in a tone of guarded admiration: 'Not bad lassie, though I say it myself. You'll pass in a crowd, so you will.'

So here she was facing her fears. She had invited him home.

From the kitchen the smell of the sea bass, slowly stewing in its own juices with lemon and white wine, reminds her that she is hungry. She hasn't eaten since breakfast. She checks the progress of the meal: home-made mushroom soup, fish stew and a crème brullee, which she would caramelise before serving, just to show off, with one of those blowtorch contraptions James bought her as a stocking filler at Christmas. She makes a final check that the fire in the living room would not need more logs, then opens a bottle of red wine to let it breathe in the warm air around her.

'Okay I'm ready for the fray,' she says out loud to the missing Elvis. And looks around at the assorted pieces of non-matching furniture she had assembled into the room from various auction houses and junk shops in what she hoped was a harmonious collection. When the doorbell rings, she is ready.

He looks almost as nervous as she feels as his large body steps into her tiny hall. Expensive coat as before, another scarf, the same well cut denim jeans. A brightly coloured sweater, probably bought for a golfing trip, draped over a pale blue shirt beneath. The smoky scent of his aftershave clings to her as they embrace: two kisses lightly placed on both cheeks.

'Something smells gorgeous,' he says. 'I haven't tasted a home-cooked meal in ages.' His smile is warm as he hands her his gifts: a bottle of sparkling wine and some flowers expensively wrapped in tissue paper.

'Cheers!' she says, handing him a glass.

She watches as his gaze takes in their surroundings. Such a contrast to his own lifestyle she suspects. His eyes fall on photographs of her family. 'This must be your other daughter Iona. Evie has told me all about her. Quite the high flyer I hear. And that's your son Tom? My, I can see you in him.'

He picks up the photo that Don had taken on the day after Tom's graduation. Her son in his old sports jacket and muddy corduroy trousers. He had taken them all punting on the river Cam and they had got stuck in the reeds. Tom waded onto the bank and in doing so ruined, as his grandmother would have said, a perfectly good pair of breeks. Don catching their boy perfectly in his tousled innocence, Bella thinks, and her heart does a skip of pride.

'Yes,' she says, 'That's Tom. He's in Canada now working on an environmental project as part of his Masters degree.'

She takes a deep breath before continuing.

'And how about you Freddie? Have you got any children?'

She sees him hesitate before replying: 'Three girls. But I hardly see them I'm afraid.'

'Oh,' Bella replies, careful to check for an inquisitorial tone in her voice.

'Unlike you Bella, I was never any good at nesting. I married Adele a couple of years after I dropped out of university and we had two daughters. Didn't last. The girls live in France with their mother.'

'And the third?'

'Oh Sonia?' His voice is casual. 'The product of another misadventure. Last heard of backpacking somewhere in Thailand. I just get her credit card bills.'

'I'm sorry.'

'No need to be.' He looks at her ruefully, then sighs before taking another mouthful of wine. 'My girls are all fit and well as far as I know and getting on with their lives. What more could I ask? I'm afraid my fathering is not something I can boast about. I should have been born a lion or some other creature, great at being there when the mating is going on, but no good when the cubs are born. A bit like my parents in that respect, I suppose.'

'You never talked about your mother and father when we were together Freddie. I always imagined you were an orphan somehow, albeit a very exotic one.'

'As good as,' he responds. My mother was French, like my first wife. Married my dad who was a big shot in an oil company. He was never at home, so ma mere high-tailed it back to Lyons and they dumped me in prep school when I was seven. You know the scene. This country is run by men like me, spawned on the playing fields of Eton or Harrow or some such upper class orphanages we call public schools. We all knew our locker rooms better than our kitchens at home.'

The smells from her kitchen entice them to eat. He was the perfect guest; appreciative, attentive and gracious in his compliments to her cooking. Bella begins to relax as they talked on. Present topics mainly with only the brief forays into the hinterlands of the past. He tells her about his passion for collecting. He loves modern art. He likes Julia's painting. He owns a few originals of people she has never heard of: up and coming painters, he boasts lightly, good investments for the future. Bella makes a note of the names. She would talk to Julia about them later.

'As a matter of fact, I am off to see the Kandinsky exhibition at The Tate next week. He's a real favourite of mine. I've got to be in a meeting with a fashion designing team that will be kitting out the Olympics as I've put in a bid for the sportswear. Fancy coming along for the ride?'

The casualness of the invitation takes her by surprise.

'Well, what can I say? Thank you but...'

'No pressure. I got the message from your letter. Just friends and in the Now as you would like it to be. I can book two rooms if you like, or a suite? It would be good to have your company Bella, that's all I ask.'

No pressure, no sweat, she thinks. Who is he kidding?' When was the last time he had invited a woman away with him without the crisp folding of several fifty pound notes in her hand? A girl from Thailand perhaps, where his daughter is now? Or the Philippines. It didn't matter, as long as she was young and brought up to be grateful and well-schooled in the art of pleasing men like him. Men who could afford to indulge in sex without the complications of a relationship. Bella stops. She checks her thoughts again. Is she wrong to think this way? Could it be different with her?

THE JOTTER.

20TH JANUARY 1921.

No one could accuse me of being sentimental. My life has been too real and too raw for that. But I confess to enjoy succumbing to a weakness in my reading. I have become fond of following the serial story printed monthly in the Hospital Gazette.

It provides a quiet time of solace during the long afternoon hours in the Linen room and takes me to another world that I long to inhabit; a world that I once briefly had a glimpse of in my youth. Lily has asked me to read it to her as she only has the rudiments of ability to read for herself.

The heroine Ethel is beautiful and rich and as misfortune would have it, she is also an invalid, suffering from a disease that has wasted her legs. Ethel spends most of her time in an elegant drawing room that reminds me of the one that Miss Elizabeth Barrett would have lived in when she wrote her sonnets of love for Robert Browning before escaping from Wimpole Street and eloping with him to Italy.

The latest instalment of the story begins to hold me in its thrall.

'Edward turned and slowly came to her side. Her eyes met his as Ethel spoke and she saw the bright colour flush into his face. In an instant the truth dawned upon him; she loved him! Why then did she insist that he walk out with the foolish Gertrude whose prating voice caused him oft to wince.

For a moment his heart leapt high in his breast then fell again as the shadowed outline of Gertrude rose from her embroidery.

"Ah Edward, you are just in time to walk with Gertrude whilst the sun's heat is not too fierce. We have been wondering what kept you from us and feared that you may have been avoiding our company."

"You mistake me Ethel dearest, I have no wish to be parted from such loveliness but God's duties make such demands on my time. I can only apologise for my lateness and seek your forgiveness in this matter."

As he spoke, he bent over Ethel, tenderly parting her hair and placing upon her pale forehead the chasteness of a kiss."

Oh to have such a chaste kiss placed so lovingly on my forehead, rather than the rough and rude embraces that I have suffered in my time. I know that I am little better than my mother in her choice of 'Penny Dreadful' material for reading , but some of my day dreaming now rests in the beautiful drawing room.

I savour the scent of the over-bloomed roses that fill the vase on top of that grand piano. I imagine Edward lifting Ethel gently over to the piano and hear her flawless playing of a sonata float over the summer breeze coming through that elegant drawing room window. However I must be mindful that Cupid's arrows can wound as well as embrace.

The stuff of my day dreams contrasts greatly to those terrors that visit me unbidden at night and the literature in the Gazette is altogether more pleasurable than the solemn tomes of Sir Walter Scott. I much prefer the sedate life of Ethel to the wilful laments of the maid of Lammamour. Besides we are only allowed into the library once a month and are not permitted to remove books for private reading.

Maggie Lennox has found me back copies of the magazine to savour from the janitor's store so I have hours of pleasure to come in the dark winter months ahead.

I will keep them amongst my threads if the good lady Niven will grant me permission to do so.

~

They stand together in front of a large canvas: 'Composition V 1'. No clues here, Bella thinks. Swirls of colour: black and red, white billowing on various parts of the painting. Lines that look like musical staves slashed across the upper part. A blob of purple (could that be a frog or a bird?) sploshed at the side. Pink and white frothy curves splashed over the centre of the piece and a wave crashing into the expensive frame at the bottom.

'WOW!' he exclaims.

Bella is dumb. She feels foolish. Her eyes seek out the caption at the side. She reads slowly, her lips moving to the words written in an effort of concentration: 'Composition is a statement, formed slowly over the weeks, deliberately depicting the inner world of imagination and feeling. The pivotal (inner) motive of the Flood (apocalyptic atmosphere preparation for the drowning of the spiritual age) is completely assimilated by the abstract means of expression and is transformed to an inner, independent, objective entity of pure painting.'

She feels the panic rising inside her.

'You don't like it, do you?'

'It's not that,' she confesses, 'I just don't understand it. I feel like the small boy in front of the Emperor's new clothes. Only I know there must be something there. It's just me. I am a bit thick, Freddie.'

He takes her by the hand and leads her around the gallery. She hears him mouth the same phrases that Julia trips off her tongue when describing abstract art… "fluidity of colour and form, the importance of emotional sound, aesthetic spiritual experience'… and so on. Then he takes her to another painting called 'Cossacks' and talks to her as if she were a child; a small girl in her pigtails trying to make sense of a grown up world that she did not yet understand.

'Look, can you see the artist straddling both worlds here? The representational and the abstract. See the rearing horse, the mauve swishing of the sabres and the soldiers with their orange hats. But is is the overall effect you should strive to see: those wonderful patterns, those urgent lines and patches of colour. Marvellous, don't you think?'

'If you say so.'

She smiles in agreement but her eyes wander back to the other rooms, into worlds she did understand. The peasant scenes of Russian life, the lovely portrait of someone called Gabrielle Munter, the artist's wife perhaps? The singer by the piano with those lovely red roses in here lap.

'Look!' He was evidently not going to give up on her. 'You love jazz, don't you? When you played me that piano music the other night, who was it, Keith somebody or other?'

'Jarrett. Keith Jarrett.'

'Who ever. He begins with a melody of an old fashioned tune, doesn't he? And then he goes off on his own with those wonderful passage of improvisation. Can you not see parallels here in these paintings?'

'Yes. But he always comes back to the tune again before he ends the piece. He takes flight then he comes back home, into the familiar and I know where I started from. Sorry Freddie, it's probably not knowing where I am going or if I'll ever get back to myself that may be making me feel uneasy about these paintings. I have a real need for some kind of certainty at the moment. Everything inside me is a bit chaotic. Maybe that's the difference between you and me. I like taking off into the unknown but I have to have my feet on the ground as well, whereas you…'

'Whereas I?'

She feels flummoxed but carries on.' I might be in danger of making assumptions here, but I see you as someone… oh I don't know, forgive me. I don't know what I am talking about. I'm out of my depth. You should be talking to my friend Julia now. She would be on your wave length.'

'You love poetry, don't you Bella?' he continues as they walk along the Embankment. 'You once said that a good poem was like a three dimensional sculpture: solid, yet at its heart elusive. I can hear you now with your school marm voice, in that pretty little Mary Quant dress that I used to love. I was most impressed.'

When they get to his suite, he pours her a whiskey; a large one, and a larger one for himself.

She settles herself into the overstuffed armchair. From the picture window the river Thames stretches before them in the evening light. In the foreground the round silhouette of the London Eye, no longer moving on its slow circumference. Across the water, the blurred outlines of the Palace of Westminster shimmer. And off to the right the dome of St Paul's is almost shrouded by the black columns of the City.

'When I close my eyes, I can almost see what Kandinsky would have made of this scene,' he says. 'Resurrection and Light'; God and Mammon in Material destruction? Black and yellow for the Big Wheel, a few shadows in the background, bold stripes of blue and red for the river stretching out at a distance with maybe a few distorted pound signs in smokey grey bursting into flames at the edges. How about that?'

He looks serious for a few seconds and then bursts out laughing.

'I think I can almost believe my own bullshit!'

Bella smiles. She puts down her glass and sits beside him on the leather sofa. She begins to kiss him, first lightly on the cheek and then, as he sought her out, openly on the mouth. She could feel a small knot unwind itself in her belly, loosening its grip on her inhibitions.

Then pulls herself back. What is she doing?

'It's been a lovely day Freddie. Thank you for bringing me here.'

'What's the matter Bella? Why the sudden change?'

'Nothing… and everything,' she stammers. 'I want to, but I'm scared.'

'Of what? Me?'

'Oh no not you. It's me. All me. I'm petrified of revealing to you or anyone I want to get close to. I just feel so fragmented. I may fall apart again. And worst of all I'm afraid you might feel sorry for me. A look of pity would just finish me off.'

'Me, pity you?' He gives a short laugh.

'Yes.'

'Have you ever thought that it could be the other way round?'

Now it is her turn to look baffled.

'Bella my dear, I'm getting on a bit. I drink too much. I've got high blood pressure. I could do with losing a pound or two. And sometimes I have to rely on little blue pills to get me going. You were the therapist, you should know what I mean.'

'But,' she stammers, 'all those girls Evie told me about. The ones you take to all those posh occasions?'

'That's the easy bit,' her interrupts her, folding one of his big hands over her trembling wrist,' if you're a man and you have the money, getting a girl on your arm is no problem. Finding someone who cares for you is another matter.'

Silence.

Bella swallows hard. She takes hold of his hand and clasps it to her. She feels the tension between them slow and stop in her grasp.

Seconds pass. Then she begins to giggle; little chuckles hiccough between them. He bends down towards her and she kisses him on the forehead, tasting the salt of his tears that have started to flow down his fleshy but still handsome face.

'Let's got to bed and see what happens Freddie. Lights off if you don't mind. And let's trust these bodies of ours to look out for each other. Then in our heads,' she begins to kiss him again, 'we will be on that boat on the Trent, under a willow tree, with the sound of Chuck Berry singing…'

NINE

MISS BARRATT

JANUARY 22nd 1921

Time passes. In the latest edition of The Gazette, Ethel has suffered a set back.

Edward has been called to his missionary vocation in Africa to follow in the steps of Dr Livingstone. She has given him her blessing and now awaits his correspondence with great anticipation and some trepidation. Her man of God has been laid low with malaria and Ethel longs to be with him to soothe his fevered brow. In the meantime her father, the retired army general, has heard about a cure for her condition.

Since Edward's departure Gertrude has not talked about him and Ethel is secretly glad that she may no longer favour his suit.

Lily has been unwell again. She is no longer kept in

the locked ward but has been removed to the sanatorium. I fear that I may not see her for a while. Elsie Macpherson tells me that Lily has a hacking cough. I hope that this does not mean what I think it is. Lily's lungs have been weak since her childhood.

I will pray for you Lily. I will make my way to the Chapel and offer up my supplication for your swift return to health for my sake

The hags in the ward are missing Lily. There is no one to help them with their food any longer. Elsie says that there is new training for nurses who work with mental afflictions and I have seen two of these women in their brightly starched uniforms bustle about the place. I hope that they will not be under the jurisdiction of Sister Jewell. Maybe her days are numbered. I will pray for that too with all my heart.

February 12th 1921.

"And how are you today, dear lady?'

I am again unready for his kindly inquisition. The woollen skirt I found for the day's wear has a ragged hem. My hair is in a disorder. Elsie came for me whilst I was in the kitchen garden, bringing in a crop of turnips for the cooks to make into a stew.

'I feel unprepared , sir.'

'Good. Unpreparedness is the best preparation for this work of ours.'

Dr. Scobie clasps his hands together, seemingly pleased with this remark.

'Sister Jewell tells me that you were upset after our last meeting. You spent several nights crying out in troubled sleep. Is that not so?'

'It must be so if she says so, sir.'

HAUD ON JEAN! HAUD ON TO YERSELF!

I make my way to the couch as he gestures me to do so. I sit holding myself stiffly and notice that the old man looks paler than before. There is a tremor in his right hand as he takes out his fountain pen. I take off the brooch pinned to the darned wool cardigan that serves to keep me warm and clutch it in my right hand. The stone digs into my flesh and bids me keep alert.

'Have you had any dreams since our last meeting Jean?'

I see him take his watch from his top pocket. I can feel my heart beat faster through the ragged raiment that I am wearing.

'If I do have dreams, I cannot remember them sir,' *I lie.*

'So shall we therefore find a way of bringing them into your recollection?'

'NO SIR!'

No Jean. That is not the way, I upbraid myself. He'll see through your protestations. Distract him. Take him somewhere else…

'But I have been thinking a lot about my schooldays, Dr Scobie.'

'Have you indeed?'

He begins to consult the buff file.

'You were quite the scholar, Miss Logan. Dux in the school, yes?'

'Yes sir.' *I feel my grip relax a little.*

'Was this a happy time in your life?'

'The happiest, sir.'

'Then tell me about being happy. Attend to your happiest times.'

~

Attend! Attend. My mind races to attention. And I am back in that classroom. I cannot wait to get there in the mornings. To climb up the steep wooden steps to my place high up on the back row; the first in the class position, and then the voice of Mr Morrison...

I close my eyes.

'Now let's us see children how well you have been attending to me.

What is the longest river in the world?'

He scans the classroom; up and down the rows in front of him.

First to the dunces on the right hand side with their snottery noses and their looks of vacant stupidity. Then the middle section: the mediocrities. My sister Meg is there. A few hands are up. Then swiftly his eyes mount the steps to the back row on the left where my arm is straining out of its socket.

'Jean Logan. Have you got an answer for me?'

'Yes sir. The river Nile sir, which rises from Lake Victoria and flows all the way to the Mediterranean sea.'

'Well done! And where is this lake that is named after our great Queen?'

'In Uganda, Mr Morrison. In the vast continent of Africa.'

'Excellent! Regard this model pupil, class three. If you were all like Miss Jean Logan my job would be the best in the world.'

I cannot contain my joy. I exult in it! I feel the blood rush to my cheeks as I gaze down at Mr Morrison, Mr Eustace Morrison, the loveliest man in the world.

The rest of the day passes in a dream. I fill the inkwells for him. I gather up the slates and place them neatly in their stacks. I fetch the register from the office and count all the scabby heads that wriggle and fidget in their benches behind the desks.

'Where is Wilma Cuthill?'

'She had to go hame and mind the wains, sir.'

'Wains!' he says in disgust. 'Don't you mean 'children'? This dialect of yours must not be spoken in this school. The old Queen would be turning in her grave to hear her language so barbarously used.'

I write '65' on the attendance slate kept by the door of the classroom.

Under that number I copy out the date in my meticulous copper plate handwriting:

Afternoon March sixteenth1903.

When he rings the brass bell on his desk I hang back and let all the other children go. My sister Meg waits for me to follow her out. I ignore her. Instead I wait for Mr Morrison to gather all his books together and then I step down from the wooden tiers to the front of the classroom.

'Have you any homework for me sir?'

I see his eyes light up as he looks down upon me. He takes from his pocket a small leather-bound book and he regards me again.

'Yes Jean, as a matter of fact I have. I thought you might enjoy reading these poems. They are by Elizabeth Barratt Browning. I believe you have heard of her.

I see you in her in so many ways, my Miss Barratt. Not in your station in life of course, Miss Barratt was a wealthy woman of standing in Society, but it is in the yearning to escape that you both have. That is the resemblance. The desire to be awakened!

Read some of the sonnets from 'The Portuguese' and tell me what you think of them.'

I am floating on air along the cobbled streets on the

way home. Besides me Meg prattles on. She is dragging our wee brother, sorry Mr Morrison, our smaller sibling, and chiding him for losing one of the laces from his boots. One of our other brothers has run ahead of us, kicking a half inflated ball. He'll be the first in.

He'll be the one to go and run the messages for our mother who has got two small babies to look after.

I hug the book to my chest and plan for the evening ahead. Can I escape from all the chores and go to the other room in our house; our best room where mother keeps her ornaments on the mantelpiece and the old clock that her father gave her when she married? There is a table in that room and a chair beside the folding beds where five of us children now sleep. If I can't find my way there before the others go to bed, then it will have to be the cludge lavatory on the landing.

That is if there is no one desperate to use it. I'm sure Miss Barratt would not mind.

She wouldn't see it as an irreverent place to read her poems.

'Come away Jeannie, into the kitchen wi' you this minute. You've got the tatties to scrub and the bairns to mind before your faither gets hame from the shipyard.'

I work silently, sloughing off all the uncouth words that fall from my mother's mouth. I pray that my father will be in a good mood when he gets home. I can often find favour with him.

'Let the child go ben the hoose,' he tells her, 'she's a clever wee lassie. They tell me they might keep her at yon school next year after she's supposed to leave. A pupil teacher, that's what they say she should become. We should be proud of her Aggie and help her in her lessons.'

' Aye and a fat lot of good that' ll do her in the long

*run. It'll just gei her ideas above her station. She'll be
raising wains like the rest of us afore long. Then what use
will her high and mighty education be to her?'*

I shudder as I close the door to the temporary
sanctuary. The room is mine for a while. Father has lit the
gas lamp for me. I open the small book and tremble.

'How do I love thee
Let me count the ways
I love thee to the depths and breadths and height
My soul can reach…'

*In bed I struggle for possession of the blanket that serves to
keep my sister and I warm. I continue with my recitation:*

I love thee to the level of every day's most quiet needs
By sunlight and candlelight…'

*'Will ye stop yer mutterings and let a biddy get to
sleep? Meg sighs 'It's that man again, isn't it? Useless
Eustace! You're smitten Jeannie. I don't know what you
see in him wi' his peely wally face and his wee ginger tash.
He's got a limp as well you know.'*

'So had Lord Byron,' *I whisper defiantly. And he's not
peely-wally. He's just pale and interesting like all the poets.'*

*I needn't have bothered keeping my voice down low.
In the other bed Alec and George are snoring loudly. Next
door I hear my mother sigh and my father swear as the
twin girls start up their hungry midnight cries. Oh yes , I
long to escape… to escape with Eustace Morrison and be
awakened by him!*

*Next day I am top of the class again. Mr Morrison
has written a problem on the board:*

If it takes John ten minutes to walk to the station and it takes his father five minutes, how long does it take if they both walk together ?

I watch the class struggle. Various pupils say 'fifteen'. The boy beside me, second in the class today shouts out: 'seven and a half sir.'

I wait for him to respond.

'Now let's have a sensible answer. Jean Logan if you please.'

I give him the answer and my reason for it. If the boy couldn't walk any faster, then his father would have to slow down and it would still take ten minutes to walk to the station.

His lovely smile is my reward. Better than all the gold stars in the kingdom!

Later when it is time to go home and I can feel dread engulf the whole of my being, he comes to me.

'How did you like the poems, Jean?'

'I loved them sir.'

I hear him clear his throat. 'Jean I was wondering, in fact Mrs Morrison and I were both wondering if you would like to help her with her sewing after school?'

'Oh yes please sir!'

'You are sure that your mother would not mind?'

'Oh no, she'd be delighted,' I lied.

And so on Tuesdays and Thursdays from four o'clock until six, I sit in his mother's drawing room, with their elegant water colours on the wall and her two Chinese vases by the fireside. She is teaching me how to make lace by hand and to do petit-point for the tapestry samplers she is making for the church vestry. It is the best time of the week! Sometimes we sew ordinary things. She'll show me how to take up a hem or mend a seam in one of the pinafores that the children wear at school.

Once she let me replace a button on Mr Morrison's shirt. I fancy she may have seen me blush with delight as I threaded the needle for that task. I have almost to be wrenched out of the chair when my time is up and she calls her son to see me on my way.

But there are a few moments of joy when he walks me up to the end of Shields Road and wishes his Miss Barratt a pleasant evening before turning back for his high tea and scones, served up on the lace doilies I have helped his mother to make.

'I love thee with the passion put to use
In my old griefs, and with my childhood's faith...'

I take to following him around. Secretly of course, so he doesn't know.

I watch him go to the library on Saturday mornings and I hide behind the shelves as he take out another volume of poetry, a travel adventure and the works of Sir Arthur Conan Doyle. I track him to the chemist's shop where he picks up

Mrs Morrison's tablets for her heart condition. I see him sometimes take a tram up to the West End of the city. I have never got the penny needed to follow him there but I imagine him going to a concert at the Kelvin Hall or buying his favourite sweets and tobacco from one of the big shops in Sauchihall Street.

Then I grow bolder. I start to creep out in the evenings when I am supposed to be doing my homework. I stand outside his gate and gaze into his window. After a while I open the gate and hover close to the window. As the evenings lengthen the curtains are open and I can see him reading or doing one of his massive jigsaw puzzles on the table after the tea things have been cleared away. Mrs Morrison continues with her sewing or maybe she will play the piano by the fireplace. I think it is Schubert that she plays because she once told me that he was her favourite composer.

How I long to be in that room! To find that bit of sky for him so he can complete the puzzle. To turn the pages for her so she can continue playing without interruption.

And now I am being jolted into the present. Dr. Scobie interrupts my tale. He is again reading from the file.

'According to these records, Miss Logan, Mr Morrison left the school later on that term. Before you became a pupil teacher, I believe. Can you account in any way for his departure?'

I close my eyes. Shame begins to burn into my cheeks.

'One night they saw me sir. They must have heard the scrunch of gravel outside. When Mrs Morrison stood to draw the curtains, I noticed that she gave a signal to her son. He was outside in a flash asking me what business I had in being there. I heard the tone of his voice change: concern, then irritation and finally anger. I said nothing, Dr. Scobie, I was so upset.'

'I see,' he replies.

I am now anxious to check HIS tone of voice. Is there a vestige of sympathy within its cadence to help me carry on?

'Carry on Miss Logan,' he continues, in a voice that is unmistakeably stern.

'When next Tuesday comes sir,' I falter.

'Yes, when Tuesday came...'

'He made some excuse and said that his mother was unwell.'

'And you said?'

'I think I must have said something like: 'can I sit with her awhile?'

I was desperate not to lose his good favour, Dr Scobie.'

'And so what happened then? Go on child.'

'I saw Mr Morrison become harder towards me. His eyes looked at me without their usual warmth. He said: 'No that won't be necessary, Miss Logan.

She won't be requiring your services any longer. She has asked me to tell you that she has taught you everything that she knows.'

'He could see my tears, Dr Scobie, and he looked away muttering something about marking some schoolbooks and wouldn't my mother be wondering where I was.'

'And how were you feeling when he said this to you Jean?'

The doctor's tones are much gentler now.

'I am mortified, sir. I weep. I rail against my stupid relations with their common ways. My father loses patience with me and threatens me with his belt. I no longer have the room to myself. And then one day I wake up in the bed I share with with my sister and see blood trailing down my legs.

I have been punished for my wrongdoings. I cry with shame when I wash and wring those soiled rags that keep me clean. I stay at home. I wish I was dead!'

Dr Scobie has stopped writing. He leans towards me. The arrival of my menses seems to have interested him. He bids me continue.

'When I sit down again in class three, I have lost my place. I am now in the third division with the mediocrities.

Sister Meg is now a row ahead of me. I watch Mr Morrison put up a problem on the board.'

How often can a jug which holds one and three quarter pints be filled from a fourteen gallon tank?

I see him look at me.

'Seventy two sir.'

'Not correct.' His 't's are hard. The expression on his face is the same.

'Wilma Cuthill, have you an answer?'

'Sixty four, Mr Morrison.'

'Excellent Wilma. You can go to the top of the class. Learn all you can from this bright pupil. **She** is the example you should all be following.

Now explain Miss Cuthill how you came to arrive at this impeccable answer.'

'I knew then it was all over for me, Dr. Scobie. Miss Petrie came to the school shortly after this time and it was she who arranged my pupil teacher appointment.'

'And that was the end of your happy times Jean?'

'Yes sir, when Mr Morrison left, he took my happiness with him.'

There is a pause. He has put down his pen. He sits for a while as if lost in thought.

'You know Jeannie, I have a feeling that you were just a little bit in love with Eustace Morrison, foolish man that he was, pandering to a young girl's infatuation. But he paid you attention did he not my girl?

Attention that you craved for and never got elsewhere. He gave you a notion of romance and you were carried away with your Mr Browning. You got so carried away you didn't know where to stop.'

I am surprised that after all these years I can still blush with feelings that are still warm inside me.

'Yes.'

'And your bleeding, wee lassie? Did no one prepare you for your journey into womanhood?'

'No.'

'I thought as much.' His voice almost a whisper now. 'And now I think we will leave off for today. If that is alright with you, dear lady.'

I am in a daze when I make my way back. For the first time in years I am shaken by pulses of feeling which threaten to overwhelm me. I am dissolving into air…

'I love thee with all the breath
Smiles, tears, all my life and if God choose
I shall love thee better after death.'

TEARS

There is such a swell inside me. I feel it rock and sway. I am sick.

Floating and rising and falling and gulping for air.

In my dreams I am a ship bound for the shores of the New World.

I am being launched on a fanfare of pride. My father waves his goodbyes.

So does Mr Morrison. I see them looking at me, inspecting every inch of my body as the bottle breaks on the bowsprit and I am named.

I glide my way into the cold river, unfitted and unfinished, held in place by great chains on either side of me. They guide my progress down the water, 'steady as she goes.' Then without warning the chain snaps.

I am losing hold, pulled by the swelling of the tide

beneath. Soon I am out of reach. My father is no longer there. Mr Morrison, just a figure on the strand.

I snap back into conscious thought and find that I am soaked by my own tears. I am drenched by them. My eyes are matted by their salty spume.

Around me many voices babble. They urge me to quit sobbing.

Faces above me loom. I catch the twisted mouth of Sister Jewell as I am carried away. Swaddled in white linen, I cannot move. I can hardly breathe.

And then a white light. Shipwreck. Driftwood. A great pain from somewhere, and still my tears are flowing.

When I finally rise, I am helped to dress by Maggie Lennox who is gentle in her regard for me. She has found me a paisley shawl and I am grateful for its warmth and colour. Maggie brings me the broth that is kept for the poor souls who have no teeth. I make my way into the Linen room and resume my former occupation. What day is it? I dare not ask.

Mistress Niven watches me with gentle concern but asks me nothing of my recent ordeal as I strive to keep the stitches from dissolving in my grasp.

'I've missed you, Jean. You have been away for eight days.'

I remember nothing of those days. God could have created another world in that time and I would have missed it all.

'But you haven't forgotten how to sew, I am glad to see. These lawn handkerchiefs you are embroidering have proved to be a great success at the Sales of Work. People have been asking who the little artist with the needle is.'

'I had a good teacher,' I tell her.

And there she is. And there I am in that lovely room with the Chinese vases and the water colour paintings on the wall and the sheet music by the piano, just waiting to be played.

Schubert, always Schubert...

I sweep away the next batch of brine as it spills from my eyes and then ask the good lady if I can stitch up some hessian sacks for coal.

Rough work to do for my chapped and undeserving hands.

PART THREE

SPRING

ONE

TOM AND TAM

Dearest Tom,

How lovely to get a letter form you in your own inimitable writing, full of news telling me what you are up to. I now feel that I have much more than a glimpse into your life.

You sound really happy. Is this put down to the beautiful Eloise? Iona tells me that she is staying on in Whitehorse and not moving back to Montreal after her contract has run out. Tell me if I am being too nosey, but does that mean that she could be looking for a job in British Columbia when you move there in the summer?

You also mention that Dad is coming over next month. On his own, without Brenda.

I must send my spies out and see what the jungle drums are saying in Sleaford.

Evie has gone a little coy on me recently. I think she

found the pair of them, plus dogs, a little hard work over Christmas.

I'm feeling much more like my old self you will be pleased to hear.

No doubt one of your sisters has told you that there is a new man in my life, well not so much a new man but an old flame. I'm not sure how you would get on with him. Freddie is larger than life. He's just won a deal to kit out the British team at the London Olympics, so you can imagine that James is very impressed. But despite his swagger I like him a lot. He makes me laugh, Tom, and he does my ego the world of good. Freddie has a house in France and a cottage in Cornwall and he is taking me to the cottage with Julia and Hugo in a few weeks, that is if Evie's babies behave themselves and don't decide to arrive early. Julia gets on with him like a house on fire. They both like modern abstract art. He bought a painting of hers recently, so naturally she approves.

I've no idea how long the relationship will last, but for the moment I'm just content to go with the flow. Evie has given her blessing because she sees a change in me, but I am not sure about Iona now she's met him. We all had drinks together before a concert last Tuesday and the atmosphere got rather frosty. Freddie was trying hard to impress her but the more he showed off, the colder she became. I know deep down she is missing her Dad, but they are both as stubborn as each other. Which one will make the first move, I wonder? Rosie was fine though. Good old Rosie.

She gets along with everyone.

I am still missing Elvis for all his grumbling ways

and I feel rather guilty for having him moved here. I'm not sure I'll get another pet. If I did get one it would have to be something like a rotweiller! Two nights ago there was an almighty fight outside the house. No doubt gangs of local kids again on some turf war, perhaps over drugs. The police are never interested when I ring and I am left feeling vulnerable again. Young Vik Chakrabatti was beaten up on his way to school after Christmas and they never found the boys that attacked him.

That incident helped me in my decision to give up counselling at the Children's Centre, as I am never sure who I may be working with any more and I can't go on suspecting every lad I see could be the one who waylays me on the way home.

In the meantime I am busy. Did I tell you I have acquired a new friend called Shirley? Shirley spends her time doing charity work and she's taken me under her wing like a good mother hen. On Wednesday mornings I help her sort out the jumble at Barnados and price up the goods that bare worth selling amongst all the rubbish. You would be surprised at some of the treasures that people throw away.

Talking of which (treasures that is) I came across an old book of Burns' poems that my Grandfer had when I was clearing out the last of my boxes. He had thumbed down a page and put a big exclamation mark against a stanza of 'Ae Fond kiss'

'Had we never lov'd sae kindly
Had we never lov'd sae blindly
Never met, or never parted
We'd had ne'er been broken hearted'

Don't you think that is so sad? I wish you had known him, Tom. You would have loved him as I did. There is so much of his life I never knew, and probably will never know now, but evidently he was no stranger to a broken heart. But enough of that! I found myself signing a petition to the Canadian Government about the clubbing of seals. I thought you would approve. You say that you are planning a trip to the Arctic regions when Dad comes to see you.

That sounds a great adventure. I bought Josh a story about a rainbow polar bear at Christmas. It was very sweet in a whimsical way. Next time I read it I'll talk about Uncle Tom being there when the cubs are born in the spring. I'm taking him to a panto on Saturday. Aladdin I think. God knows what he will make of it.

And then he is coming to stay with me for a few days to give Evie a bit of a break.

He's a lovely wee boy but prone to tantrums at the drop of a hat at the moment.

Heigh ho!

Do send me more pictures Tom. Have you any more of Eloise and her family? You'll have to be brushing up on your French when you go and visit them again! In the meantime,

A Beintot,
    With lots of love,

        Mum x

THE JOTTER.

February 16th[h] 1921.

'And Tom, or was it Tam? Tell me about Tam. The harbinger of your misfortune, dear lady.'

I squeeze my eyes tight and will myself back in time. To Elder Park, a spring day in 1912, with the sounds of Mr Johann Strauss dancing their way through the tightly mown grass and the flower borders filled with red tulips all standing to attention to the precision of the music.

Da da da da da dada dada

Da dum da dum da dum dumdum

De de de de de dede dede

De do de do dedo dumdum...

The voice behind me humming 'The Skater's Waltz' in correct time: one-two-three-, one-two-three-,one...

'How do you like this music from Vienna?'

His voice is soft, the vowels open. A man from the country is speaking to me. He is being presumptuous of course, opening up a conversation with a stranger, and a lady stranger at that, but there is something in his curious question that draws me to him.

I look around and see a man of some height, with regular features, an open brow and thick red hair. His clothes are those of an artisan but they are clean and well pressed. He holds his bunnet in one hand and draws from his pocket a white linen handkerchief to soak up tiny beads of sweat that have gathered round his upper lip.

'I like them well enough, but they cannot compare to the classical masters:

Schubert and his like.'

He raises an eyebrow of enquiry.

'I see that I am talking to an educated lady. Music of the bandstand not quite good enough for the likes of thee.'

A formal way of speaking, not like the rough dialect of Govan. He speaks of 'thee' and 'thou', taking me in with his gaze. I am glad that I have chosen to wear my matching skirt and blouse and my gloves of soft grey leather. These pale colours suit my complexion. My hair is piled high and neatly coiffed with pins.

'So a common man,' Dr Scobie butts in. 'Your Tam was a man of the people?'

'But is not a man a man for all that?' I reply.

'I stand rebuked,' says the doctor, but I detect the faintest of irony in his voice.

'I am just a little surprised,' he continues, 'that you made the choice of a working man to be your husband. Here you are now, after all, a professional woman. There must have been suitors from a higher class to engage your interest?'

'There were no Mr Morrisons if that be what you mean, sir. And no Mr Browning to take me off to Italy. This is Govan, Dr Scobie, not Wimpole Street.'

'Just so.'

'So,' I respond, 'I am five and twenty. I enjoy his company. He shows much consideration towards me. And do not presume to think that all workmen are ignorant about the finer things in life. My Tam was a great reader of philosophy and a follower of modern political thought. He used his talents well in the shipyards for the betterment of his fellow men.'

'A man of conviction?'

'Yes. And passion too.'

I find that I am becoming bolder with my interrogator who seems determined to dislike my choice of mate.

'He educated me in the works of Tom Paine. I took minutes of meetings that he arranged with workers in the shipyards. I also volunteered to teach their wives and daughters the basic skills of reading and sewing. In exchange he came with me to concerts at the Kelvin Hall. We joined a choir together and sang all of Handel's Oratorios; my Tam could carry a tune well enough. But it wasn't all worthy causes, sir. This man could make me smile. He loved the music halls and we were regulars at the Theatre Royal in Hope Street. 'Gie me a song and a dance to keep me going,' he would say. And although he loved the common man, we never sat with the 'shawlies' up there in the gods. It was always a clean white shirt and sitting in a Box for him. It must have taken all of his money to treat me so well.'

'The son of a crofter, I believe, for all his fine ways?'

I am becoming aware, perhaps for the first time, that Dr. Scobie has little concern for the advancement of the working classes. What is he doing here, I wonder, when he could be treating the fine ladies like his hero Dr Sigmund Freud? What is he doing here with me when he could be in the West Wing of the asylum?

'He did, as you say, have humble origins, with none of the advantages that you possess, but he did take care to better himself. Moreover,' I am becoming a little red about the face as I stand up for my husband, 'he did not drink. He was a regular attendee at the Band of Hope meetings in the town.'

'You make him out to be a saint,. Dear lady. Had this paragon of virtue no vices at all?'

'Well he loved his football, sir, a real Rangers man. But apart from that he was all mine. He opened my eyes to many things, including the beauties of the world.'

'Really?'

'I mind once we left the theatre and he walked me right through the city.

Hours and hours till we got to Milngavie and saw the sun rise over the Campsie Hills.

Me with my many blisters on my feet and the cold air about us. But he always had a yen to return to Fyfe. He talked a lot about his home and the croft and the purity of the air in the country as we came back into the city on the tram in contrast to all the dirt and grime we were used to in our present lives.'

'And so you married him, Jean? Your peasant poet. What did your parents think about your choice?'

'My mother was dead by then sir. Worn out as you said with all her childbearing. But my father liked him. "Yon man of yourn will stand up tae ye, so he will, ma lass. He'll tak yer heid oot o' the cloots of heaven and bring ye fair doon tae earth." He recognised his good qualities, Dr Scobie. For all his uncouth ways my father was a man of discernment.'

'But he pulled you right down under the earth did he not, with all his demands on you. From the cloths of heaven to the depths of despair?'

I feel a change in his voice. I am being reeled in my his tone. I stiffen on the couch; I am almost roused to take flight. The doctor must sense my discomfort for he continues with what sounds like an apology.

'I have no desire to distress you, Jeannie. Please do not mistake my intentions, but you must have known that your marriage would bring an end to your career and with it your independence in life.'

'I think, sir, you exalt my status. A spinster woman, sharing lodgings with others like herself, in charge of sixty or more ill fed and poorly clad children of the slums. Day after day drilling them the seven times table and how to use an apostrophe, with a war soon to beckon them into the trenches, when what they really needed was good food in their bellies and shoes on their feet. That's what independence brought me, if I was being truly honest with myself.'

'Your Tam never went to the Great War?'

'He didn't believe in that war, Dr Scobie. The only war he was interested in fighting was the war against poverty and exploitation of the working people.

We stopped going to the music halls when the white feathers were being given out.

Besides wars need ships and my Tam was a master craftsman.'

'I see that you were determined, Miss Logan. The man of Fyfe had quite captured your heart.'

He pauses. A long while this time before I hear the next 'ahem.'

'Ahem... so did marriage,' pause again, 'disappoint you? I mean to say...'

I regard him as he smooths down his moustaches.

'What I mean to say... the physical side of things...'

A faint tremor of colour rises in those waxen cheeks. His feet begin to shuffle beneath that well polished desk.

'The physical side, as you say Dr Scobie brought no surprises. My sister Meg and I often heard what happens between men and women in the night hours.

I had brothers too, don't forget. Meg used to tell me when we were young that men had big worms in their trouser pockets that could grow and grow. She told me that a man's worm likes to come out in the darkness and search for a place inside a woman's body. There it could wriggle a while before spewing out what it had inside it.'

'Ahem, a colourful analogy. And did you believe her, dear lady?'

'Worms are blind, are they not, Dr Scobie, with instincts of their own.

My Tam had a worm like any other man and it sought its place within me and spat out its innards like any other man would.'

'You gained no pleasure from this experience then?

'Is there pleasure to be had sir? I thought it was just a man's desire. But I am thankful it brought me less pain with a sober man than one who was drunk.

I suffered a lot less than my mother did in that regard.'

I see the doctor look down. He folds his glasses and places them on top of his buff file. I sense his internal discomfort and imagine his worm, now uncoiling lightly in its blind curiosity, before taking rest again in the deep folds of his Harris tweed trousers.

He clears his throat and summons himself to continue.

'You know to what purpose those nightly experiences were for?'

'For the creation of children sir, a clever man like you should know that.'

But now I think I have gone too far and may trespass into his bad humour.

He will feel chastised by that remark; his worm will have shrivelled up to the size of a walnut. I must seek to divert him.

'Besides, as you may be aware, sir, there were other things on our minds at the time. When the Great War started there was an influx of labour from all over Scotland brought into the shipyards. Housing became scarce and our rents went up.

Ours was one of the first tenements that went out on

strike against landlords for doing this wicked thing. Tam and I were busy.'

'You were living near the shipyards again?'

'Yes. In Linthouse sir, near the St. Stephen's yard, close to where I was born.

But I had a bit of money saved by then. There was good china on my dresser, not the common wally dogs that my mother had and Tam was handy with the furnishings.

We were, you might say, a cut above the rest.'

'But not so much that you weren't threatened by the strike. You could have lost your home.'

'But we didn't. I helped the women in our struggle and the landlords finally gave in. That was the real pleasure in our early married life as far as I was concerned.'

'I see. I see. Indeed!'

But I can see that with some disappointment that politics bore him.

He does not care about my little victory. It's the sex that excites him.

He wants to get back to the worms!

'Yet despite, or perhaps because of all this drama, you find yourself pregnant Mrs Anstruther. How did that take you?'

'Badly, sir.'

'Badly?'

'I spent a good time with the sickness. My body was no longer my own.'

'Were you not pleased to bring another life into the world?'

'I had seen too many children brought into the world. And my youngest sisters were barely ten years of age themselves.'

'Your sisters? Oh yes, the twins.' He consults his notes again. 'Fiona and Isabella. Pretty names.'

'Maybe but those pretty names did not keep them fed or clothed. When I finished my teaching I could no longer keep supporting them at home.'

'And so?'

'And so they went into the service of a milliner who took them to her home in Millport. My sister Aggie, the one who lived, arranged it all. I have not seen them since this time.'

'A sad story indeed. But your man could afford to keep you and your new bairn you were carrying into this world. What do you remember of the birth, Jean?

The birth of your son George.'

His voice begins to pound inside me. I am feeling cold. The afternoon light casts strange shapes over the desk; the photograph of Grace is in shadow, the old man is becoming blurred. And now two other outlines appear as if in a mist in front of me: two wee girls in their new pom-pom hats that I bought them from Daly's. They hold each other by the hand and wave with their other hands.

Waving... waving...

Whilst I stand at the Bromilaw quay and see them take a boat down the water and out of my life forever. Their cries are caught in the spittle of rain rising from their young mouths and carried away to Dunoon is spumes of steam.

My legs leaden. Stumps of metal walking slowly back. One foot in the front of the other... such a effort to get away. To get away from him!

I have left Dr Scobie at his desk. His Conway Stewart pen still racing along the white paper.

I no longer care about being in his good grace. If a man is a man for all that, then it must be for a woman too. Why is he raking the coals of my life?

Clinker and ashes…

Ashes and dross. Grey like him. His face is grey. His worm is small and grey; no cave inside a woman's body for it to go any more. Only his daughter Grace to give him some joy.

And is there any grace for me? The grace of God which is supposed to pass all understanding.

Will I be forever damned?

I pinch my skin and discover that I have no feeling. No sensation of pain within. No taste but the dryness of my mouth. I prick my finger with a needle when I get back to the linen room and am surprised by the redness of my blood. But I do not feel a thing.

There is blood, but no tears.

At last!

It is better this way. I can turn my face to a blank wall and feel nothing.

Like before.

Only this time no squalling bairn to suckle.

No man to bear down on me.

With his purple worm.

I am sealed off from all that.

AND EMPTY!

TWO

GRANDMOTHER'S FOOTSTEPS

Bella cannot take her eyes off the white-faced line up on the evening news. The woman on the screen, with brown crescents of fatigue beneath her eyes, was telling her story.

He was a good man, her Gary. The best! All he did was go outside and tell them, these lads, to play elsewhere. When they'd finished swearing at Gary, they ran their bikes over the flowerbeds. Her little girl, Amy, was too frightened to go to the school or the shops. They called her names. She was Downs, you see.

A little moon child sat beside her mummy, holding hands with the police officer. A pretty little thing, her too rounded face emphasised by two bunches of hair tied behind her ears. 'Then the knife seemed to come from nowhere', the woman said. 'And no one', the policewoman joined in, 'not one person on that busy inner city street raised so much as a finger to help them.'

Bella checks the front door, then the back, and all the catches on the windows before she puts her coat on. Thankfully she has been busy recently with her mother's old sewing machine. All the curtains were up and drawn tight. She puts the hall light on and leaves the television with the sound turned low; the pictures playing to an empty room.

Then takes out the invitation card from her handbag and reads:

> Julia Rathbone invites you to celebrate the success of her recent exhibition 'The Rites of Spring'.
>
> Please wear something that Stravinsky would approve of (and bring the odd bottle to add sparkle to the evening)

Would Stravinsky approve of the paisley shawl she had restored for the occasion? Too bad if he didn't.

Hearing the 'peep-peep' of the taxi outside, Bella picks up the bottle of Spanish wine from the kitchen table, hoping that Julia would not notice the cheap supermarket brand on its label.

She was ready for the fray!

~

'Look at you! Where have you been hibernating?'

Bella looks round at all the guests assembled in Julia's drawing room. She need not have worried about dressing up; all the women there seemed to have had the experience of a Gaynor makeover. Only the hostess had obeyed her own instruction by sporting a fascinator hat with peacock plumage at the rim.

'This is the oldest friend I have in the world,' Julia is saying. 'Bella let me introduce you to Jane. Jane owns the gallery where I exhibited my latest masterpieces.'

'Hello Bella, do you paint as well?'

'No Bella is a scribbler. She puts pen to paper every now and again and produces some quite remarkable poetry, don't you sweetie? She's just moved into one of those little houses near the Hockley.'

'Oh my! You're brave!'

'And this is Andrea, a fellow splasher of the canvas. Andrea has met Hockney, you know!'

'Just a line-up at an exhibition, nothing special, darling…'

'You are too modest. Isn't she Jane? You always get more red 'sold' stickers on your paintings than I have on mine. Anyhow, I mustn't neglect the others. Connie here is a JP, sits on the Bench at Ruddington. And you may have heard of Sue, or Lady Middleton to give her a correct title. Sue's old man is a big cheese in Boots.'

'Really? I used to work in the Boots factory at Beeston when I was a student…'

'But we won't hold that against her? Sue's a peach! She bought my 'Symphony in colour' for an outrageous amount, didn't you Sue?'

'It was worth every penny Julia.'

A woman with an apron on, and no make-up on her face, comes in from the kitchen looking flustered.

'Oh Linda! There you are! Linda has been helping with the catering arrangements for tonight.'

'My pleasure, Julia.'

Linda does a little bob to the hostess and goes straight back to the kitchen.

'You are not going to miss me out are you Julia?'

The drawl from the shadows behind the bookcase is insistent. Julia seems rather intimidated by it. Her next introduction begins as an apology.

'I am so sorry Gina. How could I forget you, especially as

you were the inspiration to the theme of tonight's gathering? Bella meet Gina. She's a journalist, often on television as well. Late night programmes on the Arts.'

The body, when it emerges from the shadows seems to go well with the voice. Slightly sinister, Bella thinks.

Gina's eyes are everywhere. The left one has a slight cast to it and wanders off at times, independent of the other. Bella follows it now, a camera scanning an opulent room; now up to the high ceiling with its elaborate cornices and down, roaming over the faces of the invited guests and finally fixing its focus on her.

Click! Click! Blink!

'I'm always interested in meeting Julia's friends, especially her oldest one.'

'What is interesting is the project that Gina is working on now. She's got this idea of exploring the past through the x chromosome- the female gene and its influences in post modernist, post feminist society-'X Ray Eyes'.Isn't that right, Gina? She tells me that she is particularly interested in the role that our grandmothers played and, wouldn't you believe it, we are all grandmothers in this room. The latest to come into the fold is Linda. Her daughter Tracey has just had a little boy. Brian, is it Linda?'

Hooray! There were still a few Traceys' around.

Linda, bringing in a tray of vol-au-vents, blushes with pleasure.

'Ryan, actually Julia.'

'Well anyhow, Jane's got four grandchildren. Two in Australia, isn't that right, Jane?'

'Three.'

'And Connie here has been busy. Six at the last count, Connie?'

'My, you have a good memory Julia. Not all of them are mine though. Terry's been married before.'

'That doesn't matter. Sue has the sweetest granddaughters. That photograph you showed me of you all in Wollaton Park is lovely. I've got three myself, and one more on the way. Can't remember about you, Andrea. Remind me.'

'Just the one.'

'Like Bella, although she has twins coming soon.'

Gina, whose patience must be sorely tested by now, edges her way into the monologue.

'What I need to know from all you ladies is what is it like being a grandmother? And how different is that from the experience of your own grandmothers?'

Here we go, Bella thinks. Why is it we always have to sing for our supper at Julia's?'

They sit down at the expensive fruit wood table to the starter course – Linda's creation: scallops, prawns and greenery and something that looked like strawberry jam but was called a coulis, splattered haphazardly round the plate. The whole effect reminds Bella of a road traffic accident; seared flesh and blood and her fork picking up pieces like a rescue lorry. It did, however, taste delicious.

Well done Tracey's mum!

'So where shall we begin?'

It may have been Gina's brainchild but it was Julia's party. No show without Punch, Don would have said if he were here. Poor Don. Bella wonders if he has heard about her trip to London with Freddie? How will he feel when he hears that she has slept with someone else?

Julia was on a roll.

'My grandmother was a suffragette. Great material for your documentary, Gina. I've got a photo of her with Asquith; all fox furs and a very stern face as I recall. Can't remember my mother's side. Nothing remarkable there, I fear. What about yours Connie?'

'Oh both my Nan's were lovely.'

Bella winces. She hears the voice of Ailsa chide Evie when she once called her 'Nan'. 'Don't you ever call me by that name: 'Nan,' 'nanny'. Nannies are goats. I will be no one's nanny, if you please.'

'What do you mean by 'lovely,' Connie?'

'Oh they knitted and sewed and baked cakes. That sort of thing. Lots of treats on Sundays… steam puddings to die for.'

'Not surprised by the look of her,' Gina whispers to Bella.

Bella smiles. She begins to revise her first impression of her neighbour at the table. Gina might just have possibilities.

'Mine drove an ambulance during the War. A real heroine in the blackout by all accounts.'

'Gosh yes! My father's ma was a land army girl. That's where she met Grandpa, getting her hands dirty by picking up sugar beet in Norfolk.' One of Lady Susan's well-manicured fingers was in her mouth, picking up the remains of a stubborn scallop that had got lodged in her teeth.

'Very romantic,' the whispering continued.

Bella tries hard not to giggle.

'But what kind of lives did they lead? It sounds like we are saying it was the war that got them out of themselves and gave them a life away from the kitchen sink.'

'Not mine,' Andrea intones, 'she was a debutante in the thirties. She didn't go to war or do anything plucky like yours Sue, just had a good time by all accounts. One party after another and after she got married she farmed out her children to be looked after by staff she and my grandfather employed in that big house of theirs in Wiltshire.'

'Lucky her!'

'I'll go along with that.' Jane was having trouble with the next course, dropping chunks of slippery pasta from her fork. 'My Grandmama, we had to call her, was a diplomat's wife.

She spent all her time travelling around the pink parts of the globe with her exceedingly pompous husband we had to call Grandpapa. They dumped my mother and her sister in boarding schools when they were five years of age. Imagine doing that now, I ask you?'

'Lots of people still do,' Bella adds quietly.

'Did anyone have a real Giles granny? No teeth, a battered umbrella, the sort of battle axe that could make your life a misery?'

No one had.

'That was long before the National Health Service, you know, and way before the pill. Some women of my grandmother's generation, especially the working class ones, were dealt a tragic hand in life. They saw their fathers and their uncles go off in the first World War and then said goodbye to husbands and brothers in the second. I'm glad I'm a grandmother now and not then.'

Linda was coming into her own.

'Talking of taking the pill and not taking precautions,' Connie interjects, 'I see too many single mums and their families with rent arrears in my line of work. Getting pregnant just to get a council flat. And their habits get passed down to the next generation. I had to tick off a young grandmother when I was on the Bench the other day. She was only thirty five years of age, and really irresponsible. Fancy being a grandmother at thirty five!'

'Dear Lord, deliver us from our sins!'

Bella was choking into her napkin.

'What about you Bella? You've not said a word about your family.'

She was now caught off guard, without a defensive cover that would staunch any further curiosity about her past.

'Oh,' she stammered, 'I never knew mine. I guess they were

from the working classes that you talked about Linda. My mum's mother died when her youngest was two. TB I think. There were eight children in a room and kitchen in Glasgow, so it's not surprising.'

'Sad though,' Gina empathises, 'and on your father's side?'

'All I know is that she disappeared off the family radar somehow. No one knows anything about her except that her name was Jean and she was a beautiful seamstress. My Grandfer told me that. I could talk about him if you like. He was a lovely man.'

'Not allowed Bella. No talk of men tonight.'

No men? This was becoming a habit.

But now she has the floor, she decides to take it.

'I do love being a grandmother though, don't you all?'

'Why?

'I guess it gives me the chance to relive the whole experience of motherhood again and perhaps get it right this time – all the mistakes you made with your own, she adds quickly. 'Like the Larkin poem: 'They fuck you up your mum and dad…' Stuff like that, if you see what I mean.'

What she didn't say was how much she ached for that tiny bundle of life that Evie had brought into the world. Love without responsibility, a freeing concoction, holding no boundaries for her. At first she had been uncertain as to how to be with Josh. She didn't want to be like Ailsa, a dominant presence in their lives. But whenever she was asked to babysit, her heart quickened. She played with him until they were both exhausted. She took in the sweet smell of him at bath time and snuggled close as he fell asleep. No other relationship was that special; with her grandson Bella felt that she could truly be herself.

'Tell me a story Bamba with your mouth…' and she was off! An invitation for her make-it-up-as-you-go-along tales was all she needed to hear. Grandfer had left his loving mark on her and she felt his hand touch her and pass down its benediction to the great grandson he would never know.

Talk flowed all around her; little bursts of boastful bubbles dropping lightly round the room. Then a switch in tone; criticism about their own children as parents.

'The thing is, they are all so neurotic. And they know far too much, rushing off to the internet with every sniff and snuffle thinking it could be meningitis.'

The languid voice of lady Susan was becoming a whine. 'And they all have these gurus who tell them what to do.'

'Oh I do agree. None of this sending them out to play and don't come back till tea time that we had when we were youngsters.'

'There is this guru,' Lady Sue persists, 'who gives orders about what to eat, how to potty train, what boys and girls should wear, and they all follow her religiously. Whatever happened to common sense?'

'I'll go along with that,' says Jane with feeling. 'I have learned the hard way that a mother's place is always in the wrong and it is a grandmother's duty to hold her tongue and smile. Smile and indulge, that's my motto.'

'Mine too,' agrees Bella. She liked Jane.

'Gina Ford, I think that's what she is called.' Linda, who has been struggling to keep pace with the conversation on her journeys back and forth to the kitchen, adds her bit with triumph. 'Tracey's got her book and all her friends with children read it like a bible.'

Bella sees Gina put down her fork. She leans forward ready to claim her space.

'You know all this talk of child care reminds me of another guru, Dr Truby King. I bet none of you have heard of him, but he was on our mother's shelves when we were growing up. 'Feeding and Child Care of Babies' the book was called: everyone's manual between the wars. And what did he say?'

Gina looked round. Everyone was paying attention.

'Breast feeding every four hours on the dot, never mind if the baby cries in between. Then outside for plenty of fresh air, rain or shine. Cold baths in morning, bed before six in the evening. Every mother,' she takes on one of those clipped BBC voices heard on old newsreels,'has a duty to the British Empire and the race to have lots of children and to stay at home and look after them.' That was the voice of Truby King and his Plunket Society was very influential in Government circles. It's the voice I hear in my namesake and all those other super nannys that you see on the box. Things come round and people like to be told what to do in bringing up children as well as everything else besides.'

'Oh I don't go along with that prescription.' Julia puts down her spoon. They were eating a rather rich chocolate pudding that Andrea had brought. Linda didn't 'do' deserts.

She doesn't like to be upstaged, thinks Bella. Back off, Gina, while you can.

'My parents raised me and my brothers to do our own thing and I did exactly the same with my boys. They ate when they were hungry and slept when they were tired. Motherhood never stopped me from doing what I wanted and I am proud to say my little granddaughter is following in my wake. She is only three and travelling the world with her parents, having a wonderful time. I had an e-mail from them a few days ago on their way to Bhutan.'

'But your bible was Dr Spock, Julia, the last hero of the permissive age.'

Ouch Linda, you have overstepped your mark with that comment.

'I don't believe in bibles. All that dogma stifles the creative spirit. Don't you all agree?'

Various members of the company raise their eyebrows. They were well used to Julia's pronouncements. She had given birth to three sons by three different fathers, without, as she was so fond of boasting, breaking her stride. Her boys had grown up in an atmosphere of careless indifference to any rules and regulations that may have been imposed on them. People dreaded asking Julia round with her latest partner in those days, for invariably her kids came too. They sat at the table with the adults, they had no manners and dominated any discussion, refusing to go upstairs when the hosts own offspring were sent to bed with cries of : 'It isn't fair!'

Bella much preferred her own battery raised brood to Julia's free range chicks any day. Eliott, the eldest had not surprisingly dropped out of public school. He formed a rock band and had a brief moment of fame in the punk era. Then he met Willow. They were travelling now with their child in tow, on the proceeds of his grandfather's legacy and no doubt would continue on the road until the money ran out. The middle boy, Nathan was a potter in Wales. He was currently living with a male partner and according to Julia they were sponging off the system, quite happily, she would add if anyone enquired further. But she broke the mould with Troy, a childhood friend of Evie's. This little chap worked hard at school and got a job in a Building Society when he left the local comprehensive. Now he was in charge of a branch and lived with his wife Polly in a brand new house on an estate. They were expecting their third child in May. Julia didn't talk about Troy very much and from what Evie said, Polly did not welcome visits from her mother-in-law.

'Do you remember the game called 'Grandmother's Footsteps?' Gina was taking another tack.

'Remind us,' Julia's voice was beginning to lose much of its animation.

'Well as I remember, it's all about sneaking up on our grandmothers and taking them unawares.'

'No it's not!'

The hostess had spilled some red wine on the tablecloth and was signalling for Linda to pass the salt. She started to rub the linen fabric with a ferocity that was way over the top.

'Someone who is IT stands by a wall with her back to the rest of everyone and they all take tiny steps towards her without her noticing. Then the one in front becomes IT. It's a stupid game about winning and losing, that's all.'

Gina's voice in reply is soft and compelling.

'But don't you see the whole thrill of the game was creeping up ever so slowly inch by inch without being known by the one in front. She could turn round, remember, if she thought that anyone had moved a muscle. Then you were back to the starting line. She had such power, that grandmother.'

She pauses. Everyone has stopped eating.

'Let's be playful for a minute. Supposing all those dead grandmothers you have been talking about stood in a line and crept up on you, what would that be like? They are in their fox furs and their false teeth and their permanent waves and all that invisible baggage that they have handed to you without you ever knowing… Inching forward, ready to take you unawares…Imagine…'

The mood at the table had changed. Bella feels a cold shiver run through her. Someone was passing petit-fours. She looks at her watch. Her taxi would be here soon. She begins to make her 'goodbyes' avoiding the stare of Gina who is now standing by the mantelpiece lighting up a black cheroot.

She is aware that she is carrying out with her a feeling of unease. That night she takes that feeling with her into her dreams. She is in the playground in that little school in Keyworth. It is a cold day with frost on the ground. Beside her in a line are Julia, Kit Horton, Deirdre Wright and someone whose name she has forgotten: a snivelling little girl who was often bullied and always wanted to be her friend. The girls' breaths hang in the air as they step forward one at a time towards the shrouded grandmother figure ahead. Bella finds herself at the head of the pack. She places her hand gently on the grey shoulder in front of her. At her touch, the body melts away. But the head is still there. It turns round to face her.

And the face?

Gina's face. Her two eyes had merged into one cyclops.

The giant orb stared right through her and into a landscape beyond her reach.

THREE

'WHEN YOU WISH UPON A STAR'

THE JOTTER

23rd February 1921.

*I have taken some time to recover my wits after my latest
session with the doctor. Lily is there for me, as always. She
sees to it that I put what passes for food into my mouth and
bides with me till I finish eating. Then she collects a decent
set of clothing for me to wear from the bins at the end
of the ward. Today she tells me that she overheard Sister
Jewell say to Mistress Niven that Dr Scobie has gone to
Austria for a 'rest cure' she calls it, in the fresh mountain
air. I choke back the words that I want to say; there is
plenty of freshness in the air he left behind, but I do not
wish to sound uncharitable. Since the coal strike we have
been on rations and although this is the first day of spring,*

there is nothing on the ground but snow and slush. I heard Mistress Niven whisper to Elsie Macpherson, when she came by with pillowcases to mend, that the good doctor is not getting any better. The tumours that have invaded his body are not responding to medication so they say, so this holiday may just be a respite interlude, poor man.

I am sorry for this turn of events and quite surprised by my reaction. I have pangs of regret that I may have added to his pains. For all his 'indeeds' I feel that he cares for me. Then a panic grips my whole body. I want to see him again.

I must have one more chance to gain his good favour.

Better news comes from the lips of Sister Jewell. She is to retire at Easter and go and live with her sister Dorothy in Dunfermline. Her arthritis is stiffening her joints and she says it is now time to live a less taxing life. I hear Mistress Niven say that she is sorry to hear the news, but I sense that her voice seems to lack sincerity.

The Jewell catches me as I linger by the door and she scolds me for nothing at all. I bite my lip as usual but fancy that a small smile is forming in the valley behind my gums.

25th rd February

I read from then latest edition of The Gazette that Ethel has just been told of the death of Edward. The malarial fever overcame him and he was buried in a clearing in the jungle alongside the mighty Zambezi river. There was little time for ceremony in the African heat but one of the converts conducted a simple but reverent service. Ethel imagines her lover now, his body mouldering beneath the lush tropical heat whilst his soul climbs heavenward on the *wings of his faith. She has borne the news stoically. Her legs are stronger now and she has been able to take a few steps with the encouragement of Dr Lennox. She tells him that she will now devote the rest of her life to the poor within the parish and set up a Foundling school to educate orphans and bring them into the way of the Lord for Edward's sake. It does not surprise the reader to learn that her friend Gertrude has left her side and married a Dragoon guard.*

As I struggle to turn over the pages my fingers are chapped and red raw. It is so cold here that I almost envy the fate of the hapless Edward. His dying words uttered in the foetid fever of agony longed for the coolness of Ethel's hand on his brow. Oh that a drop of sweat would fall on the ice that grows inside my body and threatens to snap my bones!

Some feeling has returned to me, but it is not warmth. It is the persistence of a dull ache that never leaves me now. I take longer and longer to pull together my unravelling self after I see Dr Scobie but only he can bring back some feeling to me. Then he drains me of it and I am left as if I am naked and as cold as stone.

~

The next morning, as expected, the call comes, right on cue.

'You left early you sly old thing. What did you make of last night?'

'Well Julia, it sure was interesting!'

'Why is it you always say 'interesting' in that interesting tone of yours? How about Gina? Wasn't she something else?'

'To tell you the truth I found her a bit creepy. What was all that stuff about Grandmother's footsteps? I really felt quite spooked.'

'Search me sweetie. I didn't really warm to her either, but she seemed quite taken with you. She asked for your telephone number before she left.'

'Julia, you didn't!'

'Felt very pressured, sorry. Anyhow it got me thinking, perhaps she can be useful in finding out those missing bits in your past. That mysterious grandmother of yours for instance, we were all intrigued about her. Come to think about it, she could even track down your pa. You have no idea where he buggered off to when he left hearth and home, have you Bella, and now your ma has gone there is nothing to stop you finding out.'

'I'm not so sure about that.'

She could feel a slippered tread of doubt tiptoe into her thoughts. From somewhere deep inside a voice of caution was telling her to let sleeping dogs lie.

'No! I've made up my mind, Julia. I'm not going to allow myself to be one of those women that you see on those dreadful kiss-and-tell- shows. If she rings me up I'll put her off I think. Besides I've got Josh coming to stay for a few days, that's enough to occupy me for a while.'

'Everything alright with Evie? She's not due for a few weeks yet, is she?'

'No she's fine. She just needs a break.'

'Don't we all? Can't wait for that trip down to Cornwall with you and the lovely Freddie. I'm not sure what to pack. What's the weather going to be like at this time of year? But are you sure we won't cramp your style Bella? It's early days in the romance isn't it? We don't want to be playing gooseberry.'

'Believe me, honestly, he has especially invited you both to come. He says he's got bags of room at the cottage. You and he can blether on about art on the way there whilst Hugo and I can giggle on the back seat. And it is a business trip remember?

You'll be good company when he's off setting up his franchises or whatever he'll be doing. It will be fine. Just don't trespass where you are not wanted Julia, that's all. I know you of old.'

'Wouldn't dream of it sweetie, not now I know you are fully operational beneath the sheets again, though I must say you have been a bit coy in telling your best friend all about it.'

'And that's the way it will stay. Bye Julia!'

'Have fun with the little fellow.'

'Oh I will, indeed I will.'

~

'What doing, Bamba?'

'I'm just taking some pills Josh. They are not sweeties.'

'What's pills?'

'Medicine, pet, a bit like calpol that mummy gives you to make you feel better when you are not well. Bamba has been feeling a bit depressed for a little while and these pills help.'

'What's 'pressed?'

Bella stops to think.

'A mixture of being a little bit sad and a little bit tired I think.'

Would that do for an explanation?

She looks down at the small puckered face beside her. They are walking on the banks of the old gravel pits, now converted to a nature reserve. A squally wind was coming from the river and filling her grandson's romper suit with gusts of sir. She holds tightly on to his hand, fearing that her little Michelin man could blow away and topple into the water.

She is also aware of holding down something else within her. Bella struggles to find a name for it. Fear? Dread? The prospect of those creeping footsteps tracking her down. She managed to control these feelings when the insistent call came shortly after

Julia's. Gina was upbeat. Wouldn't it be marvellous to do a bit of detective work on her behalf? After all she had access to all the resources: archivists all lined up for the chase, money no object and Bella could have a say in the editorial presentation. It would make wonderful television wouldn't it? Perhaps give others the courage to investigate their own family trees. And what about her children and all those who come after. Hadn't they the right to know about their ancestry? Wouldn't they be angry for withholding what was after all their heritage?

But afterwards, after she had said 'NO!' in as many different ways as she could muster, she felt herself give way.

She was a child again. A shy little girl on the stairs, peeping through her fingers, wanting to look, dying to run away...

And hearing Ailsa's shouts...

'I should have heeded the warnings and seen this coming. What do you expect coming from a family like yours?'

Then her father's slap...

'BITCH!'

The front door crashing off its hinges...

The shadow of his face on the frosted glass...

And he was gone!

~

'Bamba! Bamba. You're hurting my hand.'

Bella looks down and unclasps her tight fist. She rubs the small white hand inside it until the blood flows freely again.

'I'm sorry my wee pet lamb. I didn't mean to hurt you, Bamba was just thinking of something else.'

He looks up at her.

'Is Mummy 'pressed?'

'What? No Josh. She's not depressed. At least she is not sad but she is very tired. Her two little babies are growing inside her and she needs a lot of rest to help them grow big and strong before they come out and meet their big brother.'

They cross the wooden bridge that led to the car park. A group of ducks waddled in their wake, loudly quacking at their ankles.

'Give them the rest of the bread Josh. The ducks want their tea.'

She helps him to shred the remains of a loaf they have been carrying.

'Give them to the lady ducks; the brown ones over there. The ones with the green heads are men ducks. Bamba doesn't like the drakes.'

'Why not like drakes?'

'Well...' Bella swallows hard. She feels an overwhelming anger against the pecking beaks at her feet. Drakes were bullies; men were bullies, George Anstruther had pecked away at the little brown body of his wife until she was beaten. He hadn't even noticed his downy duckling left there on the stairs. What did he care?

'Because,' she says, striving to keep an even tone in her voice,' soon all the lady ducks will be laying their eggs and they will be sitting on them till they hatch out and won't be able to go to the shops. We will give them lots of bread to help keep them strong. The drakes can fetch their own tea. Come on, let's go home and have ours.'

After his bath, she puts him in her own bed. He sits up, hugging the pillows, pulling all his soft toys around him.

'Make sure you've got some room for me when I get to bed,'she says.

'Who day?' he asks, pointing to a photograph beside them.

Bella picks up the gilt frame and holds it closer to him.

'That's me Josh, the little girl with pigtails in her hair, a long time ago. And that's my Daddy. We are going sledging in the snow. Can you see me clinging on to him as we slide down the hill? Your Bamba was very happy that day. Not 'pressed like now.'

She looks closer at the faded black and white image. How old was she then? Four? Five? For a moment she can capture the emotion of that day, holding on close to her father like a parachute on his back; joy and fear like a trapped bubble bursting inside her.

Where **had** he gone?

'Tell me a story with your mouth Bamba. About that little girl. And I want Solly to be in it and Hector and Pingu and Ollie as well' he insists, lining up his collection of toys on the bed.

'Gosh, that's a tall order. Just give me a minute and let me see.'

She closes her eyes and lets her mind drift until a narrative thread takes her by the hand and leads her down an unknown path. She looks at the photograph again and begins.

'Well, once upon a time there was a little girl with pigtails in her hair and a scattering of sun kissed freckles on her nose. What shall we call her, Josh?'

'Give her your name Bamba. Call her Belle.'

'Well this little Belle always wanted to fly away. Every morning she would wake up in the attic in her house, that's a tiny room inside the roof by the way, and stretch out her arms, like this, and jump. But when she did she always landed on the floor one second later with a big bump and sometimes a splinter in her knee. And that made her cry.'

'What's a 'plinter?'

'It's a little piece of wood from the floor that gets into your knee when you fall over. Look do you want me to to tell you the story or are you going to ask me questions all the time?'

She watches as his thumb lifts from the duvet and follows a familiar route to his mouth.

Then her story telling self took over and she was away...
away into the land of make-believe that took the little girl Belle
and her soft toys on an amazing journey into space where they
rested on a cloud and ate popcorn before travelling up to a
distant star where they sang 'Twinkle twinkle...'and wished a
wish, and then came back via the planets and a passing plane
on its way to Australia. Back into the attic room and into the
safety of her bed.

'Night little man,' Bella whispered. But her grandson was
already asleep. She lifted his head from the crook of her arm
and felt it tingle as it slowly came back to life.

FOUR

'IF ONLY...'

'Did I ever tell you folks, I'm really a Cornish man. A Penhallighan on my mother's side, or so I have been unreliably informed. Probably descended from a long line of smuggling stock, I'll be bound. 'Ill met by Moonlight,' and all that. Any moment now I could come tap-tapping on your door and asking each one of your good selves to keep a few barrels of brandy for me, till King George's men get off the scent.'

Here he goes again...'putting on the agony...putting on the style.'

And before he knows where he is, he is off into an elaborate mime, rolling his eyes around and doing his best Long John Silver leer.

'Arrr arr, me hearties!'

It's working! Julia joins in on the act. She starts to wring her hands, doing a possible imitation of the ghost of Rebecca at Mandalay. It's a good dumb show. They're a good team, him and her: Julia and Hugo, Hugo and Jules.

Bella is laughing. She is spread out on the sofa, feet up and looking a lot more relaxed than when they arrived. They are all full from the fine meal she has cooked and the wine has done its mellowing job. Mein host looks on indulgently from his leather wing-backed chair by the fire. Hugo sees the smoke from his fat cigar coiling up to the ceiling and trailing to wispy vapours over their heads.

It has been a good week for Hugo. Hugo, the court jester, that is, at the beck and call of his mistress and her friends. Good old Hugo! Back slapping, joke telling, there's-a-tale-for-every- occasion Hugo. It's a role he mostly enjoys. He's spent his time wandering round art galleries and various artisan workshops with Julia, listening to her prattle on, catching her gushes and gurgles of praise for some painter or potter, always with a ready smile, a nod, a 'fancy that' or a 'you don't say?' when the need arose. It has kept her happy.

And he set his expression to 'fair' when Freddie regaled them with details of his latest business adventures. Yesterday he had set off before seven. Up and shaved before Hugo opened one eye, and off to finalise a new deal for a retail outlet near Penzance; some franchises for his shorts and vests or those leotards that Julia would sometimes squeeze herself into for her Pilates classes in the gym. Once or twice he managed to slip off the leash and slope his way into a bar somewhere. There he opened his mouth in friendly conviviality, hoping that others would open their wallets to return the favour. Some did. And yesterday there was that nice undemanding walk with Bella. Over the cliffs and far away and into a little tea shop where two old dears, straight out of 'Arsenic and Old Lace' served them up with Earl Grey tea and freshly baked scones. The pair of them played their parts well, crooking their little fingers in gentle homage to the occasion.

'Do you ever come off stage, Hugo?' she asked him.

'Whenever I see a pretty girl in the wings, my dear.' Then seeing that she looked serious, he continued, 'What's up Bella? You've been quiet all week. Some might even used the word 'pensive'. Is there something not quite right in the state of Denmark?'

He sees her face lose some of its tension. The fine lines round those blue- grey eyes relax and soften.

'No, actually Hugo I'm feeling much better. Tired perhaps, but then, I'm always tired these days. However, less burdened I think. Some things have lifted inside me and that feels good. And haven't you noticed that I'm also standing up for myself a little more? I won't let Julia push me around so much.'

'Good for you. I approve of that. But there is nothing of you to push around. Come on let's have another scone. Let all that clotted cream do its magic.'

She smiled indulgently at him, but he could tell that she didn't want to play.

'I gather you saw Don a while ago. He told me you had been to the races together. How do you think he looked?'

'Well if the way to a man's heart is through his stomach, he should have no complaints.'

Her eyes fix on him.

'Level with me Hugo. How was he?'

'Fine. The word 'contented' springs to mind – what you and I might call a little bit boring. Very different from Sir Freddie Adidas, Bella. Chalk and cheese I would say.'

'You don't like him very much do you?'

He drained the last of his tea and put his hand over hers.

'Bella, I don't mean to change the subject, but what do you see in Mr Reebok? I know he is very urbane and attentive and prosperous and I'm the last one to complain about his hospitality, but is he really the right man for you? To misquote a line from an old song: if you showed him a sunset, I doubt whether he would stay with you till dawn.'

She took her hand away and signalled to the waitress for the bill.

'Well I'm not sure what he makes of you either. And you must stop calling him those names Hugo.'

'What names?'

'Mr Reebok, or Nicely Nike or all those variations on the Adidas theme. They are starting to wear a bit thin and I don't think Freddie shares your sense of humour.'

But Julia likes him!

And he has an eye on her!

Hugo looks across at his partner, now spread-eagled on the soft leather sofa. In her element she is. Look at her! She's got that red dress on, the one with the cleavage on show; Elizabeth Taylor in 'Butterfield Eight', the slinky temptress that she is. He wonders if it ever crosses her mind how Bella must be feeling with those two udders heaving in front of her. And old Adidas over there is interested – very keen. He can't take his eyes off them tonight. Hugo is willing to bet any man's money but his own: odds on six to four, that if Bella wasn't here, she'd have bedded Freddie by now. She would never see it as an act of betrayal, just a bit of an adventure; a story to tell over coffee and croissants at breakfast the next morning.

'But I'm always true to you darling in my fashion... I'm always true to you in my way.'

Besides, as she often likes to tell him, where could she find another man who could make her laugh like he does? That could make her laugh in bed!

She is talking to him now, bending over him in fact, telling him how they met. It's a good story, worth tuning in to. He pours another glass of his host's single malt as the tale begins.

'... in a bar of all places. I saw this ever so tall man with ever such a slight stoop, Peter O'Toole in another guise. And there you were nursing your disappointment, weren't you sweetie? Some audition you'd been to for a voice-over ad. You had to say in that smokey, after dinner sort of way: "drive your way to perfection", is that right? Well it did it for me, even though it was John Hurt or some other smoothie that got the job, and Christ knows he didn't need the money, not like you did. But it didn't matter somehow, you'd worked your magic on me and it wasn't long before you moved in.'

She's honed that script to perfection over the years. Nicely Nike was in the palm of her hands.

'And you should have seen what he brought with him to the flat! A suitcase of old sweaters that his Granny would have knitted and a box of long playing records that Blind Lemon What's-his-face had dumped on him in Mississippi in '63.'

''65 Julia. And it was Missouri. If you are going to tell that story, for Pete's sake get it right!'

'Missouri, Minnesota, Miami? Who cares. And we've been together off and on I have to say for nearly eight years. I've got that right at least.'

'If you say so my love.'

'Oh I do say so! I do. I do!'

He reaches out to take her glass. She has had enough – way over the limit. But there is no stopping her tonight. Hugo cuts in before she skitters off into another saga that will see them all in the embarrassing zone where there is no turning back.

Time to start up one of his stories.

'High time we went to the Minac theatre again. My word what a marvellous place.

We all should go to a play in the summer. And wasn't that old lady wonderful? To have a vision of constructing a performing art space out of sheer rocks. WOW! What an achievement! I once bought a picture of her, sitting there in an upturned wheelbarrow way into her nineties, script in her hand, making sure that all the actors were word perfect. Amazing!'

'She wouldn't have had much time for you then,' Julia slices in with one of her many put-downs. 'You could never remember your lines when you were on stage, you said. Mr Make-it-up-as-you-go-along, weren't you? In all those plays by Terrance Rattigan and Noel Coward, with your cigarette holders and your fancy silk dressing gowns. Couldn't be bothered with daft lines, could Mr Hugo, king of the bit parts Lindsey, just a few 'Dahlings'… in that expensive drawl of yours. That was in the good old days, before the angry young buggers in their regional accents took over and put you out of a job.'

Ouch! Steady on old girl.

'STOP IT!'

Who said that?

Bella!

Bless her heart, Bella!

'Stop it Julia! Stop showing off!'

~

She's had enough. She can't stand it any more. Hugo holding the floor is one thing. He's amusing; he doesn't trespass beyond the bounds of civility. But with Julia- a few drinks in her and its another matter. Her mouth will go anywhere. If Hugo wasn't here, it would probably be on Freddie now, and he wouldn't mind that, she thinks. He wouldn't need any of his blue pills to rise up inside those big red lips of hers.

'And for goodness sake will you stop putting Hugo down. He may not have been Lawrence Olivier but who cares about that? He's been the perfect guest, don't you think Freddie?

And such a good friend to me. Thank you Hugo. Thank you for your walks and all the fun we have had together this week. And thank you for considering things that are not just all about money. About getting and spending… I'm sick of it all. Go on Hugo. I'm interested in what you have to say.'

'Well,' he resumes, for once now lost for words.

But inside he is singing! He is singing: 'I love this woman. Go on my sweet!'

'What's got into you, Bella?' Julia snaps.

Hugo sees Freddie put down his cigar.

Are we in for a mud wrestling match?

Front stalls for Hugo!

But she backs down.

More's the pity.

'I'm sorry,' she says. 'I'm just tired of all this chatter; empty chatter, making so much din. When are we going to say something real for a change?'

'So it's to be one of your 'meaning of life' conversations, is it? Is that what you want? Well go on then, you start. Mrs High and Mighty Bertrand Russell over there. You are the clever one with the fancy degree!'

'Don't rubbish what I have to say before I have even begun Julia. That's not fair. Hugo was talking about that remarkable woman who created the Minac theatre, what was she called?'

'Rowena Cade,' he feeds her gratefully.

'That's it. Rowena Cade. Now she created something special in her life. Something beautiful. She left a legacy, just like the man who started the Eden project we visited the other day. They both had a dream and they worked hard enough to see it through. Which one of us, hand on heart could say we've done the same?'

Hugo puts down his glass. He smiles to himself. This has got his lady's dander up, good and proper.

'I don't know how you can say that. People buy my pictures all the time. I've just had an exhibition in Hampstead, for God' sake!'

'Yes, alright, I'll give you that. You've got talent Julia. But you have squandered such a lot on your rich clients. And you never sponsored those kids in the school that Nathan went to. You know, those autistic youngsters who could have been so creative if some one had just spent time with them and helped bring out their potential. You had the money Julia and you could have found a space in your busy schedule to sit alongside just one of them and reach out to help. You could have made such a difference.'

'And I did!' she rejoins. 'I was always popping in to see how things were.'

'But you never stayed long enough to find out what was really going on, did you? That's just it. You pop in and you pop out. A great one for talking the talk. I've listened to it for years, like I listened to your father and never answered him back either. All high words and loose sentiment, the pair of you. Armchair socialists they would have called you now. Remember the time when we walked with CND all those years ago? You couldn't quite make it to Aldermaston when you found out how far it really was. You had a date back in Art school. Surprise! Surprise! So you hitched a lift home.

And all those Labour Party meetings you and your dad took me to? Where were you on the picket line for the miners back then? It was me who was left to hand out all those leaflets about the class struggle that your old man had written. And then I had to walk all the way back to that stinking high rise that Ailsa and I called home. But not you. Oh no! You just swanned back to Edwalton; tea in the library, crumpets on a tray, congratulating yourselves that you had done all you could for the poor and the needy. I could go on... Greenham

Common? Yes? Standing beside the fence with your wire cutters, then saying; 'it wasn't me', it was her over there, when that burly Yank bore down on us. Oh yes, meet my friend Julia, the brave suffragette.'

Hugo can't help it. He clasps his hands. What a speech! And Julia? His bright bedazzled Julia hasn't got any answer to hand. She seems to be winded. Those two great boobies sagging in their scarlet sack.

Round two! Seconds away. She's off again!

'Anyhow, it's not just you I'm getting at. It's you as well Freddie. You could do so much more with all your wealth.'

'You mean you want me to make another million, then give it away,' he quips. 'Well I could learn to paint. Do you know anyone who could teach me Julia?'

The boobs were resuming their inflatable swell. Julia replies with just a hint of coyness that makes Hugo want to hit her.

'Well just maybe I do.'

Then he sees Bella shrug. She looks defeated. Knocked out by a careless come-on jab way below the belt and landing in the soft regions where cheap excitement grows. He sees just how much this outburst has cost her and semaphores some more encouragement for her to carry on.

'Freddie that is such a selfish thing to say. What's your money for anyway? What happened to that idea we talked about when you took me to London. You know, the charity you were interested in setting up. A sports academy for disabled kids, wasn't it? Somewhere your niece could enjoy doing archery even through she is in a wheelchair? You could bring such pleasure to lots of people if you would just slow down and think things through. Or are you another one who is generous with his mouth but not his wallet?'

Ooops Bella! He won't like that!

Hugo fears she may be treading into dangerous territory with this remark. Old Adidas, if he is not mistaken, does not do altruism. Nor does he put his whole self in as far as relationships are concerned. He has seen him first thing in the morning, when he could still be snuggled up with Bella, pouring over a spread sheet, always with his eye on the next conquest: another killing. Mr Oki Koki Koki that one. He'll put his right leg over my love, then his left arm out, pretty sharpish too if Uncle Hugo is not mistaken.

No putting his whole self in for anyone. Rah! Rah! Rah!

Freddie is pouring another glass of wine for Julia now. There is a complicit smile between them. It seems to revive her.

'Well we all know what you have done with your life, don't we, Miss Virtuous Anstruther? Been at the beck and call of everyone else. Meet my friend Bella, the patron saint of lost causes. Crack heads, down-and-outs, no-hopers every one. What kind of legacy is that I ask you? You've spent your life listening to the dregs of the world when you could have been someone of influence in that precious Society you keep banging on about. A Head teacher, a professional writer, someone like your daughter Iona perhaps? But oh no, not you! Or that mousy husband of yours, for that matter. Dr, hard-done-by Cavendish, passed over again and again in the promotional stakes because he wouldn't speak up for himself and you wouldn't push him hard enough.'

'That's not fair Julia. Don's research did make a difference.'

'Well, whatever, he certainly scuttled off when things got tough at home, didn't he?

And where is he now? On some god-forsaken fen with his binoculars, I expect, with the 'brisk-and-bracing' in tow. Not with his wife, not where he should be, that's for sure.'

Ding dong it goes! Shoves and jabs and no limits on where the punches land. Not a Queensberry rule in sight.

'Girls! Girls! Please break it up!'

But Bella can't. She won't back off. But when she next opens her mouth, she can feel her tongue flailing inside it, freed from the laces that have kept it in check. But the words she wants won't come out.

Then she hears a warning voice, in another accent, erupting deep within her.

'*Haud yer tongue lassie, for fear it will unravel you.*'

Who said that?

It wasn't just the drink was it?

But the voice carries on.

'*My loose thoughts running…*
I must not loose my head
Loose ma heid
I canna gie mysel away!

The room is warm but Bella is shivering. She clasps the paisley shawl tighter round her shoulders, then looks up. Julia is repairing her face – another slash of carmine red being plastered on her lips. Hugo is looking at his watch. Time for bed, Hugo; too much good food and all that free booze taking its toll, no ready quips now to rescue this drama.

~

She takes her time to regard the man by the fireplace, hoping to find something of the boy she once knew by the river. He wasn't there now. Was Hugo right about Freddie after all? In all their lying together, Bella felt they had never been close. There was always that sense that a sentry was posted between them, to keep guard on his emotions and not give too much of himself away.

She sighs. Then says: 'You know I once wrote a poem, one of the many I scribbled off in waiting rooms not long ago. No magnum opus I'm afraid, but it scared me so much that I threw it away. I think I could hold on to it now if I felt brave enough.'

She closes her eyes and wills the words to come back to her.

'If only...
if only
one day
we could sit down
besides our own selves
and hold our own hands
in a trusting clasp
then
we could grasp
the world'

The phone rings. Nobody seems to be taking any notice of it. After a few minutes Freddie stands by the door. He looks serious.

'Bella, that was James. It's Evie. I think I ought to be driving you back home.'

FIVE

DAFFODILLS

THE JOTTER

March 3rd 2021

He's back!

Elsie Macpherson has seen him when she was serving in the staff canteen.

She tells me that he has lost much weight and most of his hair is now gone.

What is left of it, she sighs, is sparse and grey, making him look like an old baby bird. When he walks he has to have two sticks to aid him in his locomotion.

Daughter Grace has returned to her studies in Edinburgh University but her Aunt Clara has come to look after him in that big sandstone house of his in Jordanhill. Sister Jewell now positively sings in her work. Her transformation from harridan to heroine is a sight to behold. She is now the one to arrange all his appointments, so he is able to rest between consultations.

Will he ever fit me in?

March 6th.

Morning.

He has asked to see me at half past two this afternoon!
After his lunchtime sleep; his siesta, as the Jewell has come
to call it.

I make my way to the sewing room and ask Mistress
Niven to select some clothing that may suit me better. We
find a pleated skirt of a pleasing tartan pattern that just
requires some alteration at the waist. The doctor is not
the only one to have lost so much weight and my daily
apparel, randomly sought from the basket of mendings is
often held together by way of safety pins. We continue in
our rummaging and come across a green woollen jumper
that has still some softness in it texture. I sew two buttons
at the neck. The good lady says that they add a finishing
touch to the ensemble. The stockings that I wear now will
have to do.

Now she finds me the latest box of shoes that were
donated by The Friends of the Asylum, those rich wives
from the West End of Glasgow who give their time to the
poor and the destitute. I am sure that my heroine Ethel
would count herself as one of them and indeed I may even
have caught sight of someone like her at one of the monthly
sales of work. There are rich pickings today, unlike the
usual batch of throwaways.

I take out a pair of cracked patent leather shoes in a
size that would have fitted my father and I am temporarily
transported back in time. My father and mother are
getting ready to go to the Palais dance hall. He picks up

his shoes and buffs them till they shine. Then he puts them on and lifts me in my stockinged feet and places me down on top of his own and we go dancing: one-two-three, one-two-three, our feet lifting off in a perfect waltz. It is one of the few happy memories of my childhood.

Near the bottom of the box I spy a pair of fine kid boots in a soft pastel grey; high insteps and laces to match. And they fit! I am Cinderella. I shall go to the Ball!

We find a clean comb and some pins to tie up my hair. I am shocked when I see myself in the looking glass. Much of the lustre I once possessed has now gone.

My crowning glory, which used to have a russet hue, is now pure white, like the driven snow which has surrounded us this hard, long winter. Only my eyes have kept their almond shape. They have also held on to their colour: a steadfast blue-grey.

All is not gone.

'Good morning Jean Logan. Where have you been?'

Mr Niven comes in from the garden with a bunch of daffodils in his grasp.

Their yellow trumpets are as yet too small to sound out the triumph of spring, but Dorothy, for yes that is the name Mr Niven calls her, wraps them is strips of cloth and bids me take them to Dr Scobie.

'They are heralds of hope Jean, and will open up in the afternoon sun.'

~

They sit side by side in the motorway cafe drinking weak black coffee from paper cups. On a carelessly wiped table there is a vase of plastic flowers. Someone had stabbed out a cigarette on one of the yellow blooms.

Under the glare of the artificial light Bella looks over to the face of the stranger besides her and sees the pallor of age seep through his tan. He needed to stop, of course he did, driving all that way without a murmur of reproach. She ought to be grateful. She is grateful. She should really reach over to him now and offer up her thanks.

Outside, the first rays of a new day stir the feathers of a few ducks huddled in the rocks beside a newly dug pond. Her eyes take in the litter that has gathered at the water's edge: bottles, cans, plastic bags, a few bits of stale crusts of bread. One of the drakes swims out to some reeds in the middle of the pond. It picks out a chunk of bloated pizza in its beak and takes it back to the shore. Nearby is a play area for children. Bella sees a young mother yawning herself into life as she helps two small boys clamber up the peeling paint of an elephant's plastic trunk.

She thinks of Tom. She longs for Josh.

And says: 'I don't want to hurry you Freddie.'

But she does.

Then ventures the question. 'What will you do when you drop me off?'

She hopes that this enquiry will land kindly upon him for she wants him to say something pleasant in reply. She longs for him to volunteer to come home with her, perhaps help her look after Josh, after all she will have her hands full, won't she?

He says: 'I'll have to get straight back if you don't mind. I've still got things to tie up in Penzance. And Julia wants me to take her to the Tate.'

Bella feels an old heaviness return.

'Of course I don't mind.'

And strains her lips into a smile.

~

THE JOTTER

AFTERNOON

I have taken an extra portion of stew to give me strength for what is to come.

When I walk along the corridors with Elsie at my side, I squeeze my cheeks with my fingers to bring some colour into them. I do so wish to return to the doctor's kind regard.

'Miss Logan, my dear lady, welcome. I have missed you.'

He looks at me with eyes that have sunk into his skull and a rush of blood percolates through to my face, now sore with the many pinches that I have given it.

'Thank you sir. It is good to see that you have returned to us. I hope that the Austrian air has revived you.'

And then I add, to show off my knowledge, 'I believe that Austria is the place where Dr Sigmund Freud has his residence. Perhaps you were able to pay him a visit there?'

'Alas no. But yes indeed, he does. In Vienna.'

And then he begins to hum the tune: 'Vienna, city of my dreams,' and stops as suddenly as he began. 'But I did not leave my calling card. Dr Freud I fear would have little time for a humble practitioner like myself.'

'I think you underestimate yourself, sir,' I reply. And stretch my mouth into the shape of a friendly greeting.

I give him the flowers and see him return the favour with a smile.

It radiates from his gentle mouth and it is the one feature in his expression that seems to still hold on to some life. The skin on his face is papery pale and those sunken eyes...

'Miss Macpherson, will you be so kind as to fetch a vase for these brave blooms?

She obeys him swifty and I can see the yellowing buds being placed carefully by the photograph of Grace. He then signals to me to sit where I am used to.

I tell him that there is no need of his watch to lull me into reverie. I am ready for his enquiries. I lie back on the couch for the first time and notice that the tartan of my skirt seems to match the Royal Stuart Plaid beneath me. We lie together in accord.

'Miss Logan, I mind well where we left off last time. You were lying-in after the birth of your first child.'

'Yes, Dr Scobie. I believe this was so.'

'And you were not at all well at this time. You could not rouse yourself to feed your infant, so a wet nurse had to be found. Am I not right?'

'Yes sir, her name was Janet.'

Janet. Janet McIver. Wee Janet, barely seventeen, so recently delivered of a stillborn child. The milk flowing from her, pouring itself into my bairn, in love and grief and the payment of four pennies a day. She stays with us for some time and sleeps in a truckle bed by the sink, rising at night to suckle and soothe my boy; my wee boy George, a stranger to my heart.

'How long were you indisposed, child?' Dr Scobie enquires.

'I cannot mind exactly. The whole of the spring months and into the summer of that year, I fancy. Until he was weaned and my sister Meg could tend to his needs.'

'You took no part in the care of your child?'

'Little , I confess. I roused myself rarely and then it was just to wash and sup for myself.'

'And yet within a few months you were with child again. How was this when you were so clearly ill?'

'A man has his needs, does he not Dr Scobie? And I did not want my Tam to take up with one of those painted girls from the Gorbals to satisfy his desires.'

When I say these words I see the doctor look down. Is this perhaps a glimpse of manly shame? He is a man after all and must surely know about the flesh that parades itself for a few pence down by the Barrows. I start to wonder if he ever visited such haunts himself as a young man. That is before he became the respectable Dr Archibald Scobie with all those letters after his name. But he returns to my past and starts to probe once more with the scalpel of his questioning.

'And did the same condition of lassitude appear again after your daughter Margaret was born?'

'Worse, sir. But by then Meg had moved in with us and the new baby was fed with a bottle.'

'She was fed by your sister?'

' I had not the strength or the will to do it myself.'

Margaret. Little Meg, my first wee girl.

Such a long birth, arriving in a rupture of pain; bruised and blue and taken from me. Meg who is now so musical my sister says... sitting by the piano, her little fingers outstretched, maybe Schubert one day... Meg...

' Tell me Jean, what did Tam make of this new baby and your continuing sickness? That dashing young fellow from Fyfe! The man you said who was so attentive to you during the months of your courtship.'

'I barely saw him by day, so busy was he in the yards, and by then he was making a name for himself in the Union.'

'For the betterment of Mankind, no doubt, but paying little heed to the needs of his wife and his family.'

What would he know? I close my eyes and see the

bewildered look that Tam gave me when he rose up from our bed every morning.

'What ails ye, Jean?'

The look of a man that is truly lost. Family life had only brought a bitter cud of disappointment to my Tam. Better to work harder at other things that would bring him joy.

'He did his best, sir, that's all I can say.'

And now I am aware that I am tired. The same familiar wave of lassitude is coming upon me. I feel it spread throughout my body. I just want to be left alone and to sleep.

There is a long silence in the room. I can hear the sound of my own breathing steady and strong and the uneven rattle and wheeze of the old man behind his desk. He takes out a small bottle. I squint from the couch to see him as he reads the label and then uncaps it carefully, tipping into his palm four round white tablets. In one swoop they are in his mouth. The Adam in his throat, as old and wrinkled as a russet apple, rises and falls as he swallows them down.

He takes a while to rouse himself again and now I am awake and alert, concentrating on his every move. Stay with me Dr Scobie. Don't leave me now.

I see him put the bottle back, deep into the recess of his jacket. He clears his throat and once more I hear the familiar: 'Indeed.'

He has returned to me!

'Indeed your husband may have done his best for all his colleagues in the shipyards, dear lady, but what he could not do was restrain himself from his own conjugal needs. He went on and on and within another year another mouth to feed, only this time it wasn't to be- a miscarriage in your fifth month it says here on your records.'

'So it was Dr Scobie.'

But it was not so. It was something else. A word that I cannot bring to my lips. Only the old biddy that brought me the needle would say the name out loud and she was too feart to stay till the pain came upon me. And all that blood!

And somewhere in the wrapping that I brought to the bin, the ghost of a babe that could have been born.

'But that wasn't the end of your troubles was it? No indeed! So we come to the crux of the matter, Miss Logan. Mrs Anstruther. The twins!'

~

Evie's face is wan and weary when she turns her head to look up.

'Where were you, Mum?'

'Come on sweetheart, Bella wasn't to know that your blood pressure would go through the roof. You had ages to go.'

'I came as soon as I got the news. I don't know how many times Freddie must have broken the speed limit to get here love.'

'And she's here now darling.'

One of James' large hands was pressed to Evie's forehead. It was clammy with sweat and stuck hard to her skin. Bella could see her daughter recoil under its touch.

'But don't you see, she wasn't here when it mattered James.'

Evie's voice is flat and cold.

'I'm sorry Evie, I did my best.'

Somewhere in the space between them they could both hear the unspoken words: 'But that wasn't good enough.'

'You know who I really wanted?'

'Tell me love.'

'Gran.'

'Yes, I thought it might be her.'

'She wouldn't have gone gallivanting off to Cornwall so near my time. She'd have had my bags packed and ready to go, just like when I went off to Guide camp, remember? A new set of undies, my best nightie ironed and folded and some of those little cubes of lavender that she loved so much.'

'I don't know what to say, love. I can't bring her back.'

Bella looks up at James. He raises his shoulders and they fall with a slump.

'Perhaps it would be best if we both leave leave and let you rest for a while darling. I'll get the nurse to put these flowers into water. That'll cheer you up. And I'll take your mum along to special care to meet the babies. They are so tiny Bella, I can't tell you. The little boy, weighing in a four pounds and the wee girl a few ounces less. But they'll be fine; they keep telling us they'll be fine. They've got them under these cloche things with tubes in their noses to help them breathe. How they can do all that now beats me. It's amazing!'

Bella looks down. She says nothing but her hand stretches out in an offering to move a few damp hairs off her daughter's face.

But Evie had already turned her head to the wall.

SIX

'HUSH A BYE BABY'

'I'm calling her Aisa mum. I think you'll understand why.'

'I do Evie. She'd have been so proud of you, and so pleased with her wee namesake.'

'And the little boy will be Edward, after James' pa. We'll call him Ned for short.'

'Ailsa and Ned. I like that. They go well together.'

'We'll get on to the middle names when they grow up a bit. I think we might even get Josh christened when the time comes. Gran was pretty religious, wasn't she?'

'Well, she had a funny 'eye for an eye, tooth for a tooth' way of thinking if that's what you mean. I'm not sure that the notion of forgiveness was ever one of her strongest virtues; she liked to keep hold of a grudge did your Gran. Anyhow, no matter, it it's a Christening you want, a christening you will have. Your Dad and I will just have to keep our fingers crossed behind our backs… that is of course if we are both invited.'

'Bath time, Mrs Sawyer.' Amanda, the Norland Nanny with her ever-ready smile and the uniform a little too stretched over her ample body, had moved in and was making her confident presence in the nursery.

Bella wonders what school of child rearing her latest grandchildren will be subjected to. Amanda had a look of a Truby King acolyte in the way she briskly went about her business.

Some fiddling going on with the mixer taps. Then a great show being made of a plastic mat with yellow ducks on one side and suckers on the other, now being lowered into the water with a 'tut'. The ducks were turning red; the water too hot. They would be blue if... and just to be on the safe side a thermometer is being produced from the pocket of that double D chest.

'No rolling up your sleeves and sticking your elbow in to check, as in my day,' Bella jokes, making what she hopes will be a passing jab at conviviality.

'Things have moved on, Mrs Cavendish.'

'Nevertheless some things don't change. Thankfully babies are still the same.'

Bella reaches over and picks up the warm bundle from the cot, carefully cradling her granddaughter's head in the palm of her hand as she does so. Under her middle finger she can feel the steady pulse of life beating through the dip in the baby's skull. A fleeting thought comes in and out of her head. If she just pressed her finger harder on that spot, would the beating stop?

The idea makes her tremble.

Where on earth had it come from?

She loosens her grip and passes the other hand over the downy surface of growth on the skull, moving in a motion of gentle caress. The baby girl opens her eyes and strains to focus on her grandmother's face.

'I think she could well be a red head, Evie. Look at that

golden sheen to her hair. The Anstruther genes may be coming through in this one.'

'As opposed to those mousy little Cavendish ones that I got lumbered with, you mean?'

Bella flinches under this rebuke.

'No love, but it would be nice, wouldn't it? My grandfather Tam had a lovely head of red hair when he was young. As of course did I.'

'You bath her mum, I'll get Ned ready. And Amanda, perhaps you can fix up the feeds for when we are done.'

The ritual of bathing brings them closer. Mother and daughter entering into an unfamiliar territory with one another, just for a while. Something about the gentle splashings of water over these small bodies; trusting hands at one with their task.

'Were you ever able to bathe me when I was tiny, mum?'

Bella strains to remember.

'Sometimes, love. When I felt up to it. I wanted to though, believe me.'

'I know you were ill. But it did cut us off from one another in those early days, didn't it?'

'That's what depression does, Evie. It cuts you off from all your joys. I can't describe exactly what it was like for me then, but I remember my counsellor saying that depression was a bit like indigestion. It lay like a suffocating blanket of pain all over me for a while, never letting me experience the feelings of being alive. I thought she was being a bit fanciful at the time but it's not a bad analogy. Indigestion of the soul I would call it now.'

'That sounds like it belongs in one of your poems.'

'Does it? Is that so bad? Anyhow I'm so sad that it came between us.'

They are so close now; their heads together, their breaths joining in a single plume over the steam…

And then it starts to get scary in that narrow space between them.

Evie turns away. She lifts up her baby son and wraps him in a towel, handing him over to Bella to hold.

Now she turns to the baby girl, holding her tight in a slippery grasp.

'But I don't want my little girl growing up loving her grandmother more than me. She's mine, mum. Not yours.'

Bella feels herself in retreat and some of her old heaviness returns.

'Of course not, Evie. I understand. You will be a wonderful mother. Much better than I ever than I ever was.'

And they are back into that familiar place that keeps them separate. Their moment of intimacy evaporating in the chill of the air that now surrounds them.

Bella sighs.

'I thought I could take Josh for a walk in the park this afternoon. Get rid of some of that energy before James comes home.'

'Good idea.'

'And maybe later on in the week I'll take him to play with one of Julia's grandchildren. Troy's son is nearly the same age as Josh.'

'I thought you weren't talking to Julia. You and she had that spat in Cornwall, didn't you?'

'Well we've kissed and made up since then. We both agreed we'd said a few things we shouldn't have. Stuff we've been bottling up over the years. But it was good to get it off our chests and clear the air, especially before my big birthday bash next month.'

'God! Imagine being sixty! You'll be an old age pensioner mum. You'll get a bus pass, save you a fortune coming over here.'

'There are some compensations I dare say.'

Evie's brow is creased.

'Perhaps we should do that sometime, you and I?'

'Do what Evie?'

'Clear the air between us.'

Bella can feel the colour rise to her face.

'Maybe, love, maybe…'

Push and pull: closeness then distance. They both feel the strain in the tow and tug of the tide between them. Bella loves her daughter; she knows Evie loves her.

But they can never be easy together.

~

THE JOTTER.

'So, my dear lady, we get to the crux of the matter. The twins.

You are fruitful again, no surprise in that, only this time two lambs to be born in the spring without a mother to tend them.'

I nod. My memory of that time does not serve me well. My body no longer belonged to me. It chewed the food I was compelled to eat; it expelled its waste, and when the time came for me to deliver, a force came from I know not where and played its part. But I scarcely lifted my head from the pillow when the new cries of life hit the air and my baby girls took their first breaths.

'But they were sickly, those babes of yours, Jean. They bore the yellow jaundice for some time. Wee tadpoles of babes they were, born before their time and so thin and frail they could hardly suck any nourishment into them. They were taken from the house for a while and put into the hospital. Now let me see…'

I hear him turn back the pages from the notes in his buff file.

'Aye, they were in the infirmary for three months. Were you able to see them during that time?'

I shake my head. I still cannot speak. Something furls up my tongue.

Where were the words? Only sensations come back to me. The feelings of the days and the weeks passing... the blood caking between my legs... my breasts hard as boulders, seeping stale trails of milk binding me fast to the bed.

But he continues with my story. I have heard it spoken by others many times before, from the policeman who manacled me to him, from those men got up in their horse-haired wigs, parading every detail to a gawping crowd. And more bitter still from the harpies in the prison who spat out their venom full on my face.

I tell myself that I must take my mind elsewhere. I must rise above myself as I learned to do at the time of my trial. Rise so high that I can look down upon the body that lies beneath and regard it as someone else.

This is not me! I am not here!

Where is Ethel with her faltering steps, leaning on the arm of Dr Lennox? Ethel in the school she set up for the foundling babies. Preaching out of her kind mouth the word of God to all those children who have known no love. And Edward, poor Edward, now lying in his grave on the banks of the Zambezi river, his ghost looking down in pious appreciation.

But although I have striven to detach myself when the story of my life has been regaled in many places, I have not heard it spoken the way it is now. Dr Scobie's voice is not angry. It is not curdled in the tones of disgust, or grown hoarse with shouts of fury. It is quiet; calm and in its cadence it has the whisper of compassion. I feel that I am now safe to lower myself back into my skin.

And listen to him.

'Jean, I cannot imagine what must have been going on in your head at this time, but I sense most strongly that you were tired. You hadn't the strength to cope with the demands put upon you. You were weary, were you not?

Is that the right word, my dear? A terrible weariness had been put upon you.'

'Yes sir.' My voice escapes from me in the breath of a sigh.

He sees me nod.

'Your melancholia, for that is the word I would use to describe your condition, may even have been a gift from your psyche. Your soul would have spoken to you without ever you knowing it. 'Do not participate in the life that you are leading my, child. It demands too much of you, more than you can bear.

Let me instead wrap you up in a cocoon of numbness where you cannot feel a thing, where the world can go on without you and leave you to rest alone.'

What is this man saying? How has he crawled inside me. Beneath my skin, under the bones, right into the blood flowing round me now? Into those thin trickles... his voice pulsing weakly under the pale green jumper, through the tartan skirt, holding fast to the darned woollen stockings and into the laces of those pale grey boots with their high insteps and soles scarcely worn. I cling to the brooch that Tam gave me and feel it pierce my palms. Droplets of red fall on to the Royal Stuart tartan. I will stain it with my blood.

'Yes. That is exactly what I felt, sir.'

'So when your babes are taken away...'

'It is something of a relief, sir.'

'I thought as much. They leave you unmolested.'

'In peace.'

'Not quite the peace you longed for, though. There was still Tam with his nightly needs. And your sister Meg filling you up with guilt for the neglect of your other two children and all those household duties waiting to be done.'

I mouth the words: 'Please don't go on.'

But he does not hear them.

'So when these babes are returned to you, bairns that you hardly recognise, you do not want them back.'

'No!'

'They are strangers to you.'

'With all their mewlings.'

My voice returning. I am shocked by the force of its vigour. It cleaves the still afternoon air in that hot stuffy room.

'Wanting you...sucking the life from you... and George and little Meg with all their petty squabbles... Tam claiming you again and again... it's your duty to submit... more bairns will be on the way, sure enough.'

'Enough! Dr Scobie, please!'

'Not quite Jean. Let's hear it spoken.'

His voice is urgent now. It too has found a force from somewhere within.

'For one day you wake up and summon the energy to rouse yourself.

You know what you will do. Tam is at work. Your sister has taken the children to play in the park. They will not return for a while.

Permit me to stand beside you on that day, Jean. You rise and bathe yourself, cleaning all the grime away from you. You find the babies in their cribs.

You dress them in the clothes you have managed to launder yourself. You change their soiled napkins. You wrap them tightly in the shawls your mother left for you.

Swaddle them so tight that their arms will not flail or their legs stick out. You may even have kissed them and called them by their names: Fiona, the first born with her dimples and bright blue eyes, Isabella with her curly red hair.'

'Just like Tam's, when I first knew him in Elder Park.'

'I dare say you said a prayer?'

'Suffer little children to come unto me.'

'A fine prayer indeed. Then you placed them on your bed.'

'Side by side, to be near one another sir.'

Side by side on that cold April day. But first I made sure they were naked. I wanted to see their bare little breasts rising and falling with the life still in them. And my heart thumping against the weak wall of my chest. It would break through my body by the end of it and leave me for good.

Now I hear those women's shouts.

'She hasn't got a heart!'

'How could she?'

'Heartless bitch!'

'If it were up tae me, I'd cut oot her heart and fling it tae the dogs.'

Steady my beating heart. Hold on to those trembling hands. Careful whilst you wash them clean, those two naked souls; they have to be clean, don't you see, not a speck of dirt to be left upon them.

First fill the tub – not to the top for the water to spill, cold with the hot, so their skins won't scald. Now gather them tight as you lower them in.

Check their heads rest secure in the crooks of your arms.

Play with them Jeannie, gie them a song.

'This little piggy' with their fingers and toes.

'Hush a bye baby on the tree tops
When the wind blows the cradle will rock
When the bough bends the cradle will fall…

Have you washed behind their ears?
And all those wee nooks under their chins?
Whisk up the soap to a nice frothy foam
And blow them bubbles to make them laugh.

Then up and out, their wee bodies slithering in the wet. Mind you don't drop them! There, down by the fire to keep in their warmth. Pat and press to get them dry. Some cream smoothed in to the red raw chaps where the napkins have rubbed. Talcum powder to keep hold of that sweet smell.

Can you feel yourself falter as your hands do the work, Jean?

Don't let a wavering pull you from your purpose.
You know what to do next
JUST DON'T LOOK INTO THEIR EYES!
They have to be dressed, remember.
First the vests over their heads
Then the gowns
And the bindings that will keep them close
The dresses have daisies stitched on them.
Hours spent with the needle on the smocking and the hems.

Clumsy fingers must not fail in their work
Steady with those tiny mother of pearl buttons at the
neck.

'Down will come baby, cradle and all.'

'So Jeannie, you put them next to each other. Fiona and
Isabella, flesh of your flesh, for the comfort of each other's presence.
You bound them together so their arms wouldn't flail.
Tight together side by side.
Then you took up the pillow beside them…'
'AND I HELD IT DOWN!'

SEVEN

AFTER

THE JOTTER

I recall that I could not move from that couch. I lay like a stone when the good doctor carried on with his story. He told of my leaving the babies on the bed and then my search for Tam's sharp blade; the one he used with such diligence every morning for his ritual shave before going to work. First the soap worked to a lather on the brush. His face white with the suds. Then the razor sharpened on the leather strap before its long sweeps of motion on his jaw.

No need for soap for my purpose.
I took up the blade and let it cut into my wrists
And found such joy in that pain!
Cries from Meg as she finds me…
The rich red blood pumping in my ears.

Someone takes me from the couch and carries me whence.
And I am lighter!

I lose track of time now, days and dates and only a few pages left.

Sister Jewell is gone. I hardly notice her departure. Not much fuss made of her Dorothy says, after twenty eight years of service to the asylum. Just a small ceremony with invited guests. Naturally I did not attend. And Dr Scobie?

'Passed away', Elsie tells me in that big house of his in Jordanhill, with his daughter Grace by his side and my secret heavy within him.

How heavy is dread, I wonder?
What is the weight of fear?

Sixteen ounces to the pound
Fourteen pounds to the stone
After this there are hundred weights

I could not carry a ton!

PART FOUR
SUMMER

ONE

THE PARTY

DON'T FORGET!

*3 Doz vol-- au vents (take out the bacon and mushroom
   ones from the freezer)*
Dips...smoked trout and tzatziki
Cheese straws
STILL TO DO!
Butter and paste blinis
Rice salad
Put quiches in the oven to warm throughout
*Buy extra paper cups and plates on the way there-if time
   allows.*

Nearly there, Rosie thinks. Just time for a shower and then I'll
chop the celery and the carrots into batons. Turn the oven to
gas mark three: vol- au- vents in the microwave for just under
one minute.

So far, so good.

'Iona!'

She goes upstairs and into the study and sees her partner still in her dressing gown, huddled over her laptop. Irritation and affection begin their familiar tussle for supremacy inside her. Rosie battles to keep her voice calm.

'Iona, I'm giving you fair warning. We're leaving for your mum's in twenty minutes time. And if you are not ready, I'm going on my own. And I mean it!'

Iona looks up. She sees the large flustered frame in the doorway and grins.

'What's the rush?'

'I'll tell you what's the rush, if you'll just pay attention for one minute. I've got food to prepare. You've got presents to wrap. It's Bella's big day and we don't want to let her down. It's YOUR family remember? This is the first time you'll all be together, apart from Tom, since your mum and dad split up.'

'And don't I know it.'

'Has it never crossed your mind that I might get fed up playing the part of Buttons when you are all together? Fetching and carrying like some lackey in a fairy tale.'

Iona laughs. She folds down the lid of the computer and gives Rosie her full gaze.

'And here's me thinking we were the ugly sisters in this family drama my love, though you can hardly call my sister a classic princess. If Evie were to play the part of a Queen, she'd be a modest little monarch, wouldn't she? One of the Scandinavian sort, I imagine, riding her bicycle through the streets of Stockholm, begging her subjects not to bow and scrape.'

'That's not fair, Iona,' but Rosie can't help but grin at this image of Evie.

'Maybe not. But at least King James will play his part well,

I fancy. His wallet will be as generous as his waistline. We'll have the best bubbles money can buy for the occasion.'

'How about Freddie? Will he be there?'

No, he won't. He's swanned off to France, I think. Evie tells me he doesn't do family celebrations.

'Poor Bella!'

~

They drive in silence past all the known landmarks of the city. Then off into the hinterlands; unknown territory for her. Narrow streets crammed with people. Market stalls, charity outlets – Brenda had never seen so many. She starts to name them out loud: Oxfam, Help the Aged, Barnados, Save the Children, Naomi House Hospice Care, the Red Cross – yes she'd heard of that one.

'Oh my goodness!'

Now the shops with blinking neon lights and the windows blackened out. Sex for sale: 'erotic fantasy step this way.' Bright shop fronts with skimpy clothes cheek by jowl with saris and veils. Here a Polish deli. Restaurants: Star of Bangalore, Peking Dragon, a Taj Mahal laundrette, two pawn shops side by side, then round past a Chinese herbalist. On the right an arcade where barrows of fruit are piled high and into the blare of a Bollywood song.

Several youths on skateboards loom into view, rattling down a pavement in an attempt to keep up with them. She can't see their faces under those dark hoods.

Brenda shudders!

What was she doing here?

At least she had brought the dogs for company.

'I think I'll stay in the car, Don. I'm not sure I want to leave it outside after what happened to Bella.'

His reply is terse. She looks up at his profile and sees the tic on his temple start up its pulse; his left eye blinking out its warning for her to stop.

'There's no need for that. The dogs will make sure that no one comes near.'

~

James waits by the door. He looks at his watch. What could she be up to now? He's done his bit and mentally ticks off his check-list: the car loaded up, wine in the boot, flowers in cellophane at the front, kids trussed up in their seats. Josh had got hold of the console and has switched on the CD. It blares out tunes from The Lion King.

'Christ, not Elton John again!'

'Evie, what are you doing?'

'I won't be a minute.'

He starts to walk into the kitchen to fetch some cold water from the fridge for the two aspirins in his hand. He makes his way round a giant stuffed panda lolling on the floor. His son had been feeding it again. James removes the sticky marmite sandwich from the toy's mouth. A few jigsaw pieces have clung to the butter. He opens the lid of the bin and the stench of rotting nappies hits him with a smack.

'Amanda!' he yells.

Then remembers it is her day off.

'Jesus!'

Evie appears in the doorway. She looks a mess. She's put on her nice new clothes and the high heels that she bought for the Partners cocktail party, but her hair hangs limp. Her make up is not right. Much too much colour for that quiet face of hers. He wants to tell her that she looks a bit like a clown that's been caught in the rain.

'Will I do for the occasion?'
'Lovely darling,' he lies.

~

'Hugo, Julia, I'd like you to meet my neighbours Mr and
Mrs Chakrabatti and their sons Sanjay and Vik. They've been
so kind to me since I've moved in and so good in lending me
some spare chairs for today.'

Two boys in neat black blazers nod and smile. Julia is
entranced. She follows them into the garden, helping herself
to another glass of punch on the way. Hugo looks down at
the small round woman with glasses to match and brings out
his charm. He watches as her shyness melts with his interest.
Oh yes, Mr Lindsay, she misses the Uganda of her childhood
days. Maybe one day they will all go back when the boys are
grown up. The winters are so cold here, don't you think? She
doesn't like the dark evenings. And it has taken them so long
with much scrimping and saving and what was left of her
father's legacy to get the boys into decent schools – private
schools – she lowers her voice to tell him this – but it will be
an investment in the end.

Hugo nods in agreement, helping himself to another glass
of red. One of Freddie's, he notes, much better than the stuff
James is peddling in the kitchen.

Rosie is moving around the room as if she was on casters.
Dispensing dips and smiles and an extra helping of welcome
to the Smolagas who have brought their children Stephan
and Hannah to meet the new babies. Josh appears from the
skirts of his Bamba. He eyes up the Polish boy for a potential
playmate.

And James is everywhere. His tight suit bursts with
bonhommie. In his hands he carries the bottles of wine and

dips the red or white into the glasses of the guests without invitation, ignoring the occasional demur. He sees Don and Iona standing together, trying hard to dissolve some of the permafrost still existing between them.

'Good to see you both getting on so well! I hear you are making great strides in public welfare policies Iona. I'll be coming to you for advice on bringing up these little monsters here.'

Brenda is sitting up straight at one end of a well-upholstered settee. She strains to hear the sound of barking, so she can make her escape. At the other end is Evie. She has taken her shoes off and looks, Brenda thinks, like a mussed up doll. They sit and engage in a see saw of monologues hoping they will pass as conversation. Evie complains that the twins are not yet sleeping through the night. This summer will probably be a wet one, Brenda predicts, but the forecasters have been wrong before. At least giving up breast feeding was the best thing she could have done, though it wasn't helping her in getting her figure back. Too bad for the dahlias if there is too much rain. And bottles are just so much more convenient now she has a nanny, a Norland nanny, don't you know...

They nod in mutual agreement.

'Aren't they adorable, Bella?'

Julia has just come in from the garden. She bends down and breaths alcoholic fumes into the faces of the slumbering babies.

'Cooochie, cooochie...sweet. I think this chap will be a stunner. Look at the length of those eyelashes. Not sure about the lass. She has the looks of your mother, don't you think Bella? Something about that expression that says: I don't quite approve of you.'

As if on cue, the little baby girl responds with the first strains of a wail.

Evie tenses. Brenda gets to her feet.

'The dogs,' she says to no one in particular.

Rosie steps in.

'Let me give you a break. I'll take one of the bottles from the fridge and heat it up.

'Happy Birthday to you
Happy birthday to you
Happy Birthday dear Bella
Happy birthday to you!'

The chorus is ragged and sung out of tune, but she doesn't mind.

Bella pinks with pleasure at so much fuss.

It has been a lovely day. Everyone has got on so well! Look at Don with his arm around Iona. Just a pity about Freddie. Her hand rises to finger the expensive amber necklace he's put round her neck before she went away. But he had remembered to ring, hadn't he? Missing her, he said and looking forward to next weekend. He was taking her to Kenilworth. The Kinks were doing a revival tour.

And Don had brought a present back from Tom. She would open that by herself when everyone had gone. A special treat saved up to savour at the end of the day.

She circulates from the kitchen to the living room, taking an interest in all her guests. Noting that Brenda is absent, she takes a plate of food out to the car and persuades her to join her in the garden. Bella is most anxious for her advice on summer planting.

They are disturbed by Josh and Stephan who have started to play hopscotch on the paving slabs. Jan and Teresa Smolaga join them with Evie and the talk comes round to Christenings.

'Yes I'm having them Christened next month. Edward Jon

after his grandfather, and we've settled on Freya as a middle name for our daughter.'

Bella stops looking at Brenda and searches for Don, still engaged in earnest conversation with Iona in the hallway.

'Evie, what did you say her middle name was to be?'

'Freya, mum.'

'Freya?'

Bella's voice is lower now.

'Yes, that's right. Freya.'

'Freya!'

Mother and daughter stare at one another. Bella now sees the eyes of a small child locked into hers in a glare of defiance.

'You knew?'

'I've always known, Mum.'

'But how?'

'Ever since I can remember.'

'Who told you?'

'Gran, of course.'

Their voices raised now above the babble around them.

'What did she tell you?'

'She told me I had a twin sister, just like me. But God wanted Freya in Heaven and I had to stay behind.'

'She told you that!'

Bella can feel the warm tug of Hugo around her shoulder.

'How old were you when she told you?

' Three, maybe four, I can't exactly remember.'

Bella hears in her daughter's voice, the inflexion of her mother's tone coming through.

'We don't want to worry your mummy, do we Evie, or God might want to take her to Heaven too.'

'Oh my Lord! She didn't say that!'

'She did.'

Hugo's grip tightens. Bella pulls herself away.

'And you kept this all to yourself, Evie. All those years...'

Julia puts down her glass. She goes into the kitchen and whispers something to James. He comes into the room empty handed, his big hearty smile now straining at its corners.

'Evie, I think its time that we went home.'

But Evie shrugs him off. She can't stop the flow coming from her mouth.

It pours out round the room in a lava of recrimination.

'Have you ever thought what it could be like to be me, Mum? The one that wasn't quite perfect enough to go to Heaven, so she had to do her best on earth? But it didn't get me anywhere with you, did it? Being good I mean. I'd have been much better off being bad like one of your delinquents you always loved so much. I even tried being bad for a bit, not that you noticed. Stopped eating the food that you cooked for me, bunking off school and living on takeaways when I was hungry. You never even said anything when I pinched money from your purse. I also tried shoplifting for a bit and longed to get caught in the act.'

'Evie...'

'No mum. Don't interrupt! Then you see I could have been sent to a Children's Home. Better still to one of those places you used to go to. What was it? A Unit for disturbed adolescents. Wow, that could have been something else, wouldn't it? I could have been one of your clients. You would have made an appointment to see me. I would then have come into your office and you would ask me to sit down. Then you would give me a big smile and say: "Evie, isn't it? What a lovely name! Tell me about yourself? Talk to me, Evie."

'Oh I would have loved that! And when I started opening up to you, you would really listen. You'd bring out those crayons you kept in your study and ask me to draw my family. I'd take the the red colour and draw the BIG people: Mum, Tom, Iona and Dad all with their smiley faces. And then a gap and two little stick figures that you could hardly see: Gran and me in a sort of whitey – yellow colour, so very faint on the page.

"Why have you drawn them like that?" you would say and I would tell you. And then you would be really interested. "What's that big space in the middle that you find so difficult to talk about?' you would ask me. "How do you feel about that space, Evie?"

The room is quiet now. All guests frozen to silence.

'What lovely questions those would have been! What I would have told you! But it was never going to happen was it? Too many of the mousy Cavendish genes in me. I couldn't even play the juvenile delinquent role properly. I never got caught by the police. So you and I never met did we mum? What a shame!'

'Stop it Evie! STOP IT RIGHT NOW!'

Don's hand catches Evie high on her left cheek. His fingers leave a smudge of make up on the angry welt that is left on her face.

But Bella ignores him.

Her blanched face is fixed on her daughter.

'So this is what you meant by clearing the air, is it Evie?'

Then gives way into the arms of Hugo.

~

Later, when other guests have made their retreat and the neighbours have retrieved their chairs; the left- over food parcelled and wrapped into tiny plastic trays by Rosie, ready for the Homeless Centre, Bella forces her mind to shut down.

But her body keeps going. Hands pick up toys and tinsel and wrappings from presents. The gifts are piled high on the coffee table. Bunches of flowers are put into soak in the sink. She gathers up the cards in their envelopes that have scattered themselves around the room and finds a sharp knife from the kitchen to open then cleanly. 'Growing old is compulsory, growing up is optional,' reads one. A collection of landscapes: National Trust views of well-manicured grounds; safe greetings from someone like Brenda. Two women in two different cards stare up at her: one in steel rimmed spectacles raises a glass: 'Lets not age, let's marinate' is the message – Julia no doubt. The other, an Edwardian woman in her garden, feet up on a chair, reading a book. I wish! A hand written message: 'Age cannot wither her, nor custom stale her infinite variety'- good old Hugo! Bright orange squiggles on a cornflakes packet with the aided hand of Evie's on her son's grip: 'I love you Bamba."To my mother on her birthday'- a posy of violets with a verse that ordinarily would make her cringe. Bella's tears run into the writing of the greeting from Canada.

She picks up each card and places it carefully on the mantelpiece, ignoring her shaking hand. But now with the tears comes another loosening. She feels the hinges she has so carefully placed on herself to clamp down her racing thoughts, give way.

Evie stands in front of her again; a small child, purple in the rags of rage. But she is not alone. Another scene comes crashing into her head. She sees the wreckage of her car on the kerb and from it young 'Picasso' emerging, his heels winking out their greeting to her. He is walking towards Evie with his hood down giving her a high five of salutation. Bella sees faces in a smirk of satisfaction. They hold hands and pose in front of her for what seems an age then their mouths open.

Their lips, perfect rosebuds of innocence...

And once again she feels the spittle of their fury land on her again.

'I've always known mum...'

'Too girly for grandma her...'

'Don't worry mummy or else God might take her too.'

'Finish her off, fucking finish her off...'

'The one who wasn't perfect enough for heaven...'

'Let's give her a face lift...'

'How do you feel about that empty space, Evie?'

'Pretty please! show us your cunt...'

'So you and I never met mum...'

'Shame!'

'Wicked!'

Their spittle joins in a river of spite. It flows right through her, dissolving her mind, weakening her body. She can no longer remember who she is.

She looks down at the knife in her hand. Underneath its hasp she can feel the knotty bulges of tendons where the keys dog into her palm. The pain had been... she struggles to find a word for that experience.

MATCHLESS!

Then studies her arm as if it belonged to someone else. The wrist so pale. If she could just break through that translucent skin, she could take hold of those blue-veined threads of life underneath.

Her life in her hands!

The thought fills her with intoxication.

She takes the knife in her right palm, holding the blade between her thumb and her middle finger, noticing to her surprise that her grip is steady and sure. Then she begins to trace a line from the top of her wrist of her left hand, pushing deeper into a crevice of flesh and freckles as it made its way to that big pool of the artery that pulsed beneath the underside of her elbow.

Before the first trickle of red ran down her arm, she could feel a sudden rush of possibilities surge into her head.

Turning away, she holds her arm above her head. She walks to the door and opens it, taking herself out of the house. Out into the night in her stockinged feet. Opening her gate and closing it again, tracing number 36 with her bloodied fingers. Along the pavement, her arm raised again, leaving little spots of red in the puddled cracks. It starts to rain. The rain cools her head. Her cropped hair clings to her skull. Drops of cold water pass her nose. She puts out her tongue and draws into her mouth the freshness of the night. Past the Chakrabatti house with the lights all on. Nearing the Patel's 'All-day-all-night' store, with its neon sign blinking and in need of new bulbs.

'Al. .ay Al.ight'

On and off!

Round the corner, into the traffic and onto the 'ting-ting' sound of a tram.

TWO

THEN...

Shapes and shadows blur and blend.

A great weight of pain throbbing behind her eyes; heavy rocks blocking out the light.

Midnight black.

Then through the eclipse, eyelids flutter open. The contours of a face emerging: dark at its centre, a halo of grey fuzz flaking in and out of focus.

She feels the warmth of a breath bring her up from the depths.

'Well my duck!'

And strains to open her lips.

'Don't try to speak love. I know how much it costs you. We've all been up to 'high doh' we've been so worried about you. Its okay. You are going to be fine. Rest now. Take it easy. But what a shock I got on Sunday morning when I came round with my trolley full of books and saw you laid out on that stretcher.'

"Do you know who she is?" the nurse said.

'And I told her I did.'

"Well," she said, "your friend was inches away from being downstairs in the morgue. Tripped her foot on the kerb, the ambulance man said and fell right into the road, she did. How she missed the tracks of that tram, Heaven only knows. A bloody miracle if you ask me. And what ever was she doing out with no shoes on at that time of night? That's what we all wanted to know."

The face now fractures into parts. The sharp edge of a nose to her cheek. Eyes behind those black rimmed glasses.'

'Shh.'

'I've let everyone know my duck. I got their numbers off that nice Indian lady next door to you. They've all been so worried. Your daughter with the kiddies, in and out all day, she's been. Such beautiful little mites, those twins of hers. And your husband has been with your other lass. A nice man — such a gentleman and so anxious about you. They all are.'

And goodness, gracious, I couldn't find enough vases for all them flowers from your friend in France. I keep telling everyone, Its Kew Gardens here. Or the Chelsea Flower Show at least! You are a lucky lass Bella.'

'Shirl.'

'That's right my love.'

The smile widening in recognition.

Then she wills her eyes to steer upwards. The pain catches her and her bandaged arm clings on to the soft knitted blanket at her side. The eyes fix on a forehead. They begin to trace the criss-cross seams of concern on the brow.

'Shirley!'

'Well done Bella!'

She manages a weak smile before here friend at her bedside continues, her voice now quietening to a whisper.

'I couldn't help but notice love. Your name on the records you see: 'Anstruther'. It fair jolted me I can tell you. I'd seen it before somewhere. So I took the liberty. I hope you don't mind. I told the powers that be in their white coats when they were talking about your arm that you had been ill. I mean not just the cancer, but poorly in a deeper down in the dumps sort of way. You wouldn't dream of... like she did... I didn't want them probing, if you get my drift, because you are going to be alright Bella. Believe me. It won't happen again my duck. You've got too much love around you for anything like that to happen again.'

THREE

'A NIGHTINGALE SANG...'

She wakes to the sound of birdsong: the gentle 'sriii-sriii' of the baby swifts, catching their breakfast from parents on the wing. They are so close to their nest amongst the roof tiles. When she extends her arm up to the ceiling, she can feel them through the peeling plaster. Their companionship lends her comfort. It gives her a sense of security. As long as this little family was close, she could feel safe.

Gradually the sun streams in. Filigree patterns of light through the net curtains by her side. First landing on her closed eyelids, then down her cheeks and soon her neck and the upper part of her body are flecked with its rays; pinpoint patches of warmth bringing her back into life. She can almost feel those freckles, so long in hibernation beneath her skin, rise up in a hymn of gratitude.

What was it Ailsa used to call them again?

'Sun kisses, my wee pet lamb. Aren't you loved by the sun, my bonny one?'

Bella smiles. She recalls a favourite memory of her mother

in her final days. Ailsa stretched out like a basking lizard on the lounger chair under the apple tree at 'Swallow's Rest', Elvis on her lap; two old friends soaking up the sun.

Time was!

And now it felt that her time could come again. At last she could savour the precious gift of every day.

Downstairs Madame Hulbert had arrived and was busying herself with the chores. She could hear the chatter of her son Guy on his tricycle as he pedals on the flagstones around the house. The burble of noise rises up to her bedroom with its old fashioned patchwork of quilting and lace.

'Bounjour Madame Cavendish. Vous dormez bien?'

'Bonjour Francine. Oui! Avec deux points fermez. Merci.'

How she had arrived here she can hardly remember now. It was still, even after all these past few months a bit of a haze. Julia's version of events is the one she likes to bring to mind if anyone asks her.

'Don't you recall darling? It was Freddie that took you from that hospital bed and purred you here in his lovely red sports car. Bundled you straight into the front seat with many an admiring glance around you, and drove for days and days till you arrived at his little 'pied-de-terre' in the Lot valley, or lost valley as I like to call it. It is so unspoilt darling. And he gave you strict instructions, my girl. 'Stay and rest and don't bother your head about a thing. Convalescence is what you most need, Bella,' he told you. 'Do as you are told for once in your life, woman.'

Bella feels an inward smile shape itself inside her head. A model patient she had been for everyone's sake, and a grateful one too. From time to time Freddie would arrive with armfuls of wine and cheese and fresh bread and they would spend their days sitting in the garden together or going for walks by that lovely river that snaked its way through the steep limestone gorges surrounding them. Only the birds seem to notice that they were there. Bella came to expect the muffled 'ooop oop oop' of the hoopoe when they ambled past the vineyards. On their return up the cobbled streets to that little house nestling under the shadow of a cliff, curlews would often give out their cries of welcome home.

Nothing was asked of her. Freddie made no demands. She didn't mind it when he no longer kissed full on the lips, but opted French style, for more gentle puckerings on each of her pale cheeks. In the evenings they would stay up and play cards, then she would read to him before they went to bed. She discovered to her joy that Freddie loved being read to, something no one had ever done for him when he was a boy. So 'A Tale of Two Cities' unfolded its cruel and romantic plot as they sat by the log fire with glasses of the best red wine she had ever tasted. At bed time, they would climb the stairs together and go their separate ways; he off to the master bedroom on the first floor, she happily taking another flight up to the little attic under the eaves to be with the birds.

'It's like having a favourite brother to stay now,' she told Julia.

'Don't you mind, darling?'

'No Julia. I don't. It's lovely just the way it is.'

'Stay as long as you want Bella,' he said to her one evening. 'I love having you here. 'Francine can come twice a week to keep the place ticking over so your time is your own. Make the most of it. And invite anyone to come and stay. The place could do with some life in it. Friends, family, anyone...I don't mind.'

So her time took on a gentle rhythm. On days like today she would rise slowly and take pleasure in her dressing. Breakfast under the fig tree in the garden. Then she would read for a while, or write long letters to Tom. Gradually the garden began to claim her attention. She rediscovered her green fingers again. In between the clumps of wild candytuft, she sowed cornflower seeds and watched the blue heads bloom in the sun. On walks around the village she would take some yellow foxgloves growing in the tussocky heaths, and on her return home plant them amongst the wild orchids by the back door. Afternoons hummed with the sounds of bees and dragonflies and a small flotilla of butterflies that seemed to follow her around, greedy for the promiscuous tastings that the garden had to offer. Every day she made her way down the narrow street to the bakery and the charcuterie and here she would enjoy spending time choosing that piece of cheese, this cut of meat, the one baguette still smelling from the sweetness of the oven.

To her delight, she resurrected her schoolgirl French and practised it whenever she could. She made greetings to everyone around the village and began to feel confident enough to narrate events to Francine Hulbert with some modicum of confidence. Guy became her teacher. His three year old chatter instructed her in a patois that got her by in company. And that was good enough for now.

She also began to enjoy cooking again, using all the ingredients around her. So when Freddie arrived, tired after his long journey, there would be fresh asparagus on the table and a hearty casserole made of local meats and soaked in the same Quercy wine that Eleanor of Aquitane had brought to England as part of her dowry.

He never talked to her about why she was here. And he never mentioned the possibility that she might at some time go back 'home.'

Then Evie made a visit. Her anxious eyes scanned her mother's face, searching for an opening. It came one day when they were bathing the twins in an old galvanised tub in the garden. Josh pulled at her sleeve and the ugly seam of purple was exposed.

'Who did that, Bamba?'

'I did Josh. Bamba was naughty. She was playing with a knife and it cut her.'

'Did you go on the naughty step?'

'No.' Bella smiled. 'But I should have done. It was an accident, my love.'

'What's accident?'

'It's when you do something you didn't mean to, pet.'

'Is that true, mum? You didn't mean it?'

'Josh go and take your bucket down to the stream and get some water for the flowers over there. They are very thirsty.'

They watch and wait until those sturdy little legs take him out of hearing.

'Did you mean it, mum? I could never forgive myself it you did.'

Bella looks down at the two naked bodies splashing in the bath. After five months the twins were growing into their separate personalities. Already the little boy was beginning to crawl. When she picked him up and towelled him dry he would be off, over the grass and into the orchard, his little head turning every now and again inviting a game of chase. The little girl seemed to prefer a more sedentary life, content to observe all around her. Her watchful eyes now fixed on her grandmother's gaze.

'I don't know, Evie. And that's the truth of it. My mind was all over the place. All I know is that somehow I felt I had to take charge. I suppose I was a bit like one of those teenage girls I used to see – the ones you resented so much. Cutting myself was a way of opening myself up in a perverse way. I had kept so much in, hadn't I?'

'I'm so sorry Mum. I shouldn't have, well not in that way, anyway.'

'Don't be love. You had every right and I needed to hear you. Funnily enough I feel a whole lot better now. Something within me has lifted, if that makes sense. What makes us keep secrets Evie? I told myself it was for the best. I wanted to protect you in some crazy way. But "they fuck you up your mum and dad..."'

'What!'

'"Man hands on misery to man, it deepens like a coastal shelf..." Larkin love.'

'But I'm not unhappy Mum. I'm glad about the choices that I made. I never wanted to be a high-flier like Iona, or go travelling like Tom. God, this sounds so corny, but I just wanted someone to think I was special. And I wanted to get closer to you. You always seemed so far away from me.'

'Fill that empty space? With the crayons in your picture?'

'Yes.'

'I know that now and I am truly sorry.'

Bath time continues. Josh plods back and forth, spilling his bucket over the much drenched flowers. Then Ned gives yelp. He has seen his brother and is impatient for bigger splashes. Ailsa raises her freckled arms for a cuddle.

'What do you think she would be saying if she saw us now?'

They are quiet for a moment; mother and daughter willing to bring the dead grandmother back to life.

'How about one of her specials?' Evie says.

'"Mercy on us!" With her hands planted firmly on her hips!'

They say nothing more. By day they play with the children. Bella cradles the twin babies close to her and watches them grow. She covers her arms and takes Josh to see Guy on the riverbank where they build dams with twigs and mud. And they laugh together, an easy laughter, as if nothing had happened.

And so the summer passes. Iona and Rosie come and go. Hugo and Julia descend with their bustle and noise. Time spent cooking and entertaining and visiting all the lovely spots around them. When they all went away, she was left on her own and her whole body sighed with relief.

Then one day, she had no idea which day it was, something unexpected happens. The sound of a car inching its way down the gravel track alerts her to the change. It wasn't the smooth purr of Freddie's car she thinks as she makes her way to the window. This was something new. Panic comes upon her again. She can feel the lurch of her heart in her chest. The unsteadiness in her limbs as she clings on to the sink.

When she looks around the stranger is standing in the shadows of the kitchen door. She summons her voice to call out.

What could it say?

'Friend or foe?'

And then squinting into the darkness of the room, she discerns a familiar silhouette.

'Don?'

She sees him straighten and push back a few untidy wisps of hair with his right hand; that absent minded gesture he's always done ever since she'd known him.

'Don!'

'Sorry Bella. Yes. It's me.'

'DON!'

She goes to him. She holds out her arms for him to enter into an embrace.

'I know you weren't expecting me,' he says, 'but I spoke to James and he said something to Taverner. I hope it's okay.'

'Okay,' she gulps, 'of course it's okay.'

'I should have let you know . Not surprised you like this.'

'No it's fine, Don. It is so good to see you.'

And she is surprised at just how much she meant it.

Then words tumble out of her: unrehearsed, confused; a babble of niceties that she cannot stop.

'...Driven all this way... how did you find the place?. off the beaten track... are you alone?... does Brenda know?... have you eaten?... you must be exhausted... let me get you a drink...'

He lets her take her time rambling on. Then he puts a finger to her lips.

'Oh, Don!' she sobs. What have I done?'

When they come downstairs the next morning, she finds herself blushing like a schoolgirl as Madame Hulbert comes through the door.

'Francine, ici, mon mari.'

The good French wife does not even blink in reply when she wishes Monsieur a good holiday and hopes that Madame becomes fully restored to health. What had Freddie said to her?

The next few days she takes pleasure in showing him all her favourite places. Gradually the shyness that had grown between them begins to disappear. They talk. As they sit on the bank of the river watching some young canoeists paddling down the rapids, she opens up to him. And he listens.

'I've made so many mistakes, Don. I know I have. Starting with the cancer I suppose. I shut you out, didn't I? But I've had lots of time to think about why I did that. That's what illness does to you. I seem to remember reading somewhere that illness was the night-side of life. Forever a dark place. And a lonely one. I think I just drew up the drawbridge in that dark place and went into myself. Fortress Bella.'

She gave a short laugh.

'It served a purpose in a way. I realise that now, withdrawing from everyone. It felt almost like a task I had to do to help me prepare for death. To make that journey on my own with no emotional strings attached to anyone, not even you. But I didn't die, did I?'

He is looking at her. His brow furrowed in concentration.

'Bella, don't say that.'

'But it's true, Don. And I can remember when I started to do it. The time that my hair began to fall out. Great hankfuls of it all over the pillow. My lovely red hair! I was like some scrawny newborn chick lying beside you in bed. And I couldn't bear your breath on my head. It was so cold you see. Warm when it came out of you and cold when it touched me; a reminder that you were very much alive and I… on a journey somewhere else. So I pulled away and like that little chick I suppose I looked for some cracked pieces of shell to crawl into. You didn't know what to do did you?'

'No. You didn't seem to want me to be there, so I let you be by yourself.'

'But I did want you to be there, Don. I just didn't know how to ask. And then', she pauses. Looking up at him for permission to go on, 'there was all that stuff about Freya which resurrected itself.'

'I know. I'm sorry. I should have been a bit more understanding about that.'

As he speaks, a few ducks waddle past them, looking for some crumbs. He shoo-s them away, then holds her arm. She lets it rest in his grasp and looks beyond the river to the steep crags on the other side.

'You may not believe this. You may think me fanciful with that scientific brain of yours, but I feel that I have been carrying the weight of other peoples sadness inside me for such a long time. Don't laugh at me please Don, even though you might find this a bit weird, but I've had this voice in my head for a long time now and it's only since Evie's little girl came into the world and I knew she was alright that I felt I could put that burden down.'

'I believe you, Bella. And I don't think you are weird.'

He smiled. One of those lopsided smiles of his, reserved for incongruous events of life outside his intellectual ambit. 'She's a miracle that one, isn't she? They both are.'

'Fine words coming from an atheist.'

'Agnostic,' he corrects her. "There are more things in heaven and earth than are dreamt of in your philosophy, Hector."

'Horatio,' but I'm impressed. She smiles.

On their walk back to the house that evening, he stops and makes her listen.

'They say that there are nightingales in the woods round here,' he tells her.

'Wouldn't it be lovely if we heard one tonight.'

Bella feels an old excitement return.

'They are only very ordinary in their way. Plain little brown birds with a song that is not quite as pretty as a blackbird I am told.'

'Don't spoil it Don. I don't care. I would love to hear one, wouldn't you? Anyway who says that their song isn't so pretty? Do I hear the voice of Brenda in there somewhere?'

'Well maybe,' he admits.

'I thought so. Let's make up our own minds shall we?'

~

'So what about Brenda?'

They are eating a picnic. Pate and wine and fat black grapes. Another day, and they are on top of one of those limestone crags overlooking ripening fields of vines.

'What about her?'

She senses his tone becoming uneasy.

'Because I've often wondered why you chose her. I mean I know you left me, but if you had wanted to have an affair, you could have taken up with someone we knew, someone like Julia for example.'

'Heaven forbid, Bella! Sometimes I think you hardly know me at all. I would have run a mile if Julia had so much as raised an eyebrow in my direction. Can't you see it was precisely that Brenda was not familiar that was the main attraction. She knew nothing about you and that's what I needed at that time. She was just there. She was getting over Eric's death. I suppose to her I was a bit of a hopeless case and she took me under her wing. End of! And she's a good sort, despite what Evie has to say. She's kind. She's caring, and as my Dad would have said, you could set your clock by her. I knew where I was with Bee. And she certainly opened my eyes to a world outside my normal one.

'And you know the best bit about her? The bit that clinched the deal as far as I was concerned at that time? You'll hate me for saying this Bella. She didn't go in for all that 'touchy-feely' therapy stuff that you brought home every day of the week... "Tell me about your feelings?... What makes you say that?... Can you share that with me?..." you know what I mean.'

Bella sees him change his expression and put on that 'no nonsense' voice that she knew belonged to 'brisk-and-bracing': 'We are put on this earth, Donald, and we just have to get on with it.'

'I can hear her saying that. You are a very good mimic, Don.'

She looks at him more appraisingly. 'She's changed you. I can see that now. I think I owe a lot to Brenda. And I love it that you can tell the sound of a nightingale.' Looking round she adds: 'I bet you can name these wild orchids as well. In Latin, no doubt. Go on. Impress me.'

He ignores her teasing tone, pointing a finger at a clump of wild flowers beside them. 'Lady's monk, if I'm not mistaken. And that speckled fellow over there could well be a Lizard. Will that do? I could be making all this up, like you used to when we went out for nature walks with the kids. We all believed you until one day Tom called you out.'

'Ouch!'

Then she smiles. 'I'm impressed. And allows a silence to fall between them. When she begins again she is hesitant, unsure as to how he could respond.

'So why Don? Why not stay with her. It sounds like the sort of life you have been craving for.'

He looks away.

And suddenly he can't stop shaking. Tears course down his face as he gives way to the grief that he has been carrying inside him for so long.

She reaches out to him and holds him until she can feel his tension relax in her embrace.

'Oh Bella!' he sobs, 'I thought I had lost you!'

~

Hours later they are by the sink, engaged in a familiar ritual of old. He is washing the dishes and she is putting away the assortment of china and glasses that she bought at the market with Freddie.

'And Taverner?' he enquires. A tentative note in his voice, still hesitant with uncertainty. 'You were very keen on him by all accounts before we met up all those years ago.'

'That's right, I was, even though I knew it wouldn't last: not then, not now. Not in that sort of way, the sort that says you are going to be a couple. Freddie doesn't do 'Couples'. But he's been good for me, Don. He helped me feel whole again as a woman, not just a patient. Someone to cherish. And I think I've been good for him too. I'd like to carry on being his friend if you don't mind. He loves being with Evie's family and there is something very vulnerable about him under all that bluff and bluster. You must admit he's been so kind in letting me stay on here for so long.'

'He won't be jealous when he knows I'm here?'

'No I don't think so. Intimacy for him is not sex. It's about friendship. I know that now. Someone he could be with where he doesn't have to put on an act. I don't think Freddie has ever had a close friend in all his life.'

'And us now Bella? The big question mark. What about Bella and Don?'

She puts down her apron and allows his words to hover for a while before landing on the soft space between them.

~

On his final day she takes him to the famous tourist spot where she took Hugo and Julia; the village perched precariously on a rocky escarpment.

They wander along the narrow streets and take pleasure in buying gifts for the children in one of the many shops on the way: a wooden toy boat for Josh, two little mobiles of butterflies and birds for the babies. In the restaurant they sit opposite a family out to lunch in their Sunday best. Mother, father, four children and their grandparents all sitting formally, quietly absorbed in the act of eating. They notice the elderly couple seem involved in everything that was going on and yet they were somewhat separate at their end of the table, recognising perhaps, Bella thinks, that they are no longer at the heart of things.

Don takes his cue.

'Is that what you want, Bella? We haven't done such a bad job as parents, despite everything, have we?'

'I don't know,' she replies, still absorbed in thought. 'I don't know what I want now. All I do know is that if we do get back together, I don't want to live the same life twice.'

She fixes him with those blue grey eyes of her. So serious now.

'What sort of life are you looking for. Have you any idea?'

'Not 'Swallow's Rest' again, that's for sure. And no number thirty six. I've got that out of my system.'

'A nice bungalow by the sea? Mabelthorpe perhaps?'

'Won't she mind Don?'

'A bit I guess. But she'll manage. She's got the dogs. Actually I think she is closer to the dogs than anything else.'

'Monty and Rommel.'

'The desert rats!'

They laugh.

Now he looks serious.

'Bella, can I say something?'

Something in his voice stops her mirth.

'Go on.'

'You said the first time I came to your house before I went to Canada. Something about us never having taken risks. It lodged in my mind somehow and I thought about it a great deal. You were right. We had never strayed off a predictable path in our life together. Then I came to realise that life doesn't have to be like that to be good, does it?'

She smiles at him. Suddenly an old refrain comes into her head. She starts up the song that took them to Leeds when Don's parents were still alive.

"Today's Monday, today's Tuesday,
Monday roast beef, Tuesday's shepherds pie…

He joins her in his gentle baritone:

"Friday's fish and chips
Is everybody happy?
You bet your life we are."

'We are not Annie and Jack, are we Bella?'

'No we are not', she replies. 'But they were lovely your parents. They lived their lives like two devoted swans and died without making any fuss and bother, just as they would have wished. I'd like to raise a glass to them, Don. I don't think I ever appreciated them as half as much as they deserved. Jack and Annie!'

'Annie and Jack!'

'Wherever they may be!'

'And I hope,' he adds, taking on his mother's Yorkshire brogue, 'that wherever they are, there is a place for everything and everything in its place.'

Bella chuckles.

'Heaven forbid! But it worked for them, didn't it?'

'I don't want it to be our motto though. One day like another, even at our age.'

'Especially at our age,' she adds, warming to his words.

'So where was I before I was rudely interrupted?'

'I'm sorry Don. Go on.'

She listens to his opening 'eigh' as he cleared his throat and knows that whatever he will say next will mean a great deal.

'When I was in Canada, I joined Tom on one of his field trips. He took me up this mountain in the Rockies and when we got to the top we both looked into space. A far as the eye could see there seemed to be nothing at all around us, except other mountains. Mountains and higher mountains and nothing in between. Then I remembered you saying that Tom had found joy in the unknown. I found that frightening at the time. Even in all my years of research there was always something known, something to build on. Other people's ideas to shape and grow. And then Tom told me just to be still and take time to really look: 'Open you eyes Dad!' I thought he was a bit barmy but I did as he said. I stood there for what seemed like forever. And then I began to see things. Shapes I'd never seen before. Patterns on rocks. Valleys where rivers once flowed. There was so much I'd never taken in. Just a glance here and there, that would do. Then move on. Move on to the next thing. It took our son to teach me to stand still and appreciate what was all around me.'

Bella feels her eyes well up once more.

'And you know what? After a while I began to feel exhilarated. I didn't want to leave the place. When we got back to the camp I couldn't stop talking about it. And then I got to thinking that you and I had been in our own sort of wilderness, you with your illness and me in that awful place when I finished work. It was horrible, wasn't it? And we each drew in on ourselves and became separate. Yet what would have happened if we had just stood long enough together instead of running away?'

She reaches out to take his hand. She can't help it, she wants to shout out loud!

'So I've been thinking. Why not do things differently? Why don't we take off for a while all by ourselves. Come back with me tomorrow and we'll spend some time going through France. It's a beautiful country. So much to look at. So much to explore. Go where the mood takes us. Drift… now that's a word we haven't encountered before. Just drift…There's no rush, is there?'

'No rush at all.'

Then the voice of panic rises within her. She recognises it immediately. Ailsa's voice. Her dead mother fluttering her wings to be heard.

'But can we afford it, Don?'

Later, when they were too tipsy to make sense of what they were saying, he holds her hand as they stumble down the few steps of the castle at the edge of the village. Ahead of them they take in the view. A bend in the river encircling a broad chequerboard of arable fields dotted here and there with poplar trees. To the north they can just see the wooden foothills bordering the distant horizon of another mountain range. And as they look to that horizon, the thought comes to her. Somewhere in those woods, an ordinary little brown bird would be opening its throat for the first notes of an aria that could only be heard if they stood long enough, intent enough to listen.

POST SCRIPT.

THE JOTTER.

'Wherever are you , Shirley?'

'Be with you in a tick, my duck.'

She comes in from the stockroom, her arms full of clothes to be sorted for the hangers. In her right hand she is clasping an old exercise book.

'Look what I found on the floor with all the White Elephant stuff?'

'Not that old thing. All that wants sorting before the next stock take. It's a good job we've still got the skip out the back. Have you found out who it belongs to yet?'

Shirley grins.

'I think so. I haven't quite lost it. Mr Alzheimer can stay away for another day, at least.'

'Well, whose is it's then?'

'Bella Cavendish. It suddenly clicked with me a while ago.'

'Didn't you find it in the lining of that crocodile handbag that someone brought in. The one that we sold to that transvestite at great expense? But who is Bella Cavendish, when she's at home?

'Bella. You know Bella. She comes in sometimes of a Wednesday to help serve customers in the shop.'

'The one that had the terrible accident?'

'That's the one. But she's alright now, I believe. She's in France with her husband. I had a postcard from her a while back from some place called Ruin, I think? Any road they have a big posh cathedral there, she tells me. And she was having a wonderful time.'

'I expect she'll be pleased to get that jotter back when she gets home. You said it was some kind of diary that her grandmother had written a long time ago. Fascinating! She'll be ever so grateful you hung on to it for her.'

'Maybe,' Shirley says, looking down at the faded red covers.

'Or I might let that idea stew for a bit before I make up my mind what to do. Like this tea…' and smiles, raising her mug to her lips in a gesture of thanksgiving.

ACKNOWLEDGEMENTS.

My thanks to all those who gave me encouragement to write this novel. Special praise for Brian, Ruth, June and Margaret for their patient readings and suggestions for amendments.

Not forgetting Isabella and Gladys whose own lives were the inspiration for this story.

And much appreciation must go to the Mitchell library in Glasgow for providing valuable information about the early history of Gart Naval mental hospital which was used for the setting of Jeannie's story.

Anna Anderson July 2020.

 Matador